THE SONGS WE SANG
AND THE SONGS OF OUR LIVES NEVER CHANGED
A Sort of Biographical Novel

David Naughton Leavy

ARTHUR H. STOCKWELL LTD
Torrs Park, Ilfracombe, Devon, EX34 8BA
Established 1898
www.ahstockwell.co.uk

© David Naughton Leavy, 2022
First published in Great Britain, 2022

The moral rights of the author have been asserted.

*All rights reserved.
No part of this publication may be reproduced
or transmitted in any form or by any means,
electronic or mechanical, including photocopy,
recording, or any information storage and
retrieval system, without permission
in writing from the copyright holder.*

*British Library Cataloguing-in-Publication Data.
A catalogue record for this book is available
from the British Library.*

This is a work of fiction. Names, characters and incidents are the product of the author's imagination and any resemblance to actual persons, living or dead, is purely coincidental.

ISBN 978-0-7223-5115-4
*Printed in Great Britain by
Arthur H. Stockwell Ltd
Torrs Park   Ilfracombe
Devon   EX34 8BA*

PART ONE: ARRIVALS

Prologue

1942

Danny Farrell and Margaret Naughton walked down the gangway carefully together. The overnight ferry trip from Dun Laoghaire had been tiring, the weariness added to by the anxiety of knowing they were now estranged from their families, both of which had disapproved of them leaving Ireland unmarried and heading to England alone to start a new life together.

"You leave and you needn't think of coming back! You'll not be welcome here! This door will always be locked against you!"

He wagged his finger in angry frustration and, with the side of his fist, thumped the front door of the cottage where Bridget was miserably cowering. Even as he said it, Peter Farrell knew in his heart that there was no future for his oldest son in Ireland; and while he outwardly chastised him and railed at him, as was his way as father to a disobedient and wilful son, he secretly admired his pluck and a resigned smile flinched in his eyes. He knew that in later years he would not be able to carry out his threat of a barred door. He watched his son heading down the road and into town, with his small leather suitcase in his hand, and then he turned to go back inside, shuffled Bridget roughly away from the door frame, and closed the door angrily behind them to shut out the sadness and regrets.

Danny was devastated. He had never wanted it to come to this. Margaret's parents considered him a 'wastrel' with no future, and he was hurt by the untruth of it. He had left school at fourteen and had worked hard for his dad on the farm and in a general store in Strokestown; but now, rising twenty-three, he wanted a better life with bigger opportunities and he was determined it would be with Margaret. He couldn't imagine a life without her.

The ferry was crowded and though they were cheered to hear so many Irish voices, and there had been an impromptu jig with music, dancing and singing, it didn't disguise the fact that they were leaving home. Beneath the music they heard the song of opportunity, steady work for decent pay and the hope of a fresh start. Many of those they had spoken to were leaving Ireland for the same reasons: more work and a better chance in a new country. They didn't want to leave their homes, but felt they had no choice; and most of them, it seemed, intended to settle in Liverpool, where the Irish community was growing daily – like a second, contrary Ireland.

So it was Liverpool they came to in July 1942, and the sight that met them was a complete opposite environment to the one they had left behind. Momentarily stunned, they had stood, after clearing the gangplank, mouths open and eyes wide-staring. There was a prevailing air of grey and dust, and everything seemed broken, tumbledown and bleak. Skeletal buildings with window frames hanging in air and with dead chimneys reaching to indifferent skies, misshapen, ugly and brutal; grey air sodden with gloom and not a tree or blade of grass in sight.

And there were people and scavenging dogs everywhere, many looking purposeful and intent on clearing away piles of rubble from fallen buildings, others seemingly shiftless and lost as if things were so desperate it had worn them down. A seething mass of grey, grime-faced and grim humanity, or so it seemed to them, and a few children with bare feet and ragged clothes shrieking and chasing among the mounds of rubble.

As they took wary steps along the dockside they were besieged by hawkers wanting to sell everything from small, misshapen vegetables to grubby old clothes, knives, forks, anything at all, none of which the couple wanted. The stalls were set out on the dockside and were hastily constructed from tables of old doors laid across house-brick stacks. They were placed closely together and jumbled with rubbish so that it was hard to tell where one stall ended and the next one began.

They stared around them in amazement and some dismay. They looked at one another, Margaret with a look of shock and Danny with a poorly practised look of cheerfulness.

The bombings in Liverpool had stopped in January, but not before huge parts of the city had been reduced to rubble. As they moved down what might have been a main street they looked at the piled mountains of bricks with timber like dead trees sticking drily from a ruptured earth, pointing accusingly at the sky. It had become a playground for children as they chased each other around or across the sullen, lumpy landscape. A dramatic, disheartening parody of the gentle rolling hills they had left behind.

Others simply sat in the midst of the dust and chaos and looked disconsolate and grim.

"Oh, Danny, what a mess! What have we done? This isn't the fresh life I had in mind. We came away from our home for this? We've swapped emerald green for grey and black. Are you sure we've made the right decision leaving Ireland for this?"

"It won't be like this everywhere, Margaret," soothed Danny. "This dockyard and the city have been hard hit and the bombings have turned it to splinters, concrete and dust. Once we get away from it all we'll be fine, I promise you. There are lots of lovely parts in England. Come on – we need to find Lime Street Railway Station and get our tickets for Coventry to catch up with your sister and her husband. We'll be married in a couple of months and then we can find a home and a place of our own to settle."

Danny knew he could only hold on to his determination to make both their lives brighter. He felt less confident than he sounded.

"What about the green hills and the crystal-clear streams? Where are they all? I can't believe this! It's so hard leaving all the good things of home behind us. Especially for this!"

Margaret's wide eyes slowly moved around the area of dockland.

"Give it time. They're here. It will get better. This is a new life for us. A new adventure, and nothing will ever be the same again for us. Look around you, my love. There are opportunities for us here. You know, as well as I do, there was nothing left for us in Ireland. There'll certainly be plenty of work here for a strong and willing man who knows how to use a shovel – especially in this country. And also for an intelligent girl who's 'the gem of Ireland's crown' – lifting his hat he feigned a bow – "and has a smile to thaw the toughest winter." He grinned in that disarmingly cocky way of his and winked.

She couldn't help smiling back as she nudged him gently in the ribs. He pretended it was a very hard elbow.

"Oh-h! It's going to be great, Margaret. I'll make it so, I promise." Then that smile again.

She loved it when he was like this. He was always so passionate about his dreams and she loved the gleam in his eyes when he stared into their future.

"You and your blarney! You're always so stubborn and determined. But . . . I know you'll get us right. You always do." And she sighed, resting her head briefly against his shoulder.

He loved her at that moment like he'd never loved her before.

It had been even more difficult for her to leave home. She had secretly left the house when her mum and dad were out in the fields in the early hours of the morning and she was expected to clean up the breakfast things, make the beds and sweep the house. She had said nothing to any of her sisters and brothers, except Mike, whom she was very close to. Quietly and secretively she had stored some basic necessities under the bed, waiting for the right time. Mike was in awe of her daring when she told him she was leaving in a couple of days. He wasn't going to say anything. Life would be hell for them all when their dad found out. Their father was a fearsome man with the commonly held beliefs regarding filial obedience and knowing your place; he ruled with steely looks and a silent authority. His anger would oppress the house for days and everyone would walk around him, keeping their fearful distance.

She caught the bus – no farewells, with only the clothes on her back and a canvas bag the size of a Bible – and, sat in a sadness too deep to leave, she allowed the bus to bounce her gently and tearfully as she headed for Strokestown to meet Danny, who would join her on the journey to Dun Laoghaire.

He thought, 'She calls me stubborn and determined!' And he smiled with pride and admiration when he realized what risks and loss she had put herself through to be with him. He determined it would be a commitment that she wouldn't regret.

Carrying their small suitcases with a firm grip, they smiled warmly at each other, kissed and moved on, walking quickly through the crowds to get into clear space, eager to ask directions to the train station and begin their new life together.

PART TWO: DEPARTURES

Chapter 1

1986

At the time, he couldn't believe he was dead.

It was such a strange feeling to be alone in this way and cast adrift from those he had known all his life. To be separated finally when he least expected it and not know where to turn.

Ronan had just had a phone call from his brother in England, who had told him that their dad had died suddenly of a suspected massive heart attack.

Some years earlier he had had a similar call, again from Conor, to say that their mum had died after a long and painful cancer. On that evening, he had simply asked if he could return the call.

"I can't get my head around this. I'll ring you back. Just need some time to think. OK?"

"Yeah, that's fine," said Conor. "I'll still be here."

He did ring back. He asked if she had been in pain at the end. How was Dad? When was the funeral? Had she just got tired and given up? He had talked about his plans for coming over for the funeral, but Conor had persuaded him that it was pointless, that he would be too late anyway and it would all be over by the time he arrived. They weren't the things he had really wanted to ask, but they were the usual ones that he could ask without having to think while maintaining a respectful flow of conversation and keeping the deep grief from overwhelming him.

He soon realized he was not listening to himself or to Conor's answers. He had really wanted to furiously shout, "It's so unfair! She's only sixty-two! That's not a full life! Why couldn't she have had some more years of happiness and ease with Dad? Is that too much to ask for anyone? How can it all just come to an end like that? Clocks stop, but mums don't! How can someone so loved just go away? Surely they can't be taken that easily? Who has the right to do that? Is that it? Is this all there is? Where is she now? Why? Why without us? Why without me?" The song refrain drifted tunelessly through his head as he inwardly railed against the unfairness of it all: 'No one in your life is with you constantly. . . .'

"I'll see to it. Stay where you are and look after your family. I can manage all this now and there's nothing for you to do here." Conor had been adamant.

It was a hard call, but there had been some sense in it and he persuaded himself that he was just so busy at school at this time as head of English and the boarding-school manager. It was the same reasons (or were they excuses?) he had used for not coming home sooner when she had first become ill. In the end, he had offered to share any costs of the funeral or Conor's travel to Ireland. Whether it was to make himself feel better, he didn't know. Was it his thirty pieces of silver? It was a tension that always seemed to be an issue for him – trying to balance work and family and never quite getting it right.

Ronan was a hard worker, conscientious and well thought of. Like his dad, he had fashioned a new life for his family, but this time in New Zealand; he was successful and moving himself and his family upwards; he had dreams and ambitions, which he shared with Catherine, his wife. His model for family life had been his own childhood and the sacrifices and love that had been so plentiful as well as some of the rituals of Christmas and birthdays, which were always made so special. They took their two boys everywhere with them, not having any family to babysit for them, but in the end it became a matter of choice and they wouldn't dream of not taking them everywhere they went. It made them very close.

Now out of nowhere came this second unexpected shock within five years; he was taken aback and devastated, numbed and orphaned by another short call. How light the touch with which it had happened and how gently his brother had spoken it, but how heavily and quickly the dark loss had gathered in his head!

Again, because it was even more unexpected, he had asked for time to think about it and now stood slumped, wide-eyed, feeling bleak and lost, by the kitchen phone. He had thought that his mum and dad would always be there to brighten and lighten their family, like hot coals in a banked fire, and he had expected to see them give their gentle, warming advice and love for a long time. That possibility had long gone when his mum died. All his images were of life and laughter, work and stress, big meals and Christmas, holidays and gardening, drinking and good company, and it was almost impossible to see a still image of either of them. He had wanted them to see their two grandsons growing up in their reflection and turning into fine young men, and them becoming proud grandparents.

Now the fire had gone out. The dream was gone and so many plans, formed and unformed, had slipped away; a part of him and a part of their family had left with them and would not be returning. Even though he was an adult, married and with two young children, he suddenly felt that now was the time to grow up. A part of him had emptied out and he knew it would fill again with new and more immediate dreams. It was time now to grow his family with Catherine and his boys, together, and reconfigure the future shape of the family, but, sadly, in a diminished form. It shattered him momentarily and he leaned against the wall and put his hands over his head.

"What is it, Ronan?" That was Catherine calling from the bedroom, tidying the room and readying the house for breakfast. "Who was it?" she asked as she came through from the corridor into the kitchen. But she didn't get the full question out before she knew that something was wrong; now she was scared when she saw him curled and vulnerable. "Ronan! What's happened?"

"My dad's died."

No more to say and no easy way to say it. It was real now and it was coldly sharp and numbingly painful. The tears came blindingly in hot streams that itched his face, but he was too distracted with his thoughts to wipe them away and too saddened to care; he simply widened his eyes and blinked stiffly, trying to disperse them. He was swiftly folded into Catherine's arms and it was like he was an eggshell suddenly crushed and everything was falling apart in front of his splintering eyes.

"Oh, Ronan," she said, and she started to cry. "I'm so sorry. God, he was only here with us a few months ago and he was so fit and seemed so well," she sobbed.

Ronan's own sadness was shrouded while comforting his wife; father-in-law and daughter-in-law had always been close, and he knew it was a bitter blow for her and she would find it hard to come to terms with it too. Briefly, while relaying the information from his brother's call, he managed to keep his sadness contained. He hadn't voiced it, not even on the phone to Conor in England, but now it was spoken it would have to be dealt with and he would have to try to explain the unfairness of it all to himself to give him some comfort.

Catherine was a wonderful mother and wife and he knew that his dad was like a father to her. Her own father she had sacrificed to be in New Zealand with him as well as her mother, also left behind. Catherine too was from a close family and he was constantly amazed that she had gone with him, across the world, taking all the risks and opportunities with him. Their lives were not unlike Ronan's parents' and they shared the same love of family.

Suddenly the sound of padded, excitable, giggly feet running down the corridor towards the kitchen. Paul and John, eight and seven years, brimful of life and out of bed and rushing to meet the new day. Ronan and Catherine separated and so did the joy from the two boys. In that way that some youngsters have, they caught the atmosphere like a concrete ball and stared wide-eyed and serious with deep and fearful questioning in their faces.

"How are you two rascals this morning?" asked Ronan as cheerfully as he could.

It didn't work. They weren't going to be treated like children; they were big boys now and they wanted a full share of family matters. They stood staring, looking apprehensively from one to the other of their parents, waiting patiently in the quiet that had settled around them. There were no spoken questions, but their eyes looked for answers.

"Grandad – your dad's father – has . . . died. He went to sleep after a long walk and it was just too much for him," said Mum; she knew they expected an answer. "Your dad's upset . . . and so am I."

She held the two boys and pressed them close to shield them from the impact as her tears fell.

They pulled away and ran to their dad to do the same, holding a leg each and looking into the future with their own thoughts – you can lose dads if you don't hold them tight. Their dad wasn't going anywhere without them – they would make sure of that. After all, Mum comforted them by holding them, so why shouldn't it work for their dad?

Ronan crouched and held them both, one on either side of him. He realized how good it was to hold his kids and how much they meant to him. It was like holding his entire world, and they were undoubtedly two of the most precious people he knew.

"Look – you remember Grandad, don't you? He loved you both very much. He was with us for nearly three months, all the way from Ireland to see us in New Zealand, just a short time ago. He was very good to you and he was very proud of you both. He was very good to me too when I was your age and even when I got a lot older. I'll miss him because he was my dad . . . and he was a great dad . . . and he was only young . . . and I expected [and *needed*, he thought] a lot more time together . . . with my mum and my dad."

He stopped then because he sensed they were making connections that personalized the event for them. So dads are not around for ever? He knew from their looks they were questioning, and feeling less sure of the invincibility they always took for granted. And it could come like that – a sudden shock to break the ties between son and father. Their eyes were full of anxiety, not knowing if this was part of a pattern in life which you had no say in until it was formed. Their grandad's past, their father's present and their own future was less secure and it was all jumbled in their heads. But whichever way they looked at it, it signalled grief that they couldn't express. He realized again how much he underestimated these so-called innocent and inexperienced youngsters, who could catch disconnected fragments of the stories of others and put them together to make it their own, more immediate and more frightening, an intruder in what you thought was your secret, safe back garden.

"Well, fellas," he said to change the subject, "it's a pretty nice day and you need to get out in as much of it as you can. Mum's got your clothes out in the front room, so off you go and get ready."

He let them go and they stood still, uncertain.

"Are you upset? We'll look after you, Dad," said Paul, and gave him a hug. He hadn't seen his dad tearful before and it upset him awkwardly.

John picked up the same feelings too and hugged him. "Come out and play with us if you want to, Dad," he said.

"No, I'm fine, guys. Really . . . we're fine," he said, glancing at Catherine. "Away you go now; it's OK," gently pushing them along. "It's OK," he said as reassuringly as he could.

They were off. The moment of grief gone; but not. They would visit it again, he knew. In the middle of stories before bed that night they would ask, in the most unlikely places, questions that he saw in their eyes as they looked, apparently casually, at him and Catherine throughout the day. They seemed to be watching to make sure they were still there. They would eventually be reassured and go to bed untroubled by the comings and goings of life on their near-perfect pages, in their near-perfect book.

As Ronan watched them go he thought to himself, 'They're the best thing that's ever happened to us.'

He looked at Catherine and instinctively he knew she was thinking the same; and they smiled brightly at one another.

When the boys were both outside and absorbed in their other worlds, Ronan and Catherine held each other and cried. It was a curious lonely feeling that two people who were so much a part of their early life were now both gone and it wasn't a dream or a story. They wouldn't have Conor phone and say that it was all a mistake; it was final and irreversible. That's what was so hard to accept. Even though they had formed their own family now, it was still like two of their closest friends had just walked out and they hadn't even had time to say goodbye. And what was worse, they would never come back again and tell all the parts of their story that were missing. Bitterly, he realized he didn't know as much about his parents as he should have done.

"I'll phone Conor back. I'll tell you all about it when I've finished. I might just sit here in the sun afterwards and have a think. Is that OK?"

"Of course it is, love. I'll get these two scallywags sorted and some breakfast going, so take your time."

Catherine went into the kitchen, glancing back before turning the corner – just to be sure.

After the phone call, which was a mixture of laughter and sadness, there were so many thoughts jostling in Ronan's head that his mind drifted back to some of the wild times when Dad's brothers – seemingly hundreds of them, judging by the noise – came on a visit out of nowhere, bursting the house with their big bullocking voices and their thunderous laughter.

Dad was always in among it – the oldest of a large family of sixteen brothers and sisters, proud of his boisterous relations, who scattered birds into flight, brought flakes of plaster floating down from the ceiling and lifted the carpet with every big breath they snatched at to get the laughing words out.

The three boys, Ronan, Conor and Euan, had wondered how they all fitted into the house as they billowed into the small lounge. Dad was the smallest of the brothers in his family, though well built and very strong, and some of his brothers were well over six foot tall. They bent like great sacks of muscle as they lumbered through doorways, occasionally nudged hanging lights with their stooping heads as they towered to get more drink from the kitchen and then came back in and sat in groaning chairs. It was a house full of men as big as trucks, puffing and roaring away. And the boys had watched their mum shining like gentle gold among the great rollicking rocks of men.

Once the drinking and the smoking got serious it was never

long before the music started. Uncle Pete brought out his fiddle, wrapped in a shredded case; Uncle Oliver, the squeeze box; Uncle Paddy, the tin whistle; and Uncle Tommy got up and went into the kitchen to get the spoons. The fiddle jumped and shifted, with hairs hanging off the bow, like a frantic insect prevented from escaping by the big bucket hand that held it; the squeeze box gasped for breath; the whistle careered jauntily through the smoke and through the instrumental sounds; the spoons galloped on knees and clattered out the beat like shod hooves on cobblestones. And Uncle Des and Uncle Mike would raise the heavens with their voices of thunder, all amid the roar of cannon laughter, explosive conversation and bellowing song. Mum would be constantly shushing them and reminding them of the neighbours, while they told her what they thought of the neighbours they had never met and what a 'bunch of miseries' they were.

And Mum – Peg, they called her – would be up on the floor and kicking her shoes off as Uncle Jimmy took her hands and whirled her around, while the room smiled and the smoke filled upwards and their faces seemed to glow in the blur and smoke of the puffing air.

Their dad's eyes shone with pleasure. He knew she was beautiful, and she was; and the giant bear danced with the fragile princess, or so it seemed to the six bright eyes staring in wonder, afraid to be noticed in case someone realized they should have been in bed at this hour and with this sort of partying going on – too grown-up for kids to understand.

"Ah, Peg, you dance like Ginger Rogers," said Uncle Jimmy as he slipped her sideways.

"And you, Jimmy, dance like you've got both feet stuck up your feckin' arse," shouted Uncle Tommy amid the noise.

The room tipped and fell about and the music temporarily wobbled and then spun true again as the laughter burst, the noise exploded out and the conversation hammered on.

Ronan remembered how he and his two brothers had stared wide-eyed and -mouthed, and nudged one another and giggled as quietly as they could, enjoying the rude adult antics and conversations they were hearing. They would normally have ended up being pushed firmly, but lovingly, off to bed, but they had squeezed themselves into a small space between a wall and a couch and sat, as insignificantly as they could, like three silent commas in the raucous text of a magical and mystical evening's grace.

Then Uncle Paddy danced with Peg, then Uncle Tommy while Uncle Mike took the spoons and the room spun out of control, smoke formed plumes and wispy curtains around everyone and the noise became more deafening as the lungs, like giant sails, filled with air and sang with gusto the songs of love, home, loss and family.

And Danny, sitting there smiling with pride written all over his face, eventually got up to claim his wife, intoxicated with her charm and appeal.

The knee-slapping and foot-tapping were started and the boys would join in clapping, as well as they could, in time with the music – again careful not to draw too much attention to themselves.

"Now, Danny, don't be tuppin' her on the dance floor in front of the boys, there's a good lad. Concentrate on the dancin' and don't be doing that erotic jiggin'," said Uncle Pete through the flying hair of the bow, and he threw his head back and roared.

And the pride of family around him joined in.

"You might learn a thing or two," said Dad, "and then you might be able to get some women of your own."

"Sure, we're after going into the priesthood," said Uncle Oliver. "That way we get to have a good time with the single nuns. Like a pint of the draught Guinness, they are: plenty of body, a good head on it, can't get enough of it and the satisfaction's still there in the morning."

And the room erupted again with irreverent drink and laughter.

The boys could smell the drink on their breath, all through the air, hear clinking bottles, hissing bottle tops and beer mumbling from bottle to glass amid the smoke-filled room, and they looked at faces half opened to sing, lined with the fun of life, eyes creased in pleasure and the winking and the smiling full of devilment and mischief as the merriment pressed on.

And the song went on to its finish with a rousing cheer and a "Good man yourself! If you keep practising with that fiddle you could become very average, Mick."

"I've never heard singing like it and I hope I never do again."

"There's been some wonderful songs sung in this house. I'd have to say this hasn't been one of them."

"You played really well, boys, but it will never replace music."

And the jokes and the laughter came like waves and crashed against every surface of the room.

The boys' eyes had stung with the smoke as the evening played on, and eyelids drooped; and they were carried off upstairs to bed and folded in the affectionate bedclothes, and drifted into sleep like clouds. And through the mists of tiredness they could hear storms of laughter and music below before they fell softly into a deep, warm, cosy exhaustion. Later on Ronan was sure that he heard the strains of Uncle Mike's voice singing 'Bless This House', which was always the finale for an evening such as this. Even when he was half asleep it raised the hairs on the back of his neck. Then he was asleep again and the house too eventually settled on its foundations, sighed and was at rest.

It was a crystal-clear, shining memory for Ronan, and they were as common as wild flowers in the fields of their childhood.

Now it was all over – or that part of it was. Both parents were dead within five years of each other and the music and the laughter were gone for the moment. He snapped out of the dream a little reluctantly and walked into the kitchen.

"C'mon, love – I'll help you with this. Let's get some things organized and patch up the day."

Chapter 2

Euan, the eldest of the three brothers, now living in Canada, had received the news of their dad's death only a few moments before Conor had rung Ronan, but for him it was just before lunchtime on the Friday while Ronan had been awakened quite early on the Saturday morning. He too had been stunned and completely disorientated. His dad had been over to visit him and his family just three years before, and he hadn't wanted him to leave; but there was no way he could stay either.

He saw the gentle side of his dad: a family man, generous and loving. Not the tough and uncompromising figure he portrayed with his passion for education and his determination to see his lads 'make their own way' in the world. Now his dad was gone, and only four or five short years after his mum had died. He felt sure he shared common thoughts with his brothers in England and New Zealand though separated by oceans.

He was devastated by the phone call, and, when he thought about it, it seemed that once again Conor was being left to handle all the arrangements for the family; and the old guilt from when their mum died had revisited. He wished now he had gone home for her funeral, and that he had been there for his dad. Maria had encouraged him to go, saying she would be fine and could handle the family things, for a few days anyway; he sometimes wished he had listened.

He had been told by Conor, "She's gone. There's nothing for you to do. Save your money, stay home and take care of your own family."

Euan was not convinced by any of this. As the oldest of the three brothers he had always had a sense, real or imagined, of his responsibility for the other two. He just felt he should have been there.

He had always been fair-minded. He thought of others first in his gentle, considerate way and would hate to offend or hurt. He had always been a decent guy, and since he had arrived in Canada he had absorbed the phlegmatic, hard-to-ruffle, 'everything must pass' attitude of the people that had attracted him to Canada and to the wife he loved. He soon learned that it was difficult to upset Canadians; so if they ever got angry, then it was time for the world to listen! He found it really difficult to take Conor's advice and he ached for days over his decision.

Both times, and it had been easy to say to himself that that was the best thing. Mum before, and now Dad would probably be buried before he even got home. What could he do anyway? The four kids were still young – even the oldest, Jennifer, was only twelve – and the family needed him at home and would be worried by his sudden leaving.

Dad had made his views on death and the fuss of burials very clear: "When I go, just bury me with me arse pointing up towards the sky to give me last farewell salute to those who really pissed me off."

It was a 300-kilometre drive to Toronto Airport (about three hours), and who knows how long he would have to wait for a plane before the seven-hour flight to London! He would phone Air Canada, but he didn't know how frequently the flights to Heathrow left; and then he would meet Conor (and maybe Ronan) and they would fly to Dublin, hire a car and drive to Galway. He couldn't see himself getting there before the funeral.

Maria would have to stay home to take care of the family, so it would be an expensive parking ticket at the airport until he got back. But she would have done it for him. Much as it upset him, it was just too hard to do, particularly just now with everything at work being so busy.

He guessed that Ronan would have been told something

similar by Conor, who, on these two occasions, seemed to assume that it was his responsibility alone, even though he was the youngest of the three of them, to make arrangements for the funerals and carry the burden for the family. And this was going to be messy for him. With no one he could liaise with in Ireland he would have to sort out all the funeral arrangements.

Later, in a more relaxed time, Conor would write, 'I didn't know a single bastard there and I couldn't even see Dad. He was in the box!' Conor's irreverent way of coping with the stress.

Dad's brothers and the rest of the extended Irish family had faded from the picture as the three boys had got older and their dad had focused on raising his own family in the north of England while most of the rest of his family had followed him over from Ireland years later and settled in the south of England near Slough and Windsor. Their mum had lost touch with her family or they had died, and so the Farrell boys and their mum and dad had concentrated on fashioning a close-knit family that was deliberately independent, making a whole new start and disconnected from the depth of family ties. It was to be both a strength and a weakness.

Euan, like Ronan, was reflecting nostalgically on the impressive figure of their dad: his determination, his hard work, his strength and the value he placed on family underneath a very tough exterior. He too was thinking of a time in his childhood which had left a lasting impression, but for different reasons.

All three of them had gone to a Catholic primary school in Latchford, outside Warrington. It was a sombre, gritty little suburb and they got there by crossing a swing bridge on the Manchester Ship Canal. They generally walked there and back, and he seemed to remember it was miles, but it wouldn't be the first time that his childhood memories exaggerated the realities. None of them particularly liked school; it was strict and disciplined, and the lessons it taught needed to be yelled and frightened into you so that you would remember. Some of the summer days were better than those in the winter, when some of the teachers were as cold as the frost.

Walking across the giant steel structure of the swing bridge, which opened slowly and threateningly, like the maw of a savage beast, came to symbolize crossing from the relatively fresh country area they lived in to the intimidating, slightly grubby, gloomy world they passed through to get to the school with its concrete playground, smell of carbolic soap and grumpy teachers scowling over the top rim of their glasses.

The best part was that just after the swing bridge, where the road passed under a railway arch, there was a small, hidden shop there – right under the bridge, it seemed – that sold sweets by the truckload, stacked on wall-to-wall shelves, all in large glass jars so that you could see all the sweets in them. It lit up their eyes and made the shop a magic place, irrespective of its hunched position in the very corner of the arch. The Cabin, they called it. Whenever they had a few pennies to spare they would go in to buy as many Uncle Joe's Mintballs or sugary pear drops as their money would allow. The smily shopkeeper was always gentle with his time and very good to them and wouldn't count the broken ones in the cost; he always made sure enough of them were broken. They loved going into the shop and wished he was one of their teachers giving out sweets all day.

Kevin Gattland, one of the big boys, all of eleven years old, at their primary school, St Augustine's, had stolen some money from the bus depot on his way to school. The conductor had left his bag with the money and ticket machine on the driver's seat as the driver and conductor got off to have a smoke and wait for the right time for them to leave on the next stage of the journey; they were about five minutes ahead of schedule.

Kevin was a tough lad; he had eyes like slate, muscles like iron palings and clothes that spoke of life at the ragged edge. He spat and swore and was rude to the girls, and the other kids thought that he must be the roughest kid of any school. He was shunned by them and, to pretend how little he cared, he broke up most of their games or casually punched people on the way past. For most it was an innocent time in a distant past, but not everyone shared the innocence. Kevin had carefully helped himself to a few of the notes and quickly grabbed some of the loose change as the two men drifted in smoke around the back of the depot. He scampered off the bus, deciding to run the rest of the way to school and so avoid discovery and blame when the two busmen came back. A bad reputation gives you nowhere to hide – a lesson not yet learned by Kevin.

The conductor knew Kevin because of his bad behaviour on the bus and his constant attempts to avoid paying the fare. Hearing footsteps running, he glanced around through the smoke and saw Kevin racing away; he wondered what the scallywag was up to now.

When Kevin got to school, at morning playtime he told everyone that it had been his birthday on the weekend and he had got money from his relatives. He now shared it out with the friends he longed to have and revelled in the attention he would get for the rest of the day and the games he would be allowed to join in. He was happy. But it didn't last. It never did for him.

Children's small places whisper big stories, and the story went that the headmaster had appeared at the door of the classroom, where Kevin sat daydreaming about joining in the football game, just before lunchtime.

The headmaster had excused himself with the teacher, Mrs O'Rourke, and shouted across the room, "Gattland! Come to my office now!"

There was a collective intake of breath, and nothing moved in the room except the eyes that followed the boy to the door.

When Pop Arden had gone and Gattland had closed the door behind them both, the class quickly unwound and the room was alive as people breathed again and the room was criss-crossed with rumours. Everyone was convinced that he or she knew what it was really all about.

"He's been throwing stones through windows on the new building site at Appletown!"

"No, I know what it is – he went into the girls' toilet yesterday and pulled Teresa Schofield's knickers down."

"That's not it. He set fire to the grass at the back of the caretaker's shed this morning. He threw his cigarette in there when the handbell went for the end of morning playtime. The groundsman and the caretaker had to get a hose on it to put it out. It nearly burned the shed down. It did! That's what he'll be in trouble for. Just wait and see."

The icicle voice of the teacher broke through the whisperings, and the class settled uneasily to work again with sly glances from under lowered eyebrows, each person sure they knew what Gattland had done and all of them simultaneously glad it was him, and not one of them, who was facing the Furies.

The true story came through slower than rumour, but it was a good enough truth for bursting kids, bloated with speculation. Gattland had stolen the money from the front seat of the bus when it stopped at the depot to get back on schedule. What was going to happen? Would he be expelled? Nobody could remember that ever happening to anyone in the school. Would he get caned? Six of the best? Would his parents be brought into the school and would they be asked to take him home?

Rumours and questions were rife, and none of them based on anything resembling fact, but the excitement of it all held the school in thrall; chatter mysteriously passed from classroom to classroom through the walls, under the floorboards, like a contagious flu in the very air they breathed, from student to student running teacher messages to the office in the corridors, from notes that circulated in books passed around rooms and handed on to other rooms when students went outside for sport. News even moved through the electrical wiring and crept like fevered draughts under every door so that the air was full of voices in the silent, whispering rooms up and down the school.

Those who had shared the money he gave away so generously, cringed in fear and dread of being called up. They hoped in vain that Gattland wouldn't tell. But when he was asked to give back the money – a lot of which he no longer had – it was too much for him to carry on his own, and he gabbled out those with whom he wished to share the blame, dilute his crime and maybe share the punishment as well.

In the end the whole truth, such as it was, came out. And several were summoned to the headmaster's office including three other boys from the senior class.

"Did it hurt?" asked Conor as the other boys walked home that afternoon.

"'Course it bloody hurt! Stupid little get! What do you expect?"

Euan was still smarting from the looks he got from other students gathered at the gates before going home. Some of the looks were sympathetic, but others were gleeful. Conor got the sharp end of his humiliation.

"How many did he give you?" asked Ronan, expecting a similar angry response.

"Six each. Bloody bastard!" Euan had got serious with his cursing by now. "I didn't steal the money. He told us it was his birthday money."

He knew he hadn't really believed it then. Why would Gattland give out money to people who scorned him and were afraid of him, except to win friends? He had simply forced himself to believe it when the money was being passed around, and he had pictured himself in the Cabin on the way home.

"Why did I get into trouble? How was I to know he was telling lies?"

He didn't expect an answer and he never got one. Everyone knew that Gattland was always telling lies.

They walked on quietly, puzzled with the complexities of fairness and justice and why it was always so unfair and unjust for some.

"I have to tell Mum and Dad and I have to write a letter of apology to the bus company and have it signed by Mum and Dad and then bring it into school tomorrow morning and give it to Pop Arden."

That news fell like a wall on them all. The two brothers stared silently at him, eyes wide, unable to hide their sympathy and unable to tough it out, because they knew straight away what would happen at home when their dad found out about this.

The rest of the journey home passed like a jail sentence.

Mum was furious and Euan couldn't remember, as he thought about the incident now, how many times she had called him a 'stupid article'; and she reminded him, as if he needed it, of how angry his dad would be when he got home from the afternoon shift at 10 p.m. that night. Euan didn't want to think about it.

Their parents were hard-working, ambitious for him and all of their boys; and while Mum was usually the one they could get around when they got into trouble, Dad wasn't. He was implacable and tough when it came to them doing wrong. Euan knew he had done wrong and no amount of wheedling would save him.

He wrote the note and Mum signed it and left it for Dad to sign when he got home. He started early shifts in the morning – away by 6 a.m. – so Euan knew he was safe until tomorrow night. His dad would be home at 2 p.m. the next day, and when the boys got home at 4 p.m. there would be a reckoning. Punishment would keep till then, he knew.

And it did come. Even as he thought about it now, grown-up and with his own family, he had a slight shudder with the memory, and with still a touch of guilt for the bag of trouble he had dragged home.

Tea was eaten in silence in the kitchen, but Dad's furrowed brow was smooth and his ears were back – signs that the boys had learned to recognize as anger. The dishes were cleared away and he remembered that they had never been so helpful and uncomplaining about clearing the table, washing dishes and putting them away in the cupboards. In his naivety Euan thought it might get him into his dad's good books and so it might not be so bad. They headed for the front room.

"Euan. Stay here. I want to talk to you."

The rest of the family trooped quietly out and Euan walked, palely flinching, to the furthest place at the back of the kitchen.

The next forty minutes were a whirling mix of confused memories now. Every argument – "I didn't know it was stolen" and "Lots of other kids got some money as well" and "Mr

Arden has already given me six of the cane" – had no effect whatsoever, but the responses he got were punctuated by the flick of the switch across the back and sides of his legs as he tried lifting them to avoid the sting of the thin branch snapped from the garden. He wondered if he got more when he tried, sometimes successfully, to protect his legs, and he thought maybe it was best to let it happen and have a quicker end to it. He tried and he cried and he sighed, thankful it was all over, and he was sent to bed early. There was nowhere else he wanted to be at that moment. He only discovered later that his mum and his brothers had had an equally distressing time listening to the crying and the pleading as they huddled uncomfortably in the front room, their mum toughing it out but heartbroken too, knowing that it was necessary but feeling Euan's pain with him.

A little while later, all three of them had gone to bed. Conor, being the youngest, had the small box room on his own while Ronan shared a bed with Euan. Mum had put them to bed and they had tried to go straight to sleep because they didn't dare to be heard. Conor never had a chance to ask anything about what it was like as he was shepherded off to his tiny room, and Euan remembered he had deliberately had his back to Ronan as he came to bed. He didn't want to talk anyway – too tired with tension and too sore. He remembered that.

And he remembered too that later that night – and it was much later because he had fallen asleep listening to the muffled drumming of conversation from Mum and Dad downstairs – the light on the stairs had gone on, and it had run a halo around the edge of the door. He woke to see his dad looking anxiously through the slice of light and into the room.

When his dad saw him awake he slipped quietly into the room, sat on the bed next to him and put his hand on Euan's head and tousled his hair.

"You all right, son?" he asked.

"I'm fine, Dad," Euan answered, not really meaning it.

"Listen – I don't care who else was involved in this. You're our lad and we want you to grow up straight and decent and true. We want you to be honest so that others can always trust you. We want all our boys to grow up to be fine young men. Do you understand that?"

Euan didn't trust himself to speak, so he merely shuffled a yes with his head on the pillow.

"We've already lost one son and we're not going to lose another in whatever way; we certainly don't want to lose you. Good night now, son. See you tomorrow."

His dad leaned over and kissed him on the forehead and left the room. The stairs light went off, and in the dark a warm tear trickled across Euan's nose and on to his pillow, but his face felt aglow and, after a few soft snuffles, he was happily and soundly asleep in minutes.

Chapter 3

Conor's memories were quite different from those of his two brothers. As he was breaking the news to them he decided on a matter-of-fact, businesslike tone to mask the emotional turmoil he was feeling at the time. He was closest to the whole sad tale, and his dad had also visited him and Tessa before heading off to Canada to Euan's family and then to New Zealand to Ronan, several years ago.

Now that he thought about it, it seemed like a farewell visit – doing the rounds of the family before moving on. Had he been unwell and not told them anything? By all accounts he had been fit and well while in Canada and New Zealand, and they had all agreed he was a picture of health. They all later acknowledged that he wouldn't have told them anything even if there had been a problem; it was not his way. They did agree now, when they looked at it closely, that it resembled very much the closing of a book. Perhaps he had known something. They would never know.

Conor had helped his dad with the planning for his mum's funeral, and now he would rather just get on with organizing this one as well. The planning would take his mind off things, and he would be glad of the distraction. It never crossed his mind that his brothers needed to be there, and he realized how difficult it would be for them to get over in time for the funeral anyway.

He was remembering the terrible summer in 1980 when he and his wife had visited their mum and dad in Longford. Mum had been ill for some time with cancer – part of the reason for the visit – and it was hard to stand by helplessly and watch her fade slowly but steadily while the pain was constant but the patience was steely and resigned.

He flew back again to Ireland, alone, the following April, when she finally died and was buried in Strokestown, near her home town of Kilteevan. He remembered the day after the funeral, his dad coming to the upstairs bedroom at the house in Longford where Conor was staying.

He stood in the doorway staring bleakly at him with bewilderment and sadness in his eyes, and asked, "What am I going to do now?"

It was not the image Conor had of his strong, confident, irrepressible dad. It was a question that Conor had no answer to, but one which he had never forgotten.

His memory was of complete but private distress – his own and his dad's. But it was always Conor's way to disguise any strong feelings with humour. In fact humour was his truth; and for those who didn't recognize it, he could appear flippant and detached. Those who got to know him well knew how sensitive he really was and how at pains he was to make sure he always seemed in control. His job had given him enormous confidence and, despite the very rare moments of uncertainty, he had a sharp mind and a magnum of wit that saw to the heart of every situation. He was the prop still standing when others had collapsed under the weight of seriousness.

In spite of his distress Danny sold the house later that year and bought a dog and a cottage in a small village just outside Galway. He had always liked Galway and he loved dogs, and he must have decided it was time to focus his own life on the things he could still love though they were as driftwood in comparison to the treasure he had lost. He needed to reduce his life down to some basic desires, and these seemed to be a roof over his head in the land he loved, and some companionship.

After a few months he had found some part-time work in a small grocery business, and it was his job to deliver phoned orders to some of the elderly customers who couldn't or wouldn't come into the village – 'that noisy, bustlin' place full of eejits who drank too much'. It had restored some of his vigour and fun after a while of being a 'delivery boy'. He would drive around to deliver their orders in his Fiesta and he would joke with them and give them plenty of cheek and blarney, and was a great favourite with the old ladies in particular.

The manager of the shop was surprised at how quickly his home-delivery customers increased in numbers over the weeks, and when it was a new customer they always finished the order with "And can you send that nice young man Danny around with the order?" The manager thought about it and realized that if you were eighty-five years or older, someone in his early sixties could be seen as a 'young man'.

Their dad had become something of a celebrity in the village and was always going for long walks with his dog and greeting his customers on his days off.

He got to have a very busy and full round of deliveries, but he had returned from his chores on this particular day in July and after a long walk sat down in his favourite chair, with his dog on his lap, and died. It was the crying and barking of the dog that had alerted a neighbour.

Conor was now thinking about a funeral and thinking about getting himself organized to go again to Ireland to bury his dad. He wasn't looking forward to it because it seemed to him, looking at it from the outside, things were in quite a mess and it seemed up to him to sort it all out. There would be no money to worry about – he was sure of that – but who should he inform about his death and who else was there to help with the arrangements?

In the next few weeks it was Tessa who helped keep things together. She steadied his planning and supported all his ideas with balanced concern. With both of his parents gone, he felt that an important part of his life had shrunk too and he was feeling alone and, to some extent, isolated. There seemed to be so many impenetrable folds in the pages of his knowledge about them and their place in their world as kids growing up in Ireland. How had they met? Why had they married in England and settled there? How had their brother, Declan, died, and how did they pull the pieces of their lives together after that? How could you? What about all the places they had lived and the jobs they had done? What was the driving ambition they had had for their own kids and where did it come from?

It was an incomplete story and it had not been copied out in full to reveal very much at all. So many conversations they had not had, and now the time and the opportunity were gone and he wasn't alone in reflecting how little he knew about the two most influential people in his early life. There were pages and pages of untold story about their mum and dad that would remain lost to all of them, and he felt strangely sad and very regretful. He guessed his brothers might be feeling the same.

The last few years should have been ideal to catch up, now that they had time. Their mum and dad had both retired and their three sons, scattered around the globe, were living their own separate lives with their own separate families. That was partly the problem – the gypsy heritage that had kept the wider family apart for so many years. But true to that heritage, his mum and dad had suddenly sold up and decided to return to Ireland, close to where they were both born. Conor's job and family grew and he found that when life took hold of him and shook him like a sand clock. The time, like the sand, rushed out.

There was never enough time or opportunity after that for full family gatherings, where family history and stories of childhood would have helped to fill in some of the gaps that turned into chasms as the years passed.

He saw the danger looming that the three brothers might, in the end, know as little about each other's families as they did about their mum's and dad's.

If both parents had lived for a few more years together, things might have been different for all of them.

PART THREE: ARRIVALS

Chapter 4

2009

Ronan sat quietly at the airport terminal, Heathrow. Why was it called a terminal? It sounded ominous, he thought. He had just got in on his flight from New Zealand (arrived at 1.15 p.m.) and he was waiting for Euan to arrive on a flight from Canada. They hadn't met for thirty-four years, since Euan and Maria had had a year's exchange in 1975 with teachers in Australia and they had come to stay with them in Opotiki for a couple of weeks with the first of their children, Jennifer. So much for good intentions all those years ago to try to see each other more often and strengthen the family ties.

It was 2.20 p.m. and he felt nervous and tired, but excited with anticipation, and there was a tension that was hard to define but borne of anxiety about whether or not they would recognize each other and what would it be like trying to reconnect after all this time? Would there be embarrassing silences? Uncomfortable jokes that didn't cross the culture barrier? Facial expressions that wouldn't match the words that came out, such as "You haven't changed a bit"?

He was, as usual, amazed at the security presence at the bigger airports, especially ones as big as Heathrow, when compared to the much smaller airports of home. He was short on recent experience of the international air-travel circuit (he and Catherine had visited Vietnam and Cambodia two years ago for three and a half weeks), and he felt uncomfortable and mildly guilty, as he always did when in the company of law-enforcement people.

It was about trying to be as normal as possible while not being able to be because of the effort of trying. He kept his bags close as the speaker on the public address system kept reminding people, and he looked around at all the strangers busily about their business or lazing around, tired after long flights and little sleep.

He was weary too, and reflective, and already missing someone to talk to. Catherine had not wanted to come on this trip.

"It's important that you meet with your brothers and do what you have to do in Ireland. I'll stay here and catch up with friends and keep myself occupied. We've discussed it on the phone and in emails and I know Tessa and Maria feel the same; you guys need to do this on your own and we'll see what comes from this. Just take care and I'll see you in about ten days in New York."

It was happening again and it was like déjà vu. Both boys had been working in America for just on three years and were happy there and enjoying the lifestyle with their partners. They had successful jobs and there was a good chance that one or both couples might decide to settle there. Wait and see. It was an irony not lost on the family.

Catherine had been back to England from New Zealand several times in the last few years to visit her mum, who was now in her eighties, and to catch up with her brother, Bernard. She had also been home one time to see her sick dad, who had died just before she arrived in Manchester. She would tidy up a few things at home in New Zealand and then fly out to New York. Ronan would arrive a few days later from England.

In this daydreaming state, with still some time before Euan's flight was due to land, he had lost focus and was not watching the arrivals line as closely as he should have been, so it came as a complete shock when a voice spoke loudly in his ear and said, "How are you, you grey-headed old bastard?"

He stood up abruptly and, for a brief second, stared at the figure in front of him.

"Bloody hell!"

There was no trouble recognizing the face. It was like his own in some ways and like their dad's, and he was too busy looking to say anything more than that.

"Bloody hell!" he said again.

"I see your conversational skills are as good as ever," said Euan in a Canadian drawl that was just not how Ronan remembered his voice.

It took him off guard, so he just continued to stare. He had heard it on the phone many times, but that was disconnected to the face; and now they were put together the voice seemed somebody else's and the face seemed to be miming. He would have to get used to it.

"How did you get here?" asked Ronan.

"I bloody walked – got my feet wet, but I'm here. What sort of a stupid question is that?"

"I meant how come you're here twenty minutes early? You took me off balance."

"Well, that's a good way to greet your big brother after thirty-something years. Hell, would you like me to go out and come in again? Maybe if I wait outside in the baggage area until the time is right?" asked Euan.

"No. Come here, you big daft bugger!"

They hugged while a lifetime of childhood memories somehow passed between them silently.

"You're right about the 'big brother'," said Ronan, pushing his brother to arm's length and looking at his close-fitting jacket. "Is the extra bulk in readiness for winter hibernation? I heard that bears do it in Canada, but I didn't know the humans do it too."

"I didn't come all this way to be insulted, you know," said Euan.

"How far do you usually go?" asked Ronan. "As far as the mirror?"

"Oh, very good," said Euan, "you smart bastard. I should have expected this after some of your emails."

"Come here," said Ronan. "It's good to see you."

And they hugged again.

"You've obviously kept well."

He hadn't changed much either – same old comedy act. Ronan

assumed there would be plenty of that though. In reality he had to admit that Euan was not fat; he just seemed to have got bigger. He couldn't explain to himself what he meant by bigger. The self-conscious stoop of a teenager had changed into the upright posture of a self-confident adult. He wasn't big as some of their uncles had been; he wasn't even that tall. It was more a bulk that was evenly spread and was carried with an easy lightness. Certainly from a distance he looked bigger than when he was up close. Conor, he knew, was tall and lanky and still slightly self-conscious about his teenage growth spurts, which came as fast as echoes.

"At least I don't look as if I've been through a famine," said Euan, casting a reproachful eye over his brother's slight but solid build.

"Maybe, but I don't look as If I caused one," replied Ronan. "I reckon your jacket weighs more than I do."

Euan ignored that one. It was early days yet.

"What's with the tin frame? Hey, do you remember when we used to call Conor 'Tin Ribs'? God, he looked like he didn't have long left. A scythe in his hand and a black hood and cloak and he would have got the part."

"No decent food or drink in New Zealand, then, I see?"

"No properly sized jackets in Canada either from the looks of it. You look good and it's great to see you," said Ronan with a tone of repentance. "I've thought about this day and these next few days for a long time, and now it's happening. I can't believe it."

"Yes, it is. All thanks to Conor. His idea to do all this."

"Yes, you're right. It's a great idea. We needed to do this," said Ronan.

"Yep. So we'd better get going. See how Tin Ribs is. He's expecting us at 4 p.m., so we'd better go and get my bags. What was it we had to do? Bus from Heathrow Central to Watford Junction and he'll meet us there? About a fifty-minute bus ride, he reckons."

Ronan nodded. "OK, the bags first."

"You haven't claimed them already and stuffed them inside

that jacket, have you?" asked Ronan as they walked off together to the baggage carousel, Ronan carrying his bags with him.

"Look at all your stuff. Why didn't you just bring Catherine's handbag for cabin luggage? You would get all your tiny person's clothes in there without having to bring a suitcase. Do you do all your clothes shopping in the children's department?" asked Euan.

"Do you buy all yours at the Over-Sized Jacket Shop?"

"Is everything about you small?" A sideways grin accompanied that one.

They were like a couple of kids teasing and laughing with each other as they headed off to claim the baggage. They were both tired and had covered something like 20,000 miles of tired flying between them, but they already felt comfortable, and more quickly relaxed than they had expected to be, in the folds again of family.

It wasn't quite like never having been away, but it felt as close as they could ever get to living the cliché.

Chapter 5

The idea for the get-together had indeed been Conor's. He had spent time a couple of years ago organizing a headstone for his dad's grave after a trip to Ireland when he and Tessa had decided to have a look at the graves as well as have some holiday time together. They were shocked to see the state of his dad's grave in the cemetery in Oranmore, though when they thought about it they realized it was twenty-three years since the funeral and some sort of change at the graveyard was inevitable. He remembered there had been an iron cross about a foot high with a round porcelain plaque covering the cross juncture. The rusted cross was still buried deep in the small stones that were covering the grave, but the porcelain was nowhere in sight. He later found shards of the plaque, after tearing at the profusion of grass and nettles, and pieced them together to remind himself of the words.

Danny Farrell
Died 23 July 1986
Rest in Peace

He had taken the pieces home and sent a piece of the broken porcelain to each of his brothers. Then he set about organizing, with a local monumental mason, to have a proper and durable headstone placed on the grave – small and uncomplicated. It had meant coming back alone to finish the job a few months later to make sure it was done properly this time. He was pleased with the result, and so were the brothers when they were sent photographs.

He knew his dad always said, "I don't want any fuss," but then he thought, 'We all say that, don't we?' Anyway, it was about him and his brothers and the memories they wanted to keep. And the new gravestone would at least give them those.

DANNY FARRELL
1919–1986
LOVED ALWAYS
Euan, Ronan and Conor

The one thing he couldn't deal with was a wild fuchsia that was growing right in the middle of the grave. In spite of his frantic efforts, and his even more frantic cursing, he couldn't manage to even disturb the soil or the small white stones at the base of the stem of the plant. He gave up after a while. He imagined Euan, 'the Sleepwalker', would be scared shitless that if he pulled too hard he might pull up the coffin and their dad with it. However it had got there, the fuchsia had an iron grip on the earth, and maybe on their dad, and was not letting go.

When he told his brothers the story, Ronan, at least, had a good laugh at his fanciful fears and his own images and fancies of how it would have looked and the state he would have got himself into. Conor was a most creative and amusing wordsmith when it came to frustration.

He had also visited his mum's grave in Strokestown that same holiday, and, to his relief, it was in much better shape and was obviously being looked after. It had almost made him feel better.

It was, then, four years after this trip that Conor had suggested another trip.

"We should meet up in England at my place, visit the graves and do whatever is necessary to bring them back to shape, though no doubt it will only be Dad's that needs attention. It will be great, apart from the fact that I'll have to put up with you two eating me out of house and home and drinking all my booze."

Ever the sociable one!

The time was right and the time for excuses was gone. It was time to focus on family. Their own families were independent. Euan was retired; Ronan had accumulated enough holiday time at his job to spend close to ten days in England and Ireland; and if they all came together in mid to late August, Conor would be on holiday from his principal's job. It couldn't have been better.

The wives had all agreed to it provided that the three of them promised to plan a holiday for all of them in England the following year with all the wives and husbands – a chance also to catch up with old college friends and other family. And so plans were drawn up. Insulting emails were exchanged; abusive phone calls were made to each other; and then it was on again off again with hesitations coming in like pelting rain.

Suddenly, out of nowhere, it settled in, and in a short space of months everything stacked close together like baggage claim and, just when it was least expected, the bags were packed, tickets were booked and it was all happening in late August 2009.

Chapter 6

"OK, that's my lot," said Euan as he grasped his last suitcase from the carousel – a big heavy swollen wreck of a thing with straps to hold its waist in and keep it from bursting.

"Look at that! Everything does come supersized in Canada!" said Ronan.

"You said it, kid! But don't get jealous!"

They caught the bus and the talk turned sad, but it was punctuated with laughter most of the way; they were trying to catch up as quickly as possible on all the things that had been talked through or were left unspoken over the years.

Euan talked about the summer he and Maria had gone over to Ireland and met Tessa and Conor and Mum and Dad, and he spoke of how ill Mum had been though she'd been trying not to show it. It had been a depressing experience because he and Maria were unable to stay and Mum died soon after and Dad was all alone. That left a brief guilty feeling too hard to overcome, and they let the chatter on the bus fill the aching silence for a while.

As they worked their way with the crowd of passengers towards the bus exit they quietened in anticipation. Would they recognize Conor?

There had been family photographs sent back and forth, but sparingly, and often they'd been taken from a reasonable distance away to spare the vanity. They had talked about Conor on the bus ride – his quirky sense of humour, his rudeness to all and sundry wrapped in playful teasing, irony and Johnny Walker, which you had to understand if you were not to be offended. Not that he cared if you were. On the phone it seemed to make him laugh even harder so that your eyes watered, the breath left you and you could hardly speak. The calls would usually start with a groan and then a terse "What do *you* want?" It was after these pleasantries that the insults started.

Suddenly, Ronan pointed him out: "That's him. Long string bean. I'd recognize that face and that way of standing anywhere."

"Yep, you're right. That's him."

Ronan went up to him first to break Conor's motionless reserve.

"Hi, Conor. How are you?" he said, and he reached up and gave him a hug.

"I'm not sure yet. I'll tell you when you've gone. Get your hands off!" he said, frantically dusting his shirt and jeans off with his hands. "I don't know where you've been." And then the mischievous roll of laughter as he pretended to dust himself free of contamination again. "You New Zealanders are full of sheep diseases. Yours has always been foot and mouth. You can't speak without—"

"Yeah, yeah, I know," finished Ronan: "without putting my foot in it."

Euan moved to grasp Conor. "How are you, buddy?" he said as he too hugged Conor.

"Don't get too familiar. We've only just met. Who are you anyway?" he asked, looking Euan up and down.

"How are you, you long streak of insults?" asked Euan.

"Oh, now I recognize you. You must be Euan. Nobody else could do such a poor impersonation of a Canadian accent. Insults? I haven't started yet. I'm breaking you in easy. Are we going to stand here all day cracking wind or are we going to move and get home? I need to start soon because it could take hours with all this luggage. It's only a VW hatchback, you know, not a furniture removal van. What's in these cases? Mountains? Lakes? Pines? Sheep?"

They squeezed everything into the car and set off, Euan in the front and Ronan in the back. On the way the conversation turned to ageing and looks – how the passing years had treated (or mistreated) them and particularly regarding hair and hair loss.

"Isn't it funny", said Ronan, playing with the back of Conor's head, "how hair grows where you don't want it to grow and grows everywhere where it's not supposed to grow and it's not wanted?"

"I know," said Conor, pushing Ronan's hand away. "A hair on the head is worth two on the brush. I've got hairs between my toes now. They're everywhere except where I'd like them."

"Yeah, like in your nose," agreed Euan. "I yank mine out all the time."

"I thought we were talking about hairs up the nose. We don't want to hear about what you get up to in the shower, you yanker," said Conor.

"Sometimes I think that hairs that grow in my ears or on my earlobes have come off my head, when I've had it cut, and grown back there; so I'm thinking of gathering up the hairs on my face and collar after a haircut and sticking them back on my head until they take root," said Ronan.

"Don't forget some of that spare bush round your arsehole," laughed Conor.

Ronan ignored that one.

Conor continued: "You must get a lot of cut hairs going down the inside of your pants and then taking root, I've never seen anything like it, as I remember. Just take some from there and put them on your head and you'll look like a haystack on a fence post!" He laughed loud and long at the joke, and it was impossible not to join in with the sheer joy and familial rudeness and cheek of it.

But the talk settled as they all knew there was too much to get through, in too short a time, to make it all a joke. They talked of symptoms of age and memories of youth and the slight differences between the two times in life; of family, of immortality through your kids and of what may or may not come after. The journey passed in no time as they talked of many things and spiced their conversation more carefully and cautiously with playful humour and avoided talking about their mum and dad. They soon arrived at Conor's place.

Chapter 7

It was a comfortable detached house in Knebworth – part of the London commuter belt – and it had a pleasant, very English frontage and a spacious back garden. Around the suburb on most sides was the countryside, the best of both worlds, and they were fortunate to have arrived during a late summer sunburst towards the end of a simmering August.

As they got out of the car both Euan and Ronan took a deep breath of the English air. It was as if they needed to breathe fully and deeply again to remind themselves of the warming nostalgic smells and sounds of what for them had been home for most of their teenage years and a portion of their young adulthood. It was strange how in a matter of seconds so many memories came rushing back in – a warm gust of air on a temperate, unsettled breeze.

"Are you always sure you made the right decision when you left this country, Euan?" asked Ronan.

"Strange question. I've only just got here. Why do you ask?"

"Oh, just curious," replied Ronan as casually as he could.

"I think so," answered Euan after a long pause, the tone of his voice sounding less convincing than the words. "What about you?"

"I think so too . . . most of the time," answered Ronan, carefully avoiding the consequences of taking too long to answer. He wasn't ready just now to have that discussion.

"I think I know now why you asked," said Euan, smiling at Ronan.

"Can you two stop blathering and help me get the gear in or neither of you'll be staying in this country – or not at my place anyway." Conor started pulling cases and bags out of the car and dropping them on the driveway. "What the fuck is that?" he asked as he pulled out Euan's case of creased leather and straps. "Is it a dead reindeer? Why'd you bring that?"

"He's so full of brotherly love," said Ronan.

"I thought it was something else," said Euan.

Conor ignored their comments and moved off to unlock and open the front door, leaving them to it. With a smirk on their faces and a shake of their heads they picked up what they could on the first shift and moved inside.

"Second right at the top of the stairs, fat fella; first on the left, hairy arse," shouted Conor. "I'll put the kettle on unless you want a Johnny Walker?"

The silence answered.

"OK. OK. Tea or coffee it is, ya boring bastards!"

"Pity Tessa isn't here," said Ronan, coming down the stairs after putting his case and bag in the bedroom. "She loves her sailing, doesn't she? Why didn't you go with her? I thought you loved Greece."

"You two took so long to make up your minds to come that she booked this well before you had sorted things out."

He didn't tell them that she had left so that the three brothers could have all the time together. She had agreed with Catherine that it was important for them to do this. There would be another time for them all to catch up.

"I was looking forward to a couple of weeks on my own, and then you decide to come, for God's sake! I wish I had gone with her now, but she prefers Clare to me."

"Very perceptive woman," said Euan, trundling into the lounge, carrying his shoes. "Aw, heck, can we get takeaways tonight, then?"

"What are you saying?" asked Conor, handing out tea and coffee with consummate ease. "Sugar? Milk? I have dinner almost ready, so like it or lump it."

"Can we go for a walk soon?" asked Ronan, sipping his tea.

"What time does it get dark here in the summer? I seem to remember it was quite late."

He couldn't wait to be reminded of the countryside he had always loved as a kid and still loved now.

"I see you haven't changed, have you? You could never sit still for long. Look – we can go for a walk if you want to, if we have to. I've got most of the tea prepared. Just have to cook it now."

Conor didn't trust microwaves and so he'd never bought one.

"Can we just finish our drinks first?" asked Euan. "I need to rest my feet."

"Sure, no rush," said Ronan, draining his tea and jumping up to grab his shoes.

Euan and Conor glanced at each other, and raised eyebrows and a resigned smile said it all.

They stayed as they were, but put their shoes back on. Conor grabbed his keys and they went out through the door and into the cosy warmth and the intoxicating and evocative fragrances of a folding summer's day: the early evening smells of newly sawn wood and freshly mown grass.

"What a glorious late afternoon!" said Ronan, and he stopped and took a very deep breath, savouring the smells of late summer that he remembered so well and that triggered so many memories of them as young boys, often fighting, always on the run, frequently in trouble and endlessly, imaginatively happy. He knew the memories were half fantasy, half fact, all polished by the brush of time into something quite precious.

Around one corner, past the end houses in the street and they were into the countryside proper, quicker than either Ronan or Euan had expected. No footpath, just a seamless meeting of road hedges on low banks of wild grasses and fields stretched out like patched cloth. It was the closing warmth of those English summer late afternoons and early evenings and the gentleness of the sun that had stuck most in Ronan's head and had, in their absence from his later experience, grown into something quite mythical and mystical – the idylls of boyhood.

He cast a sideways squinting glance across at Euan as they walked along, and he thought he saw a look of dreamy concentration and contentment on his brother's face as the waning sun, off to Euan's left, cast golden light around his features. He was staring ahead, face leaning forward, and he seemed to be daring the countryside to try to entice and seduce him with its undeniable charm and his own childhood memories.

Euan felt, rather than saw, Ronan looking at him, and he glanced at Ronan and smiled contentedly.

'He feels it too,' thought Ronan. 'I know he does.'

But he was reluctant to break the spell. He wanted to let it carry them both for a while longer. He was aware though that nostalgia was like a drug, and he had no wish to indulge it too much.

They strolled on in silence for a while – three elderly figures no longer looking or feeling their age and testing their lightness of step, the result of a slow-growing comfortableness with each other that placed them together like jigsaw pieces, a disconnected but inevitable fit. While no one admitted to it, it had taken less time to happen than any of them had dared to hope. Parts of their misgivings and anxieties had quietly drifted away like the noise of the day, and they settled gently into each other's company like early leaf fall.

Euan was actually thinking how good it was to be walking along a country lane with his two younger brothers again. They had done this often as kids, but not along the same road and not through the same countryside and not for the same reasons. It was home and had a comfortable, safe feel to it in those days. It was not a wasteful pursuit. They picked up stones and hurled them at gateposts, the gates leading to cow-shitted courtyards, the courtyards leading to barns stored with hay waiting for kids to jump around in it, the hay barns leading to mud-splattered tractors, squat and satisfied, with just a few red scratches like wounds to show that they had once been shiny and new. Then the dogs would come to the gate and bark them down the road. They would look in birds' nests as they squirmed their way up the trunks of hawthorn trees to reach inside for the little oval skies, coming away with more red on them than the tractors from the fierce thorns of childhood freedom, but feeling like explorers in the new morning landscape that was such a simple source of contentment for them.

They couldn't explain it, but it was at times like that that their spirits soared and their hearts sang. Those years together had been short in family terms as they has gone to secondary schools and made friends with others in their own age groups, and had moved on with other interests before Euan had left for Canada, Ronan had left for New Zealand and Conor had developed deeper roots in England.

They drifted along now in a silence that spoke of reconnection that didn't need conversation, and the dwindling day closed around them like a darkening wood that seemed to promise days of warmth and protection and unknown places – the beginning of feeling safe and secure in each other's company was taking a hold on them like the earth they walked on and felt anchored by.

They didn't know, and couldn't know, how alike their thoughts were about youth and how short it had been and how optimistic they all were, individually, that these few days would be a time they would all remember for a long time.

Conor stopped to pick and eat some blackberries, which were all along one side of the road.

"Try some of these," he said. "They're delicious. Nature's bounty. Don't you wish you lived in paradise too?"

If he expected a sensible answer, he didn't get one.

"Is this instead of dessert?" asked Euan.

Conor pretended to be offended. "In your case; any more cheek like that and it'll be instead of dinner and accommodation."

He wondered what his two brothers were thinking. Were they thinking now of their own countrysides and making comparisons? Did they still remember the countryside of home and how often they searched its trails and found tons of excitement? Did this fall short of what they were used to, now that the memories would have faded?

'I wonder where I would be now if I had emigrated as well. Maybe I should have done. Maybe I'm the "stop at home". Maybe that's the way they see me. Good job for Mum and Dad that I was here. I wonder if they think of that. I'm sure they do. I hope they do.'

"Mmm! Pretty good," said Euan. "In fact, very good. I love the road-dust taste," he said mischievously, slowly filling his face.

They sauntered on, easy walking, occasionally stopping, along the narrow, winding lane heaped at the sides with grasses, wild flowers, hawthorns and blackberries and interspersed with oak. They looked across fields separated by hedges and packed in places with an outburst of trees containing a density of birds pouring out a chorus of evensong; they hugged the hedges, feet tipping sideways into a shallow gully, and leaned down to hold on to the grasses as cars pushed the warm air of the evening, mixed with fumes, against their screwed-up faces; they listened to the ring-necked doves with their blunt but distinct cooing while black-rag crows flakked and arced across tumbling skies; they engaged in scatterings of conversation and pondered their own private doubts and fears and feelings as time and distance moved on and closed in. There were even memories in the indolent drone of flies in the lazy air and the small clouds of gnats that mostly broke away as they moved through the warm night in great ease and contentment. Every sight, sound and smell brought back happy times for the two visitors to their homeland.

They had been walking for just over an hour when Conor broke the mood, saying, "We should start heading home, back the way we came. We can keep going this way if you like, but it will take us further away before we loop back around in a large circle at the end of this road up there by the sign. We need to reserve some time for drinking."

"Good idea," agreed Ronan, and they headed back to the house the way they had come, taking the direct route, as Conor suggested, rather than the longer, roundabout way.

By the time Ronan and Euan had their shoes off, Conor had cracked open three bottles of beer, had taken three glasses outside to the garden table and parked his long frame in a chair. The other two joined him quickly and drank easily of a Suffolk ale.

"Great countryside, beautiful house, warm evening, fine ale, shit company. Still, you can't have everything," said Euan, bellowing, and he got a blessing of flicked ale in the face from Conor and Ronan for his sap.

After a dinner that was substantial and 'surprisingly tasty', they said, 'considering it was cooked by Conor', the evening wore on with untidy conversation. It covered many topics, mostly lightly, and it was really a scrambled skimming of a lot of things that were important for them to eventually clear. For the moment they were spoken and opened up in the early stages of their renewed relationship; but they weren't tipped out. They touched on family and what it meant, feelings of home – but they were no longer sure where that was – and was there more after life and where was it lived?

Their confidence with each other grew as the evening closed in, but there was still a sense that some topics were like thin ice on a giant lake and they really had to tread carefully as they moved out towards the middle. None of them wanted to tread too heavily or too quickly on some parts in case they would not hold the weight of memory and would send them all crashing through and everything would go cold.

"The biggest struggle for me", said Conor, "is staying alive to enjoy life, not stuck trying to answer your difficult questions about why we're here and what happens next. Who gives a fuck? Just get on with it! You'll find out soon enough!"

There was still the cheek and the insults, but they were the backdrop to the conversation now rather than the mask in front of it. They merely acted as a canvas to paint their safer thoughts on to while the real issues for them all still drifted just out of reach in the fading light of the front room.

So they played safe.

"Do you know," said Ronan, "it doesn't matter how long I'm away from England, I still think the history here is unbelievable. Do you remember when we used to cycle to Chester and we thought it was really adventurous to walk around the Roman wall of the ancient city? I never thought about it then, but I have since – a lot. We were walking in the footsteps of Roman soldiers who had watched and patrolled there 1,100 years before! I find that spooky."

"And? Your point?" asked Conor.

"You can ask that, Conor, because it's there all the time for you, so you don't really know what you would be missing if it wasn't there. You're so lucky, if you use your imagination you're as much a part of the past as you are of the present, and it's so continuous when you visit places like that."

"He's right, Conor." Euan joined in the conversation. "Canada is a recent part of the English past and so is New Zealand, I know what Ronan means about the history here. I miss it too, but I've realized that history is built up from the dreams and ambitions of people and, while neither I nor Maria will ever make the pages of history, I contribute just by being there and having family; and they too build, as well as they can, the history of the country – we all do. You can't jump into a ready-made history all the time. Sometimes you have to be part of the foundation that others will talk about and add to when we are long gone."

"I think under the foundation is the best place for both of you," chipped in Conor.

"This place is so beautiful, like so many others over here. I remember our school camps in the Lake District and how I was constantly in awe of the beauty of the place. It made it hard to breathe sometimes, and when I saw a beautiful part of the area I just couldn't find words to say what I was seeing and what I thought. I felt that sometimes my face was always up to the heavens, speechless in that way that words don't cover the wonder of what's in front of you. I got straight into Wordsworth when I got back to school after the first camp, and I've always had a great affection for some of his best poems inspired by the Lakes. He at least could find the words."

Ronan seemed lost in reflection and for an awkward moment there was silence. Conor soon fixed that, though he seemed reluctant to break the mood and damage the reminiscences.

"I've just found a few words. I think we should get to bed," he said suddenly, "before we get stuck in one of the pages of some old poetry book. We have to be up early tomorrow. Flight's at eight forty-five in the morning and we need to be there on time. We're up at 6 a.m." There was a protesting spluttering from his two brothers, but he brushed it aside: "It's a bit of a drive from here; and if you're late booking in, you don't get on the plane – simple as that. That's one of the reasons the flights were so cheap. Another is that you get no refreshments unless you buy them – they tell me you'll be paying extra for everything soon. By the way, you find your own seats, so don't you dare take excess cabin luggage. I haven't booked any hold luggage for any of us. We'll buy toiletries in Ireland when we get there. We're only there for seven or eight days, so wear the same old durable stuff and bring a coat just in case. In Ireland it's always about to rain, and when it stops it's about to rain."

"How long's the flight?" asked Euan. "Or do we pay for that information as well?"

"Na," replied Conor. "About eighty minutes."

"How much were the tickets, so we can settle up?" asked Ronan.

"Don't worry about that," replied Conor. "You can buy me some meals and a couple of drinks. It wasn't expensive."

He wouldn't take any persuading, so Euan and Ronan decided to drop it and pay it back some other way.

"Jimmy next door has offered to drive us to the airport in my car. He's an English teacher, so he should be able to talk his way through an early start with his wife even though he's supposed to be on holiday. He'll come back here, park the car and head back to bed, maybe. He'll just drop us and leave. He's offered to come back and pick us up when we're coming home. I agreed."

"OK," said Euan. "I'm away. I need my beauty sleep."

Nobody spoke.

"You should have gone hours ago, then," said Conor eventually. "Anyway, we don't have that amount of time."

"I'm off, then," said Ronan.

Another silence.

"Notice there was no disagreement," said Conor again.

They put the glasses in the dishwasher along with the dinner dishes. Conor turned it on and they turned out the lights in the lounge and the kitchen and headed up the stairs.

As Ronan was about to enter his room at the end of the landing, he said, "Hey, guys?"

"What?" said Conor with an attempt at feigned impatience.

"Really great to see you both again after all this time," said Ronan.

"Yeah," said Euan, turning in his doorway, his face beaming, "real good. Wish Mum and Dad could see this."

"They can," said Ronan.

"Yeah, yeah. Piss off to bed, both of you," said Conor. "You won't be feeling so bloody nostalgic in a few hours when you have to get up."

And he turned into his bedroom and closed the door.

"He just gets so emotional," said Ronan.

"I know. He's just like his emails: all love and warmth. He'll be asking to read your poetry books soon."

They both closed their doors, and before long the house was silent and their dreams and memories drifted in the quietness and filled in the spaces where they had been.

Chapter 8

The following morning was a race and a panic. Last-minute packing of backpacks, trying to work the bathroom and the toilet between them.

"I'm next! Have you finished in here?"

"Can't stop the bleeding, bloody shaving! Fucking hate it!"

Getting some toast and jam ready downstairs. Needing more time. Eating on the run.

"Everything's steamed up in here!"

Bodies whizzing up and down the stairs.

"Can you just move that out of the way?"

"Time's running out! Is anyone in here?"

"Always cut my face when I'm in a rush."

Moving round and through one another.

"Oh, God, who did that in the toilet?"

"Get a move on!"

Last-minute checks of passports and money, wallets and document holders. Bloody hell! Jam marks on jackets and jammy fingers. Dishwasher being emptied of dinner dishes and drinks.

"How long does a shower take you?"

Dishwasher being filled with breakfast dishes.

"Bathroom's available!"

"What's the time?"

Dishwasher filled again and turned on.

"Look at the size of that backpack!"

"Sod's feckin' law."

"Hurry up!"

Someone's knocking on the door! "Are you guys ready?" through the letterbox.

"'Course we aren't!"

"Can't forget my rain jacket."

"Got any tissues I can grab so I can dab my cuts?"

Usual anxieties: What have I forgotten? Have I got money? Have I packed something I can't take in?

"I warned you about letterboxes and intruders."

"What's the time?"

All the lights are out – check all the doors and windows are locked.

"Where's my fucking house keys?"

"Everyone out the door – quick!"

Keys to Jimmy waiting outside with a knowing grin on his face.

"How are you, Jimmy?"

"Good to see you."

Introductions: "Ronan, Euan. How are you?"

"Shit!"

"Put the bags in the back. Get in the car for God's sake."

"How should I know?"

"What a mess!"

Stopped. Stopped dead. Except for the car.

Like the noise and tumbling chaos of a cyclone it was over. They settled back exhausted and let Jimmy drive them away from the tumultuous house.

PART FOUR: DEPARTURES

Chapter 9

After a largely uneventful journey they arrived outside the terminal at Gatwick: departures.

"Always seem to be in departure lounges," said Ronan.

"Look out," said Euan. "There's an analogy of some kind on its way."

Jimmy caressed the kerb and opened the boot to start getting the bags out. They all climbed out to help, and soon they had all been piled on the ground like a cairn.

"Thanks, Jimmy," said Conor, and he gave him a manly hug. "I owe you one. See you in eight days' time: 2 September, 2-p.m. arrival. OK?"

"OK, mate," said Jimmy.

"Yeah, thanks a lot, Jimmy," said Ronan and Euan, almost in unison.

"Really good of you to do this for us," said Ronan. "Makes it easier."

"It is a pleasure because you're with him," Jimmy said, pointing in Conor's direction. "I'm glad you're here at last so I can see what all the talk was about."

Conor was unaware of the conversation. He was heading for the departure doors when Jimmy said to Euan and Ronan, "You're very lucky."

"I know," said Euan. "Waited ages for this holiday—"

Jimmy interrupted him: "I'm not talking about the holiday. I'm talking about lucky – really lucky."

"For an English teacher, you're hard to understand," said

Ronan. "What do you mean by lucky? You mean we're lucky? How are we lucky?" he asked, taking in himself and Euan and even the receding figure of Conor with a gathered-up gesture.

"Because you get on so well together and the feeling of family is so tight," replied Jimmy.

"Were you not listening in the car?" asked Euan.

"Yes, every word," said Jimmy. "And I watched you all too. In spite of all the ribbing and the insults you're great friends. He's been talking about this for weeks and he's been so excited, but of course you have to read it in his movements, his whole attitude, the lift of his shoulders. He always disguises his real feelings with jokes. It's not a refuge from the truth; it is the truth if you can see it. You have to know him well or you'd take offence. You can say anything heartless and rude that would test any friendship every time the three of you open your mouths, and all it generates is laughter and a greater bond between you. I'm buggered if I know how you do it."

The two remaining brothers stood there bemused, wondering why something that happened so naturally should be such a source of amazement.

"Here you are after half a day and you talk like old friends can talk, without offence and without barriers. I think he was quite nervous about this whole reunion thing."

"Hell, Jimmy," laughed Ronan, "I feel as if I've just been reviewed like a good poem. Do you do this all the time? Are we what English teachers practise on? A piece of poetry needing in-depth reading got in the car with me this morning, so I thought, 'I'll warm up for my day by working out its meaning.'"

"Look at him!" said Euan, indicating Conor going through the sliding doors and into the departure area to check in. "There's our great friend and brother disappearing into the terminal without even looking around to see if we've been crushed under a giant slab of critical analysis. Do you really believe all that, Jimmy? We're still nervous of each other," he admitted.

"He's a great neighbour, a good man and a very funny one," said Jimmy, smiling over his shoulder as he headed for the driver's seat. "You don't realize how lucky you are!" he shouted.

"It must be great to be able to sing the same song together so comfortably!"

"Hey, Jimmy, thanks, man. Have to go. I suspect you know him better than we do just at the moment," said Ronan, realizing Conor was out of sight.

He and Euan picked up their bags and headed across the drop-off lanes after him, amazed by what they had just heard.

"That was the strangest conversation," said Ronan, unsure of what else to say, "and we haven't even got to Ireland yet. He was serious, you know?"

"Where have you two been?" asked Conor. "We don't have a lot of time. We need to check in."

"Just being good classmates and making up for your lack of gratitude. We were having a good chat with Jimmy, sir," said Euan.

"Jimmy's an English teacher, as I told you – full of bullshit, just like you, Ronan," said Conor, eyeing them both warily, and he moved off to check in.

Euan and Ronan looked at each other, smiled knowingly and followed him dutifully. There were several things that neither Ronan nor Euan was prepared for, like not having designated seats and having to rush to get on as quickly as possible if they wanted to be sitting near to or next to each other. They realized that all the other seasoned travellers already knew this, and by the time they got through all the check-in procedures they were pretty near the back of the boarding queue anyway.

In no time at all they were on the plane and heading for Ireland. Service was brisk and cool, and it could just as easily have been a bus with a conductor. They felt vengeful and bought nothing. It was a laughter-free flight though the trumpeted boast, through the plane's speaker system, of another flight arriving on time was so unexpected, and so like a street parade or carnival loudhailer, that they smiled grudgingly in spite of themselves.

PART FIVE: ARRIVALS

Chapter 10

In just over eighty minutes they had landed at Dublin Airport and they taxied between Aer Lingus planes – the romance of the name had stuck in their heads since childhood – and came to a halt. Everyone rushed to get out once the seat-belt signs went off, as if they were glad to get back to the real world and escape the cold welcome and get into a warm arrivals lounge.

They only had cabin luggage, so there were no queues for bags, and they went through the exit doors and into the Irish air. Though it didn't, they felt sure it smelled different from the air in England: good ale, peat, farmland, drystone walls, mown hay, cigarette smoke, donkeys and happy memories. In fact it smelled of plane exhausts, cheap fatty-food outlets and, once outside, car and bus fumes and heavily smoke-filled air. But they weren't going to give up easily the memories that get rosier and brighter the further away from them you grow in age.

Conor seemed to know his way around from his previous few trips, and soon had them all on an Airlink service bus into Dublin city, which took them into O'Connell Street in just over thirty minutes via the Port Tunnel.

It took some time, once they got off the bus, heading one way, doubling back, going around a square and past the same places several times before eventually finding the hotel in Parnell Square, where they were staying. For a while there it felt like any other city: frustrating, impersonal and busy with or without you. They went to the reception desk, where they were greeted by a young lady with a pronounced European accent, who asked them to fill in a number of details. Ronan and Euan asked for their passports to be locked in a safe in a room behind the reception counter, then they all got the keys to their rooms and took the lift to the third floor. They went separately along the corridor into rooms that were alongside each other in a line.

"What do you reckon?" asked Conor. "Fifteen minutes to get acclimatized to the room and then we'll meet in my room and go into the town?"

"Sounds good to me," said Ronan, and Euan agreed.

After several tries at swiping the card and racing to get the door open before the green light went off, Ronan finally managed to get his door open. The other two had been standing, one foot inside their doors, the other out in the corridor, in growing amusement, taunting Ronan as his anger and frustration grew.

"It's a good job that you're technologically illiterate in New Zealand and you still use keys the size of crescent spanners. Imagine if you went out to your silly bloody street letterboxes to collect your letters and the front door closed behind you and you only had a swipe card to get back in! You'd end up having to kick your own door in or break a window just to get back in your own house," said Conor.

"He probably uses the cat flap," said Euan. "Do you want a hand or do you enjoy public humiliation?"

"Piss off, both of you."

With that, Ronan fell in through the door as he pushed as hard as he could to end the embarrassment. A few seconds later he came out, contorted himself to grab his bag and keep the door open with one foot, slipped back into his room like a letter into an envelope and disappeared with a cry of victory drowned out by the slamming door.

"Yes-s-s!"

The other two grinned, chuckled, muttered and shrugged into their rooms.

Chapter 11

"The top o' the mornin' to ya! Well, afternoon, then. Right, where are we going?" asked Euan, as the three of them, having unwrapped their rooms, made a coffee or three with the supply in their rooms, went to ground in the lift and waited as Ronan put some more of his valuables in the safe at reception.

"We'll go left out of here, down to the bottom of the hill, left again into Parnell Street, and then it's right and we're on O'Connell Street. We'll have a wander along there towards O'Connell Bridge – see what turns up."

That was Conor's plan, and the others accepted that he seemed to know his way around and probably would lead them somewhere pretty interesting.

When they turned into O'Connell Street they all felt they were walking in history. In their childhood it had figured in the few more serious conversations that they had heard in their home or heard in the homes of others of their dad's family when they had gone to Slough and Fareham to visit their relations.

They moved down the street slowly, taking in the sights and sounds as if it could get through their skin. The General Post Office was not to be missed, and they mingled with a handful of customers and several policemen and marvelled at the statue of Cu Chulainn in the main foyer with its black sheen and strong lines and the strength imprisoned in bronze. It had been placed there to commemorate the 1916 Uprising.

"He looks as if he's tied to that rock," said Euan. "Wonder what that's about?"

"I can answer that for you," said Conor. "It was his last fight. He died young and he is said to have been a fearsome fighter who went through some sort of physical and psychological transformation when in battle. He was dangerous to be near, whether you were friend or foe. He tied himself to this standing stone after receiving a mortal wound from a spear thrown by his enemy, because he wanted to die on his feet."

"And the bird on his shoulder?" quizzed Euan.

"That's a raven," continued Conor. "Cu Chulainn's enemies wouldn't come anywhere near his standing body even when he was so close to death. It was only when the raven landed on his shoulder that his enemies believed it was safe enough to approach. The raven was thought to be the goddess Morrigan, the Shapeshifter in Celtic mythology and a harbinger of death."

"Why the raven?" persisted Euan. "Just a symbol of death? Such an ugly-looking thing, isn't it? Why not anoth—"

"Don't misunderstand the raven," interrupted Conor. "Some ornithologists consider it the most intelligent of the bird species – very skilful in flight, a mimic, mischievous, and it mates, generally, for life. I suppose that counters the likelihood of intelligence though," he concluded.

"That's right!" said Ronan, remembering. "You used to do bird spotting, didn't you? I couldn't believe it when you said that in one of your emails. It just doesn't seem to be your thing. Do you still do it?"

"It's the only time I can watch and listen to birds without having to put up with their endless prattle," he countered ironically. "No, I don't still do it, but it's a time thing. I may take it up again when I retire."

"Well, thanks for the history and natural-world lessons, you two," said Euan, a little bit sheepishly. "I feel like I've just been put in the special class by my two top-stream brothers. Do you ever stop being teachers, you two? I gave it up years ago."

"You just happened to ask about something that we both had a small interest in, and together it sounds impressive; but that'll be the last of my knowledge about ancient Ireland apart from a few other bits and pieces and of course the Guinness." Ronan was trying to mollify Euan's obvious embarrassment.

Ronan and Euan went across to the sales counter and bought some stamps and postcards to send to their friends, their kids and their wives. They decided to write and post some of them there and then before going out on to O'Connell Street and down towards the river.

Parts of Dublin, they decided, looked like any other city – cosmopolitan, occupied and self-absorbed – but they were aware of many different accents after naively expecting everyone to speak with an Irish lilt as they had remembered it. They probably also half expected to see the tweed jackets, the flat caps, baggy trousers and creased, weather-worn faces, but they knew they were dreaming. However, the individualism asserted itself once they asked a group of guys about a particularly eye-catching object, sticking like a needle into the city air.

"That's the Spire of Dublin," replied the first and last of the serious men in the group.

"Aye," said another, "better known as the Rod to God."

"Ah, not so," said a third. "Sure it's the Stiffy on the Liffey!" And he folded over at his own joke.

Like a chain reaction it set them off.

"The Binge Syringe!"

"Erection at the Intersection!"

And they wafted away, throwing more jokes into the air like jugglers.

"Pole in the Hole!"

"Poke through the Smoke!"

The three brothers stood and stared with mouths open and eyes creased.

"Good God!" said Euan. "Ask a simple question . . ."

"No such thing in Ireland," said Conor, and they continued their wandering.

They crossed on to O'Connell Bridge over the Liffey, passing by a man clearly drunk, sitting on the ground, his legs awkwardly out in front of him, an empty bottle in his hand, with a face like a roaring fire, a nose like a distress signal and his hair thin wisps of smoke – more like eyebrows than a head of hair. Beside him was a homeless, badly dressed hat with a few stray coins in it. He seemed out to the world: eyes closed, sagging face and slack mouth. He obviously couldn't care less about the indignity of his position or condition and was back maybe in a more familiar, uncomplicated place of his own.

"He's not going to get wealthy soon, is he?" said Euan, dropping some coins into the hat.

"I don't know how anyone begging can survive in this city," said Conor. "It's expensive enough just being a tourist."

"I don't like to see that," said Ronan, pausing to look at the dishevelled clothes drawer in front of him. "It's like an exposed bone."

"Whatever that means!" jibed Conor.

Ronan didn't respond. Euan was quiet and embarrassed for the man.

"We'll just have a quick look down Temple Bar from the end of the street. The statue of Molly Malone at the bottom of Grafton Street is not too far from here. We'll look to see where Trinity College is and then we'll get back to Temple Bar and have a couple of drinks and grab a meal," suggested Conor. "Will that do you? We can do more tomorrow and come back to some of these places before we leave for Strokestown in a couple of days."

"Grand idea!" said Euan in his best brogue.

"Suits me too," said Ronan and they moved off together over the bridge.

Euan and Ronan were surprised at the number of beggars sprawled against the bridge and on the kerb and glanced back occasionally to see if it was just a game to get money. They took in all the street names as they crossed Aston Quay and into Westmoreland Street. As they passed Temple Bar they stared down the narrow cobbled streets and marvelled at the number of pubs and eating places and the jostling crowds of people in among the street vendors, seeing and hearing faintly the street musicians, the sheer thumping din and drumming of the place and the vibrant colours of the old-style alehouses.

"We have to come back here," said Euan.

"We will, we will," Conor assured him. "We don't have long in Dublin so we need to move slowly with haste. This is just a stopover, remember, before we get about our real journey. What's wrong with you, ya wanker? Why so quiet?"

"Just thinking", replied Ronan, "about the changes that have happened here, and yet because it's so long since I've been here I can't say they're changes so much as an adult view of childhood memories. Perhaps that's the only thing that makes it different. Maybe it's the same as it always was."

"Whatever," sighed Conor. "Just enjoy it; don't analyse it."

They moved off, and on into Grafton Street and College Green and a maze of streets whose hub seemed to be Trinity College. It was every bit as grand as they had expected, and they gazed silently, unable to find words enough to express the feelings of awe and an anchor in history that it gave them.

Chapter 12

He whispered loudly at the young lad he held firmly by the arm of his thin, shabby jacket: "Now, look here, you little shoite. You only get one chance at this and we can only do it once in any one place so we need to get it roight. If you don't, you'll be done like a chook in a foxes' den. Stand still and listen to me," he said, and he slapped the young lad hard across his ear. "Stop swinging around like an old sack o' bollocks. One good job and we could be in clover for a week."

"Oh, feck!" cried the youngster as he held his echoing ear and scowled at the man, whom he depended upon for a meal and a bed.

He edged closer to the tree near the statue, hoping to avoid another crack across the head.

"Now, I'll go through it all just one more time. As soon as I see someone who looks like an overseas well-heeled eejit heading into the toilet I'll go in after him. You wait out here for two seconds and then follow in right behind me. I'll pretend to use the pisspot next to him. If there's others in there, just concentrate on the man I followed in; forget the rest and watch for my signal."

"What feckin' signal?"

Smack! Ring! Ring! Another hard slap across the same ear.

"Watch the feckin' language, ya foul-mouthed little shoite. I've told you what the signal is a dozen times. If you listen I'll tell you, for the last time, what the signal is. Are ya listening?"

"Yeah, yeah," he sulked, flinching in case another slap was coming.

"I'll be watching him from behind as I follow him in and so I'll see if he has a wallet in his back pocket. You come in just behind me. Then when I get to the pisspot next to him at the same time, I'll see if he has buttons and no zip fly. I'll lift my left hand and scratch the back of my head as a signal to go. If I don't scratch my head it's not feckin' on, so just wash your hands and leave or go into one of the bogs. Ya got that? Have you got that?"

He changed his grip and twisted the boy's jacket collar, pushing his face closer, and the boy grimaced with the smell of the man's breath. He thought to himself that it must be what it would be like to stick his head down a sewer, but he decided not to say it.

"Yeah! Yeah! I got it. Let me go. You're hurting me!"

The man pushed him away angrily and then stepped towards him, peering closely at his face to be sure he was listening.

"The rest of it I've practised with you dozens of times so you know what to do. Wallet first, trousers next; three and a half seconds! Remember, that's all the time you've got."

The boy just nodded tiredly. They had been here for over two hours, gone over it all every five minutes – or so it seemed – and he was hungry and there had been nothing so far. Observant people would wonder what was wrong with the two of them – in and out of the toilet all the time. He had the cleanest hands in town, even if the rest of him wasn't up to much. The man was worried about the boy's lack of concentration. They would both need all their wits about them.

"Here's a go now! Could be one!" he whispered urgently. "Get ready! I'm going to follow this one in."

Chapter 13

Ronan had spotted the toilet sign while they were staring around at the grand buildings of Trinity College and several others nearby and across the road which looked like Houses of Parliament they were so magnificent.

"Just wait here," he said. "I need the loo. Be back in a minute."

He trotted across the road and the other two stood and stared. Surrounded by columns and distant spires, they looked up and down the canyons piled high with the stones of history.

As he walked into the toilets, Ronan planned the day while he tried to sort out the jumble of mixed feelings he had on being back in Ireland – a trip he had been looking forward to so much it had become an ache.

'At least it isn't raining, and it is quite a pleasant day,' he thought, 'especially when you hear so many jokes about the weather even from the locals.'

He moved closer to the urinal and what happened next took his breath away with the speed of it, though later, when he recalled it, it had all seemed to happen slowly like in a film. And he understood why. In that instant, when his mind was racing five times faster than his body, everything around him appeared to be in slow motion. In the next few seconds his brain was urgent while his body was dazed and dreamed dreams of action.

He felt the back of his jeans move and, thinking it was just the jeans slipping with all his buttons undone, he hoisted his shoulders with his elbows pressed on either side of his waist in an effort to get the jeans in a more comfortable position. He then realized that it was the pocket that was moving. He realized too late that it was his wallet being removed from his back pocket. There was a quick, slick slide and he knew it was gone even as he felt his pants pulled violently down around his ankles after catching on one of his knees, and his hands were too full – he almost smiled at that later – to grab hold of them to save himself from embarrassment.

It took him moments to realize what a strange fix he was in, and he was glad the toilets were nearly empty now apart from himself and one other man. His jeans were down; his wallet was gone. As he recovered his wits he turned around, reaching for his trousers to try to pull them up as fast as he could.

"Come here, ya little fuck!" he yelled, and then he stumbled and fell as the man beside him pushed past.

"I'll get him for you, sir!" said the stranger, adjusting himself quickly.

The man ran out through the open doorway and around the corner as fast as the young boy that Ronan had glimpsed a sliver of as he fell to the floor. He was on his feet in seconds, mind and body now on red alert and in synch.

"Somebody stop that little bastard!" he yelled, and the echo bounced off the tiled toilet walls.

He worked his hands as quickly as he could, though he had to stop twice to get a button done up because his hands shook and fumbled, impeding his progress, but he was soon out through the door and looking around for the youngster he had seen bolting like a young terrier round the corner beyond the entrance some seconds ago. There were so many streets he didn't know where to look to his best advantage and he was losing valuable time standing there.

"Conor! Euan!" he shouted urgently as he caught sight of his two brothers standing chatting together across the road from him. "Which way did they go?"

He saw their bewildered looks.

"The young guy running and the other guy chasing him!" he shouted in desperation. "C'mon! C'mon!" he yelled, wanting a quick answer before time slipped away from him. "The little shit stole my wallet while I was having a pee."

He stumbled across the road to meet them, grabbing them urgently to try to shake the words out of them.

They knew this was no joke, though Euan contained it with difficulty as he saw Ronan fumbling with his fly. Ronan's furious eyes told them the whole story.

"Wait! Wait! Wait!"

Those were not the words he wanted to hear.

"There was no guy – there was no guy chasing him, but a young lad just belted down that way!" said Euan, and he pointed back down the way they had come from O'Connell Bridge.

"Like a greyhound out of a trap!" said Conor to Ronan, beginning to move away from them.

"There he is! You can see him still going!" said Euan, coming up to him again and pointing.

And at that moment Ronan spotted him, 100 yards away, wriggling and darting his way through the ambling crowd like a mini twister weaving through a field of corn. With his last button done up, he was off.

"Oh, for fuck's sake," said Conor. "He thinks he's young enough to catch that young fella. Donkey and a thoroughbred. They shouldn't even be in the same race. C'mon – we'll need to pick up the pieces where he stops."

He grabbed Euan by the sleeve and they were off down the street together, trying to keep Ronan in sight.

Ronan meanwhile was in it for the long haul. He still ran a little. Had run marathons. While the bursts of speed over long distances were gone, he could lope along still. At a steady pace . . . for a long time. Perhaps he could wear this youngster out. If he could just keep the little bastard in view. He jumped to the roadside. Horns sounded, fingers were lifted to the air, people shouted and smiled, cars swerved and crowds flinched. The sky was watchful.

He stayed along by the kerb. It avoided having to bump and push and hold up people while unbalancing all those who were making their own escapes. A macabre body dance.

'The little gobshite is just a blur,' he thought.

He worked his way through the crowd, barely slowing, jumping and sidestepping, one way . . . then the other . . . all at a cracking pace . . . heels bobbing like rabbits' tails. In among the legs of the crowds on the pavement. Legs hurrying away.

If the people in the street knew what was going on they gave no signs of it – the casual, guilty indifference of the crowd. Don't get involved. At all costs. Nothing to do with me. Ronan knew it was no use to shout – he didn't want to waste his breath, their breath, my breath, our breath. He could see it on the studied faces.

'Not my concern.' A careful blankness. The indifferent face.

'Glad it's not me.' Selfish sympathy.

Something more. Ancient admiration. The daring underdog. The love of the scoundrel. You know how it is. He's me. He's probably been you – once. He's someone's son. Could have been mine.

'Why am I doing this? What if I catch the little arsehole? Thank him for the exercise? Do I want to catch him? I don't know! Stop thinking, twat! Just run!'

He blazed his way down Westmoreland Street, unable to tell if the distance between them was growing or diminishing – bodies in the way, obscuring calculation. Prevented him measuring clean, comparative lines. Between the two of them. Nearer? No, further. No, maybe not.

'Why are you trying to calculate the fastest runner? Does it matter? Keep running. He must tire soon. I might tire soon. We'll both tire soon. Then what?' He had a quick moment to take in The Temple Bar as he rumbled past.

'I will kill a pint later. Down towards the river. God, that boy can run.' Breathless admiration! 'So? You could run too. That age. Need to get over my age? Panting for breath now. He'll be old one day. How'd he learn to run like this? Won't always run like this. Yes, sometimes. Chasing buggers like you. Leave me alone, mister! It's a life. It's my food and bedding.'

It was like a breathless conversation he was planning to have with the boy when he caught him.

The boy was across Aston Quay and heading for O'Connell

Bridge. Still flying. Arms tucked in front. Prising free. Loosening. Slipping. Folding. Slowing. Hand in pocket. Middle of the bridge. Don't look back. Pursuit too close. Not far enough behind. A short sprint will have him. But breathless – bridging the distance between them. Almost stumbled on a figure sprawled on the pavement.

Suddenly. Hand in the air. A desperate farewell. Flung out in an abrupt gliding arc. Brown, square message of loss as the wallet passed over the decorated parapet and dived to meet the water.

Ronan stopped.

The boy ran on and disappeared irrelevantly. He had taken his eyes off the boy anyway and didn't even know which way he had gone other than out of his reach. He stopped and watched the wallet, which somersaulted through the air effortlessly from the bridge and into the water as he staggered quickly to where it splashed quietly before floating towards him, turned out like an empty pocket.

He stepped past the drunk and climbed on to the ledge, just above the pavement, to watch its progress. It was bouncing cockily on the water, away under the bridge.

A hand grabbed his leg, the shock nearly unbalancing him to make him tip over and into the water. Ronan looked down in disbelief at the drunken man they had seen as they first came across the bridge an hour or so before, still sprawled on the footpath, but with a spidery hand firmly grasping his trouser leg and a wary, knowing shine in his eye.

"Ah sure, I wouldn't if I were you," he said.

"Wouldn't what?" asked Ronan caught between shock and impatience, looking around, realizing the boy was well gone and, at the same time, trying to shake his leg free.

"Well now, I wouldn't be after jumping in there for whatever it was that young fella threw in there. You'd have more chance of surviving if you had your head stuck down a shithole."

"Let go of my leg. I've got no intention of jumping in after it," said Ronan, getting down off the ledge as the hand released him and peering at the man, amazed.

He was sweating now that he had stopped running, and he needed to catch his breath, which was not as laboured as he had expected. He leaned against the bridge, staring into the river, feeling helpless and frustrated.

But, surprisingly, it was the drunk they had passed on the first time across the bridge that interested him most now, almost more than his wallet. Just at that moment Euan and Conor came walking quickly towards him, also out of breath and eager to finish the story.

"What happened?" asked Euan. "You didn't catch him? Where's the wallet?"

Ronan pointed across to the other side of the bridge. "Over there, in the water, headed out towards the Irish Sea."

"You mean the little shit threw it in the river?" asked Conor.

"That's exactly what he did. That's exac— Damn! Damn! What do I do now?" asked Ronan.

"Report it to the police," said the man on the bridge, not considering it worth his while or the effort to get to his feet. "You won't get your wallet back, but it adds to their files and gives someone a job – maybe gives three or four people a job."

"We thought you were drunk when we came past here just over an hour ago, but you're not, are you?"

Euan wanted to hear him talk some more to see if he was right.

"I'm not sure," said the man. "Sometimes, if I drink enough, I get gloriously drunk and then after a few more I come out on the other side and, sure, then every drink I have after that I get more and more unpleasantly sober. It's like drinking in reverse." He chuckled to himself. "And that's where I am now: almost sober."

"Did you get a look at the lad when he came past you?" Ronan asked the old man.

"Sure, no, I didn't. I'm sorry. I glanced up at the noise of running and I saw him throw something. I had me head down most of the time, passing sadly through into sober, but not quickly enough. They all look the same to me anyway. And besides, I just listen; I don't look too much. I learn more."

"Not much in the hat," said Conor.

"Don't really care. Anyway, it's enough I've made today. But it's early and I'll have more by the end of the day if I'm lucky," replied the old man. "It's a free show on this bridge every day. Characters walking across this stage." He swept his hand in a gesture to cover the length of the bridge. "Talking about unimportant things because they're unimportant men. The stuff they care about and the miserable lives they seem to live! I lead a calm life and I don't go hungry and I don't get cold. I spend the money I get carefully and I rarely go short. My friends look after me and I look after them. We all look after each other."

Again that bright look that Ronan had seen some minutes before.

"Would you two mind just focusing for a minute? I've just been robbed in broad daylight and you are busy discussing life with someone who doesn't give half the shit that I do about my wallet and probably has more money than I do just now! I need some help here, guys."

"Listen – who's talking about discussing life? For once he's right though. C'mon, let's go. Enough of Socrates here," said Conor, and they starting walking off. "We can at least report it to the police even though it won't do any good. Does travel insurance cover money? I presume it does, so we'll have to have a report for you to make a claim. By the way, you weren't 'robbed in broad daylight'. I've been in that boghouse and there's more light in a tunnel."

"Do you know where there's a police station?" asked Euan, walking a few paces behind, still fascinated by the Jekyll and Hyde recovery of the man.

"Now, why would I know that, young fella?" said the man, and a smile parted his face. "Too far away from here. If you don't know your way around, you'd be better stoppin' the garda car yourself and they'd sort somethin' out for ya. Head up O'Connell Street and there's sure to be one come by before long."

Ronan waved back. "Thank you!" he shouted, keen to get

something done instead of just dangling. "I'd give you some money if I had some!"

The old man simply smiled and nodded. "You hang on to your money, my friend," he called. "I don't need anything from you. Too easily parted if you don't watch out for some of the thieving shoites around here. God bless ye, my friends," he said.

The three of them left him and headed off, hoping to catch up soon with the first police car to come within hailing distance.

"There you are – you've made a new friend. How good is that?" asked Conor, feeling a lot less cheerful than he pretended to be.

"At least he's not a thieving git, so don't take the piss," said Ronan.

Euan was quiet, feeling miserable for Ronan and trying to be appropriately glum. There was a stooped despondency about the group as they moved away. Anyone looking would have believe they'd all been robbed if they'd seen them.

The old man of the bridge watched them head off to the other side of the bridge and up along O'Connell Street. He climbed slowly to his feet, picked up his hat with the few coins in it, pocketed them, crossed nimbly over to the other side of the bridge and, getting more of a spring in his step the further he moved, ambled off around the corner and on to Eden Quay, hoping to get away from the crowds.

"No more work for me today," he muttered to himself hopefully.

He glanced up O'Connell Street, but the three men were gone – out of sight. He still stopped occasionally to look back behind him, even waited some moments to take in the bars (an involuntary lick of the lips in anticipation), the people and the traffic that sneaked and scuttled by, before shuffling off again, unhurried and unworried.

He wedged himself into a narrow side street and waited – but not for long. He saw Seamus heading towards him from the other direction and with him was his son, Kieran.

"You clever little bastard," he said quietly as they knotted together against a wall. "Well done, yourself!" And he tousled Kieran's hair.

Kieran pushed his hand away.

"How well did we do, Seamus?"

"Five hundred euros!" he whispered delightedly, spraying exuberant fountains of spit all over his brother while greedy saliva collected at the corners of his mouth.

"Oh, Jesus, Mary and Joseph! Thank you, God," whispered Barry as he put his hands together and looked heavenward as if in prayer. "A bunch of generous fellas those three were. Almost a shame to take their money, now, wasn't it?"

It was rhetorical and he didn't believe it, and the silence of the other two was assurance enough that neither did they.

"Still, I told them to report it to the police. A little bit of inconvenience and then they'll get the insurance, so we're all winners. Sure, isn't that what life's about?"

He looked around seeking agreement, but Kieran just looked surly and Seamus was starting to drool, his eyes distant and already dreaming.

Chapter 14

The three of them sat in the bar with the conversations drifting and surging around them. They hadn't spoken since they had bought their beers, and they sat looking around them at the bobbing heads, flailing arms and fish mouths pouring words like spilling water, caps hissing off bottles and ale handles sighing and slurping as the beers flowed freely. It had taken them over two hours to get themselves sorted out.

They had gone back to the hotel because Ronan had left his passport, records of money exchanges, his driving licence and some other valuables and bits and pieces in the hotel safe when they had checked in. He was very careful about carrying too many things around with him wherever he went on holiday so that if he lost something important he would still be able to see his way through and not be double-stranded.

In fact he had been luckier than even he had imagined because he had only had one card with him while he was out and that was his Debit Plus card, and when they had stopped to get postcards and stamps at the post office he had used his card and put it in the top pocket of his jacket – glad it had worked as easily as the bank at home said it would – to remind him to see what the docket told him and if it was different from the ones back home. He had been too shocked at what had happened to him to remember all this, but once they were back at the hotel he realized that all he had lost had been his €500 as well as the small leather document wallet; it was tough enough, but not as tough as it could have been. He had even left his English notes and coins in the safe because he knew from past experience what a pain it was when you got two currencies mixed up in your pockets and you kept pulling out the wrong notes and coins.

Now they sat in the lobby waiting for the police. They had decided against advice and instead sought help from the people at the hotel once they had got back there.

"So, what was all the screaming and shouting and huffing and puffing all about, then?" asked Conor as they stood in the hotel lobby. "Just a bit of money and a tatty old wallet."

"Might be nothing to you, pal, but I can't afford to lose money just like that," replied Ronan.

"He's only having you on, Ronan," said Euan.

He was always the one to calm the waters, which, to be fair, he thought, rarely broke. He enjoyed it when they got along well, even if at times they all sailed close to the wind. He felt it was his job to keep the peace.

"The police are here anyway so we can get this all fixed up, fella."

He got up, patted Ronan on the shoulder and pointed to the police car pulling up outside.

The hotel had been sympathetic and helpful when they heard about what had happened, and the receptionist offered to phone for the police for them and said they could talk it over with them in the hotel lounge.

They went through it and over and under it with the two policemen, like an obstacle course, one asking questions and the other making notes and then asking questions, and they'd been slightly mesmerized by the lilting accents. But both officers were thorough and, at times, it had felt like an interrogation as they backtracked and stopped them from speaking at the same time, collecting more and more detail instead of Ronan's resigned offerings. They had asked to see all the things that he had put away safely in the hotel's safe, including passport and documents showing dates, times and places of currency conversion (especially the New Zealand dollars into euros) and all his credit cards. They were only doing their job, and doing it well, but it was frustrating and, Ronan felt, a waste of time. He blamed himself and felt it was all his fault, though nobody else did – not even Conor. Ronan was always hard on his own mistakes, real or imagined. He was a bit of a perfectionist and such an easy crime had caught him off guard and made him feel stupid. He didn't appreciate that, and now retelling his foolishness to two policemen was reminding him of that.

After all the questions were over, they made their way back to The Temple Bar pub, mulling over their day and desperately trying to get their feelings and nostalgic memories back on track. Not before Ronan had distracted them into a small bag shop and bought himself a thin credit-card wallet to replace his stolen one. Then he asked a stranger for the nearest ATM, eventually getting the local gentleman to indicate to him the closest 'hole in the wall', as he called it, where he used his card again to get a small amount of fresh euros; he wasn't willing yet to carry large sums in his pockets.

Ronan and Euan both knew they had been down O'Connell Street and other parts of Dublin before as kids, but they remembered little of it except vague, pleasant memories and they felt a natural attraction to it as the land of their parents, though their parents had probably been to Dublin fewer times than any of them. Or had they? They just didn't know.

Their parents had decided to return to Ireland some thirty years ago in May 1979 and had settled in Longford. Mum didn't like it from the start, and her illness, which had first appeared in England, got dramatically and quickly worse. She was diagnosed with cancer and died just two years after they had made the trip back to Ireland. She had asked to be buried in Strokestown – Dad's birthplace – and the cemetery had a number of the family buried there, including Dad's parents.

She probably thought that was where he would be buried, and perhaps, at the time, he thought that too.

Ronan remembered being in Dublin some forty years earlier when he had a hitch-hiking holiday around Ireland with a couple of college friends. Euan and Conor thought their memories were from their time as kids when on holiday in Ireland with their parents visiting grandparents in Roscommon. They had also both been to Ireland not that long ago, though much later in life. For Euan it was to visit the house in Longford and see for the last time their mum struggling with cancer and their dad confused and angry and lost. For Conor it had been twice to Ireland to bury both parents just five years apart, and a couple of visits later to tidy up Dad's grave and then make the headstone a more permanent one. It was those collective memories which had sustained a lifetime of fondness and admiration for a country and a people that was literate, witty, talented and surrounded by green, gorgeous countryside.

Now it was the history that interested them and the feel of a country that had struggled for greatness and independence and had won and lost both. It was also the place where they suspected they would make their last visit as a threesome to see the graves of their parents. For that reason too, Ireland was like a vault with some of their greatest treasures buried within it, and they just wanted to see them and admire them one last time, maybe.

"I've read lots of stuff about the huge growth of Ireland and its new-found wealth," said Euan, but there's an uncertainty and an uncharacteristic, eh, em . . ." He struggled for the best way to express what he was thinking.

"Diffidence?" offered Ronan.

"I suppose. If I knew what it meant," said Euan.

"It means 'lacking self-confidence'," explained Ronan.

"Well, yeah, then. Perfect word because the Irish have always seemed so full of brash self-confidence, but . . . somehow it's not quite there any more. They used to live under such harsh authority, family and church, that it was inevitable that rebellion would be very wild when a sniff of freedom was in the air. Not hard to understand really," concluded Euan. "They'll pick it up in the next few years. I'm sure of it."

"But you said it yourself. You used the word 'brash' and that's exactly what it is . . . or was. It's a showy, noisy sort of confidence, but it's what kids sometimes do to hide their lack of self-confidence," explained Conor.

"I think we all see it though," said Ronan. "Laughter is

sometimes the only way to get through desperate situations, and the Irish are very good at laughter. Let's be honest – we all have that in our genes to an extent, some of us more than others," he said, glancing under his brows at Conor.

"It's a bit of a stretch to say that they only laugh because they're desperate, isn't it?" asked Conor, choosing to ignore Ronan's observation.

"No, I didn't mean that," answered Ronan. "Just occasionally it sounds a bit hollow. That's all I'm saying."

"It's true," agreed Euan. "There's a feeling about some of the people that I felt during the day. There's a feeling and a realization that the dream needs to become a reality, but I don't know when or how—"

"And the golden boy of Europe has not matured yet," said Conor.

"That's right," agreed Euan.

"Exactly right!" said Ronan. "It's that hapless, helpless look in the eyes, like rabbits feeding well on lush grass, never hearing the shots that kill and not moving until the bullets fly through the skull."

It seemed the young Irish lad had rushed to manhood, shouting his towering pride to the deafened skies, had tried to grow up independent, not wanting advice, loud and full of new-found confidence after years of playing prompt for so many others in starring roles. He had moved off daringly and flamboyantly, unaware of the signs that he was moving too quickly and too carelessly, enticed by being able to grasp the things he was told he could never have and could never afford. He wanted it all, and it seemed for a while that he had got it.

Now he was like a boy again, coming to terms with being called, scoldingly, home having played out late into the evening with his rich friends from across the river, who had got him into trouble. He knew he was in for a hiding and he was already flinching from the anticipated blows.

The three of them realized there had always been an air of the rascal about the men in their lives from Ireland, so in one way they were not surprised. Even their dad had been a larrikin.

Often when he came home after a few drinks, the twinkle was in his eye and the stories of when he was young came tumbling out and they would sit mesmerized by his antics, wondering why they got walloped for doing similar things. Somewhere his view of things changed and he dedicated himself to bringing up successful sons and loving his wife. He became good at both. He – *they* – had poured everything into the family. They were different and had done things differently and independently.

"When you think about it, you know, all the family we've met have been great characters but some were too irresponsible and too clever in the ways of the world. I never knew what any of them did for a living."

The other two nodded in agreement.

"But they always seemed to think they had life sorted."

The others nodded again and looked into their own distant memories.

"But they had money, however they came by it. None of them at the time seemed to have a relationship that was going anywhere, so they lived fairly feckless lives." Conor held out his hands at the simplicity of hindsight.

"Do you think they missed the innocent and watchful stage where they should have learnt so much more wisdom? And maybe learnt from the mistakes of others?" asked Ronan.

"I do," said Euan, "because even the jokes about the Irish suggest guile and a wiliness about the Irish character underneath the insulting intention of the joke. By mocking themselves the Irish come out of it laughing at the stupidity of the rest of the world at being so easily persuaded of their naivety. Do you remember how pissed off Dad would get when people made fun of the Irish or told jokes that made the Irish look stupid?"

"Yeah, he was pretty sensitive about it, wasn't he?" agreed Ronan.

"But then, as you said, Euan, they turned it around and told the jokes themselves and made them up themselves from their own folklore, their quirky behaviour and their unique observations of human nature. As a result everyone, in a kind of mirror-image way, began to admire their humour . . . and other skills. People certainly do now," insisted Conor.

"Yeah, but that can be a bit too clever sometimes. They make up most of the jokes themselves about themselves anyway, as you said, but who's laughing at whom? No one knows," laughed Conor.

"Exactly!" concluded Ronan.

They stared then in silence while conversations bustled around them. They had been surprised at the number of beggars along the street and on the bridge, and in the conversations they started, out of curiosity, with the shopkeepers and in the bars, they learned the truth of a country struggling in uneasy times.

They knew it was too costly for most tourists, but lower profits, lower wages and loss of jobs seemed the only real solution and they couldn't bear to talk or even think of those things, and they didn't want to return to there; they had hoped that they had left those days behind, but like a revolving door they were heading back in the way they had come out.

The three of them reflected alone on the mixed blessings of the day and thought about how well it had or hadn't matched what they had expected after all this time. They knew from their day around the city that there was still an indomitable spirit there, and they were left with a sense of unease mixed with a wish that things would be done with a little more care next time. That to be as happy as everyone else did not mean you had to be the same as them – not even in terms of wealth. It was the difference, and usually that meant the people and the culture, that gave them the edge.

Ronan broke the silence, anticipating their thoughts: "The bottom line is that we're back in Ireland to say farewell to our parents, maybe for the last time, and we're lucky to be able to do it together. I think it's magic and it's a magical place."

Euan agreed. "I find it hard not to love this place and the people when the two people that meant so much to us remind us all the time of Ireland and Irishness."

"Over the years I think we've all come to realize how much love was poured into us and the sacrifices that were made so . . .

you give love, you get love. Seems simple really, doesn't it?" said Conor. He grabbed the end of his T-shirt and pretended to wipe his eyes. "That was beautiful, guys," he mocked. "I feel so moved. In fact I can feel a motion coming right now." And he got up and headed for the toilet.

"Bloody cynic!" called Ronan after him, though he couldn't help smiling at their ponderousness.

"Don't encourage him," said Euan. "No reaction, it gets no traction. He does all his kindnesses in a casual, satirical fashion so as not to be found out."

"The more I see that cynical side to him, the more I know it's an act," said Ronan. "He does make me laugh though, and he keeps us a little more grounded. He's good for us both. I think we're all good for each other."

Euan was about to speak again, but Ronan held up his hand. "Yeah, look – I know exactly what he's like and you obviously do too. Don't worry. This is growing into a strong family unit at last. Do you know, you would have made a good Canadian Mountie, keeping the peace."

When Conor came back he decided everyone had to tell a good Irish joke to lighten the day.

"Me first," he said. "An Irishman walks into a pub and the bartender says, 'What'll ya have?'

"The man says, 'Give me three pints of Guinness, please.'

"The bartender brings him three pints and the man begins to alternately sip one, then the other and then the third until they're gone. He then orders three more.

"The bartender says, 'Sir, I know you like them cold, but you don't have to order three at a time. I can keep an eye on it, and when it gets low I'll bring you a fresh, cold one.'

"'You don't understand,' says the man. 'I have two brothers, one in Canada and one in New Zealand [that didn't make sense, but he couldn't resist]. We made a vow that every Saturday night we'd still drink together. So right now my brothers will have three Guinness stouts in front of them on the Saturday night, and it's like we're drinking together.'

"The bartender thought that was a wonderful tradition. Every week the man came in and ordered three pints of Guinness. Then one week he came in and only ordered two. He drank them and ordered two more. He drank them as well and ordered two more.

"The bartender said to him, 'I know what your tradition is, and I'd just like to say that I'm very sorry that one of your brothers has died.'

"'Oh, both me brothers are fine,' he said. 'I just quit drinking.'"

The smiles were slow at first, but cheeks filled like sails and puffed and surged into laughter.

"That's pretty good!" said Euan. "So now it's my turn – just give me a minute. Right, into a pub in Cork comes Danny Murphy, looking like he's been hit by a train. His arm's in a sling, he has a broken nose, his face is cut and bruised and he's walking with a limp.

"'What happened to you?' asks Mick, the bartender.

"'Sean O'Connor and me had a fight,' says Danny.

"'That little shite, O'Connor,' says the bartender. 'He couldn't do that to you. He must have had something in his hand!'

"'That he did,' says Danny. 'A shovel is what he had and a terrible bashin' he gave me with it.'

"'Well,' says the barman, 'you should have defended yourself. Didn't you have something in your hand?'

"'That I did,' says Danny. 'I had Mrs O'Connor's left breast, and a thing of beauty it was, but useless in a fight.'"

Again the laughter flowed and they were beginning to get over the hassles of the day.

"Right," said Ronan. "Two good jokes I'll have to better. OK, young Mick comes home from school with a writing assignment and he asks his dad for help.

"'Dad, can you tell me the difference between potential and reality?'

"His father looks up, thinks for a minute and says, 'I'll give you a demonstration. Go and ask your mother if she would sleep with Robert Redford for a million euros. Then go and ask your sister if she would sleep with Brad Pitt for a million euros. When you've done that come back and tell me what you've learned.'

"Young Mick is confused, but does as his dad has told him:

'Mum, would you sleep with Robert Redford if you were given a million euros?'

"'Don't say a word to your father, but yes, I would,' she replied.

"He then finds his sister and asks her, 'If someone gave you a million euros, would you sleep with Brad Pitt?'

"'Don't tell Mum and Dad, but oh yes! Oh, my God, yes, I would!'

"Young Mick goes back to his father, who says to him, 'Have you figured it out now, Mick?'

"'Aye, Dad, I have,' says Mick. 'Potentially, we are sitting on two million euros, but in reality we're living with a couple of sluts.'"

They roared with laughter and the mood, which was straining at the tether anyway, broke free. They were chuckling and giggling like kids, and the day was aloft again.

They had several more drinks, moving again from pub to pub and getting a feel for the variety and yet the indelible sameness of the environment. It was lively, alluring, noisy, musical and totally atmospheric, and they could see each other's smiling eyes. They knew that in spite of everything that had happened that day, nothing would change their thinking. They had been captivated by Ireland since childhood and there was no use thrashing around in old age to try to break free.

That night they all slept soundly and dreamlessly – especially Ronan.

Chapter 15

The next morning was an early start.

Today was their last day in Dublin and there was a lot to see and do. They had picked up a number of brochures from the hotel lobby when they arrived the night before, had pieced together a very random itinerary for the following day, and now they were ready to do the tourist thing. Ronan got some money from the machine as they headed once more down O'Connell Street. The machine worked, to his relief, and his new wallet and money were placed in separate front pockets of the light jacket he wore. He would never put a wallet in his back pocket again.

It was starting to rain, but there was still the promise of warmth in the morning. The mood was light, some innocent beliefs had been dealt with and they were firmly back on the path, determined to enjoy as much as they could of a trip that would have its sad as well as its joyous moments.

The day went by too quickly. They went back to the bottom of Grafton Street to see again the statue of Molly Malone, 'the tart with the cart', which was so shamelessly voluptuous and wonderfully done and which again reminded them of how often they had heard the song sung in the house of their youth.

The longer they looked at the curves of the figure, the more they wondered if they had missed the real reasons that Molly was on the streets, and they once again smiled and joked about the contradiction and ambivalence that was always there in Ireland: now, revered in song; then, reviled in life! A commoner's resurrection.

Into the steady rain and on to Trinity College, founded in 1592, mainly to see the Book of Kells, which they had all heard so much about. They now gaped at the real thing: a beautifully decorated version of the four Gospels written in Latin. Again, Ronan and Euan felt that awe when they realized it had been around for over 1,200 years.

They found the age of things and the history quite staggering, especially when compared to New Zealand in one instance and Canada in the other. Conor took it all as a given. And they wandered throughout the many fine buildings and read about the great and the good and all the folds of history that they were part of, like layers in an ancient rock wall exposed by an avalanche of recorded time.

Out into the pouring rain and catch the next 'Hop on, hop off' bus out to the Guinness Storehouse, designed in the shape of a giant pint of Guinness.

"Guinness has been brewing for over 250 years," said Euan. "That's nearly older than the history of my country!"

"A lot older than mine," said Ronan.

Conor seemed unimpressed: "It's been estimated that, if filled, it would hold 14.3 million pints."

"It doesn't divide equally by three," said Euan, "so no point in dreaming. There'd only be arguments."

"Maybe," said Conor, "but they wouldn't last long and they wouldn't be good quality."

"That's true. I'd just as happily give away my share of the remainder to the last man standing . . . or even lying down," laughed Ronan.

They made their way to the top of the building, where they were given a free half-pint of Guinness each, which they drank slowly as they looked around at a 360-degree view of the city, blurred in grey mist, and the Wicklow Hills behind, hunched in drench, but they still seemed spectacular to them because they had heard them talked about so many times at home.

Out into the torrential rain, but now protected, sort of, by a Guinness-crested brolly that cost €13 though it was barely the size of one. The great Oscar Wilde's house, Dublin Art Gallery,

Dublin's oldest building, Christchurch Cathedral, nearly 1,000 years old, containing the tomb of Strongbow, leader of the Normans, who captured Dublin in 1170.

"Why did all his followers have the name Norman?" asked Ronan.

"God!" said Conor. "He must have invented Strongbow Cider. They have everything going for them here, don't they, as well as the Guinness?"

By now it was drenching rain, so, in spite of their plan to take in as much of the city as they could, they found themselves drifting back to Temple Bar on Dublin's south side, deliberately splashing in puddles like kids as they ran past each other and into a pub, where they settled down to get dry and enjoy the company of strangers.

While the rain had sent them scurrying for cover it barely affected the other visitors, who had been holidaying longer, and locals who carried on with their music in the street. The restaurants had sent out people to stand on corners or in side streets with placards, touting for customers and pointing the way to the hearth and good food; others were idly looking in the few shop windows or just angled on building edges and ledges chatting, smoking soggy cigarettes and laughing seemingly without a care in the world. The rain dripped and ran from shopfronts and bounced when it hit stone. Rivulets of water hurried in the gaps between the cobblestones. It sat in soaking patches on jackets, coats, hats and umbrellas and ran down noses, hands and legs while shoes squelched and squeaked and soaking people splashed their way round water and made a bid for cover. But for many there was a familiarity with the conditions that meant they passed unnoticed for some, and the discomfort and whingeing around them was dismissed as the fuss of strangers.

"Sure, it's only water – it's not acid," they said. As if it wasn't obvious.

In spite of it all, the three brothers were enjoying themselves. They were growing even more relaxed in each other's company after all the years apart, and their experiences during the day had been kindnesses, helpfulness and courtesy and humour. It was still there, the legendary hospitality, and it had emerged in drain loads during their hasty trip around some of the city sights.

"So, Conor, what's on the agenda for tomorrow?" asked Euan. "Off to Strokestown?"

"Yep, but we need to get a car first. I asked at the hotel and we can catch a bus just across from reception and ask the driver for 'CarHire', eight kilometres down the road. She says the bus driver will know it, so just ask him for a nudge when you get there and he'll set you down just outside the place."

"Who's driving?" asked Ronan.

"Not you!" said Euan. "You can't even look after your bloody wallet. You'll probably get the car stolen or drive us off a bridge."

"And you're not either," said Conor, "because you'll drive on the wrong side. It's like that joke about the lady who rings her husband on his cell phone in the car and says, 'Be careful, luv. There was a police message on the radio saying there's an idiot driver driving the wrong way on a dual carriageway towards oncoming traffic.'

"'You might not believe this,' said the husband, 'but there's about fifty of them on this road doing exactly the same thing!'"

"Argh! Ha ha! Good joke." Conor's chuckle bubbled out and Euan joined in.

Ronan just looked at them both and shrugged. "Fine. I can wait until you two have made complete twats of yourselves and then you'll be pleading with me to drive."

"About as likely as God apologizing!"

"Or you growing angel's wings!"

"Or you two cracking a decent joke between you," said Ronan. "Let's move on and have a couple more drinks in another couple of places. Oscar Wilde said that 'Work is the curse of the drinking classes', and so is guilt, so let's get on with some decent drinking."

They went down the road a . paces among a heaving mass of soaked humanity and there was another warm glow magnetically drawing them in, well as music that spun and danced and sounded lively and cheering enough to banish the weather outside and the dampness inside. They ended up in at least another five places, including The Temple Bar pub itself, the district's namesake. All were inviting and all were like entering beehives.

While they were sitting in one of the pubs enjoying the music and the buzz of conversation, Ronan pointed to a black-and-white photograph on the wall. It showed three men in what looked like a pub, one playing the fiddle and the other two obviously enjoying a good joke while half-full glasses rested on top of a piano.

"Would you believe it? I have that poster at home. It's called *Fiddler's Light* by Jill Freedman. Isn't it wonderful?" The other two looked and just nodded.

"They look as rough as we do, only a bit older," mused Euan.

The other two eyed one another critically and, looking soggy, bedraggled and driven from home, they had to agree.

"I just bought it because it was such a typical scene. I reckon it's a classic. Years later I checked out Jill Freedman on the Internet. She's an interesting American photographer – mostly New York stuff before it became a great city.

"There was a song written by an Irish group based on the photo, but I can't remember who it was now. Something about 'Feel his art lift the heart, sense the spirits rise and fall, as the fiddler plays in Donegal.' I don't think I got that right," said Ronan, who, by this stage, was quite animated.

"God," said Conor, "you're a mine of bloody useless information. It is a good poster though," he agreed.

There was no stopping Ronan now: "The fiddler is John Doherty from Donegal, who is – was – very famous in Ireland. She actually (I mean Jill Freedman) had a book published in the eighties of a whole lot of Irish images, and that photo was the cover photo for the book."

"Look at the way the light coming through the window strikes the hands of the fiddler. That's quite magical, isn't it?" asked Euan, who was more taken with the photograph the longer he looked at it.

Ronan looked from Euan to the photograph and back again.

"You clever old bastard," he said admiringly. *Fiddler's Light*! Obvious. But I never really noticed. I just looked at him sitting in the light and I did and I didn't notice his hands. Well, not in the way you just did! You smart old bugger."

"Look," said Euan, "if you're going to praise me you could at least leave out the 'bugger'."

"Come on, you two – let's do what they're doing in the poster: less talk and more drinking," interrupted Conor. "Get them in, ya old git." And he pointedly pushed his empty glass across the table in front of Euan.

After a few more drinks they felt restored and content and stepped gingerly outside to head back home through the bustling crowds. The rain had stopped though the water continued to trickle into secret places as they hit their stride back to their hotel.

The next morning, slightly the worse for wear, they packed early, got a good breakfast before nine in the hotel dining room, paid separately for their stay and went to catch the bus just outside the hotel and across the road.

"Good hotel, that," said Euan, looking back approvingly as they crossed the road and stepped on to the bus. "Nice, helpful people."

"Hurry up! I have ta be goin' to stick to schedule. And the roight money too," said the bus driver. "I don't give change."

He pointed with a grubby finger to a small sign on the outside of the small counter where the money was placed and the tickets were given. He eyeballed Conor as he spoke, and Conor detected a glint, backed up by a hint of creases round the eyes to suggest a life of fun.

"Yes, it is a lovely morning and you're looking well," said Conor as he dropped the correct money on to the tray, a big grin on his face. He instinctively tuned in when he detected a sense of humour.

"He's a quare fella is that one," said the driver, nodding after Conor, who was heading down the bus after stowing his bag near the front.

"That's my brother you're talking about," said Euan as he paid and headed down to the back after putting his case on to the baggage rack at the front, next to Conor's.

"Lookin' at ya, I'm thinkin' they're your brothers too?" asked the driver as Ronan moved forward to pay.

"Only one of them," said Ronan as his coins clattered in the tray and the driver's laughter clattered in tune with it. "Can you give me the nod when we get to the LandEscape Cars place?"

"Sure, I can now. Just sit down there now and don't be going miles down the bus so that I have to yell to get you." He indicated a seat at the front just back from the automatic door.

Ronan put his bag with the two others on the rack and sat down where he was told. A few more passengers arrived, paid and took their seats. Eventually the bus pulled away from the bus stop and headed off up the road.

It didn't take long. The road was busy, with it being a working day, but the worst of the early rush was coming to a close and anyway the driver drove as if he was a pilot in open skies. And, what's more, it was as if he owned those skies. Ronan had a theory that it was slow drivers who had most accidents, not manic ones, and that was what he hoped was a sound theory as he clung tenaciously to his seat with his shoulders hunched ready for impact.

The streets were lined with trees as they headed away from the centre of the city, and some of the businesses and shops could have been anywhere in any country at this time of the day: unfolding activity, trudging in vacancy at the start of another working day, old buildings dressed in old work clothes, the colours of grey and grind and routine and rut.

"Here y'are, my friend," called the driver, looking in his large rear-view mirror so that Ronan caught a glimpse of him looking back at him as he got up to go to the platform at the front.

Ronan signalled to the two at the back that they were to get off. So they got out of their seats and grabbed their small cases. The bus pulled in to the kerb and they got off, waving to the driver, who grinned and pointed his thumb across the road to the car-rental building.

"Yer man's over there! Good luck now, lads!" he shouted as the door sighed shut, gulped and firmed its rubbery mouth for another nerve-wracking journey. They stood on the footpath, watching the back of the bus disappearing down the road. Euan stared longest, shaking his smiling head, and he was still staring at the departing bus as he stepped out into the road.

Without even thinking, Ronan grabbed at Euan's jacket and pulled him viciously so that he stumbled backwards over and up the kerb and fell clumsily on his backside as a car blurred by, horn sounding a long mournful wail, missing him by a whisker.

Chapter 16

At the same time, Ronan watched inside himself a young boy, rising five and brimful of life, smiling and shouting to his dad, and breaking free from his mum's hand, run out and forward and leap cheerfully and lightly from the kerb and the earth and on into eternal youth, and the distracted joy inside him burst like a blood-filled balloon as he went under the wheels of a truck which no one had dreamed was built for this time and this moment.

There was a screeching and screaming of brakes, and the horn keened loudly as the young mother raced out on to the road from across the street, arms raised helplessly, screaming – screaming piercingly and angrily at the truck and the indifferent fate, as on the other side a man threw his careless bicycle over and away and ran towards the body of the young boy who was covered in blood, twisted out of shape and unrecognizable except to loving parents. The lady fell on her knees at the side of what was left of her child and, picking up the broken, distorted fragments, hugged him to her breast, covering her white blouse and fawn-coloured skirt in blood while a heart-rending cry from the deepest part of her despair broke from her lips.

The man came and knelt gently next to her, unable to believe what he was seeing, shaking with the unreality of it, haunted already with sights and sounds he would never be able to forget and dreams that would never be fulfilled. He too reached out, touching what was left of the child and clinging to his sobbing, despairing wife in a desperate bid to hold her and their newly broken lives together, as she shuddered with an overwhelming yearning to turn back time and never have to face this moment over and over for the rest of her life. She wished with all her being that it could have been her instead.

But it wasn't and couldn't be, and she would always dream of him becoming but not become. The child they held would be immortal in their eyes because their years would be filled with images of the man he might have been. They knew his solid life of promise, now fractured, would be a life of unfulfilled dreams and aching sadness that would grow with them like age.

The man was stunned with grief and disbelief and guilt. It was a terrifying moment of teetering sanity that would shake them both profoundly and forever.

Chapter 17

"Oh, Jesus! Thanks, man," said Euan as he climbed clumsily to his feet with Conor's help and stood next to Ronan, who was staring absently across the street.

"Are you OK?" asked Conor. "That was pretty good reactions from an old bastard, Ronan." Then he noticed the look on Ronan's face. "Are you all right? You look as if you've seen a ghost. Ronan!" And he shook Ronan's shoulder as his confusion grew.

"Yeah, I'm fine," said Ronan finally, and he turned to look at Euan. "Just don't ever fucking do that again. Don't just step on to the road again like that without looking. Please."

Euan didn't know for sure what the problem was, though he had an inkling, but Ronan's face was serious enough to startle him into sense so he didn't argue.

"I won't. I won't. Thanks again," he said as he dusted off the back of his jeans, a little embarrassed now by the mood he had unintentionally created.

"Let's go get the car," said Ronan.

They all looked carefully before taking their chances crossing over and walking the short distance to the car-rental company. They stopped outside to decide what to do and what arrangements to make with those inside.

"Who's going in?" asked Euan. "I don't need to. I'll only drive if you guys get fed up, and only out in the country where it won't matter which side of the road I drive on. I'm pretty clueless on the road anyway, it seems." And he smiled at Ronan, who managed a diluted smile back and an almost imperceptible shake of his head.

Conor and Ronan headed for the office of LandEscape Cars and walked in through the front door.

Adding to the many surprises, neither of the people behind the desk spoke with an Irish accent. In fact, they sounded like they were from Eastern Europe though neither Conor nor Ronan could say where exactly, when they discussed it later on. The formalities were over surprisingly quickly, and they didn't even ask to see Ronan's international driver's licence, which he had been so careful to organize before coming away. In fact it seemed like only a cursory glance at his New Zealand one. Conor's processing was even quicker, and all the lines were signed, the money paid (half each) and the paperwork handed over. Then the rules were explained and they were told to have the car at Shannon Airport at the agreed date and time with a full tank of petrol.

"I'll bring it round the front," said the young man in a safely monosyllabic but slow, rounded accent, and he disappeared out through a door at the back of the office to a courtyard outside.

"Should we wait outside, then?" asked Conor of the young lady on the computer. "I'll assume no answer means yes, shall I? She wants us to wait outside, Ronan. At least that's what's coming through in the conversation."

They didn't have long to wait before a car was driven down the narrow alleyway at the side of the office and a silver VW Golf was parked outside the office and right in front of them.

"Keys?" said the man, holding them up.

"Is he telling us or does he want us to confirm that they're a set of keys?" asked Conor.

"He wants to know who's driving, you fool. Thank you," said Ronan, and he took the dangling keys from the air. "One missing wheel trim," he indicated as he walked around the car.

"Covered by the insurance," he was told. "No problems. Drop off at our rental yard at Shannon Airport," he reminded them.

"Yep, OK. Right, I'm driving. Come on, Euan. Which seat do you want?"

"I'm happy to go in the back and Conor can have the passenger seat."

"Do I get a chance to choose my own seat?"

"OK, you can go in the back and I'll take the passenger seat," said Euan.

"I don't want the back seat. I'll get car sick. I'll go in the passenger seat."

"That's what I said to start with! What's the matter with you now?" asked Euan.

"Just asserting my right to have choices," answered Conor mischievously. He was really just attempting to disperse the gloom which had briefly settled on them. "I could drive if you like?" he continued. "I'm used to these VWs, remember, and you'll struggle with reverse."

"No, you don't, Conor. I haven't come all this way not to drive in Ireland. You'll get your turn. Why can't you be accommodating like Euan? Now get in the front."

"God, it's like a school trip with the class teacher in charge. C'mon, Euan," said Conor, taking his hand, "you accommodating little turd. Get in the back." And he opened the rear door and shovelled him in. "Right, *mein Führer*, I'm getting in and we'll be away."

He climbed in and closed the door with military efficiency and put his hands flat on his lap.

Ronan walked around and got in the driver's seat and made himself comfortable, his mood lightening.

Chapter 18

Even with two navigators, and Conor had done this trip at least twice before and fairly recently, it was difficult getting out of the city. It seemed to them that they had gone round in circles at least twice before they found themselves out on the N4, heading for Longford, and with all the signs pointing in the right direction for Maynooth and Innfield and Mullingar – names that were refreshed from their childhood, though they knew nothing about them other than the names of the places and the memories of the people they loved who had spoken them. The arguments and the blame about who kept making the mistakes could stop now and they could settle back to enjoy the remainder of a journey, which would hopefully be a lot simpler than the first part.

"There's nothing quite like being lost in a strange country in a car full of bloody know-alls to make for a good argument, is there?" said Euan.

The other two agreed.

"Works every time," said Conor.

"Do you remember that song that we used to hear often when Mum and Dad used to have Radio Eirean on the radio with the Irish showbands singing? Early in the morning Dad would get home from night shift and Mum, without fail, would get his breakfast for him and he'd come into the front room with the paper and turn that old, round Ekco radio on. It was all about how you can't forget Ireland."

Ronan got no reply.

"Aw, c'mon – you do. You must do. Dad used to sing it! What

was it now?" He dug deep into his memory and he turned pieces of it over in his head. "Something about old Kerry pipers have all ceased to play . . . something, something blood runs free in your veins. . . . Help me out here, guys."

Conor handed him a tissue. "Here," he said, "wipe your mouth with this. You're dribbling uncontrollably."

"Do you find that though?" asked Ronan, undeterred. "Euan, I'm asking you. I might get something more than sarcasm from you. Have you thought much about Ireland as you've got older and further away from it?"

"Hang on a minute – I remember some part of that song: 'and the wide Shannon flows . . . da da da at all of a wild Irish rose'. That's all I've got in my head."

"'You'll never forget about Ireland,'" sang Conor to finish it off.

"See – you do remember it!" shouted Ronan. "I knew you did, you awkward bugger!"

"Might remember Ireland, but didn't do too well with the song, did we?" laughed Euan. "But to answer your question, yea, I sure have. There were so many memories to recall – weren't there? – of all those holidays in Ireland when we were younger, when Mum and Dad used to go home to visit their parents, our grandparents, in Strokestown. Hell, those were really fun times and so simple. Do you remember the year when they had bought or raised – I can't remember which – three small sheepdog pups and they gave us one each to look after during the time we were over there?"

"Yours was the easiest to look after, Ronan, because it used to sleep all the time. It could never keep up and would sit down, close its eyes and topple over on to its side as it dozed off."

"It must have been listening to that song about Ireland!" chipped in Conor. "You two didn't sing to it, did you? That would send a glass eye to sleep, never mind a young pup."

They laughed at that and Euan leaned back to clip Conor across the ear for his effort.

"Smart arse!"

"Keep still in the car, will you, ya eejit!" yelled Ronan.

"Was that the same holiday when we used to buy the small round boxes of caps for the cap guns we had? Do you remember those? Small bubbles of gunpowder on a strip of pink paper that used to feed through the gun in such a way that, as it advanced, it moved one small cap of gunpowder each time you started to pull the trigger and it placed it under the hammer just before it fell and went off with a bang."

"Yeah, and as usual that got too easy and boring so we found Grandad's sledgehammer and we used to put nearly half or more of the caps on to the stone wall around the cottage and then give them a really good slam with the hammer. All the caps would go off at the same time with a hell of a bang. We thought that was special and we knew – do you remember? – the adults were watching from the windows and the doorway with big grins on their faces."

"Do you remember the big old fireplace in the cottage where all the food was cooked? It was huge! There were metal rods that used to swing from the sides and they would put all the – they'd fill the pots with potatoes and vegetables. Witches' cauldrons!"

"And meat?"

"I don't know – I can't remember. But probably. And then they would build up the fire and swing the arms with the pots hanging from them over the fire and everything would be cooking – you know, just cooked like that."

"They must have had an oven though, because I remember lots of soda bread."

"Dunno. I think that was cooked somehow in the fire. Don't remember, but the food was good. It was good, wasn't it?"

"And what about the house – the cottage? They used to keep chickens out the back. Dozens of them, and they were fed each morning with something that Grandma used to mix up."

"Probably leftover soda bread," said Ronan.

"And then she would be outside, wearing that big old apron and those strong black shoes, chucking handfuls from a large basin, saying, 'Sook, sook, sook.' And chickens would come from everywhere, haring round corners of the sheds, jostling and sprinting and fighting as if they wanted it all to themselves.

Squawking and fretting and trampling each other on the way and complaining and cackling the whole time. If she was late they used to start peering in the two doorways and even come inside only to be chased out with Grandad's big working boot up the bum so that his curse and the birds' squawks were like a scratched symphony."

"I remember the way they used to peer inside the door – beak first, then eye, then the red rubber glove and the flourish of the head. Cheeky little bastards!"

"Some of them ended up in the pot, didn't they? She was pretty sharp, old Grandma was. One minute 'Sook, sook, sook' and the next minute 'Squawk, squawk, squawk!'"

"Yep, I never got how she did that, but she would catch the bird she wanted, tuck it under her left arm . . . isn't it amazing how you remember little details like that? She'd grab its head and the top part of its neck in her right hand and twist like she was squeezing a jumper dry."

"And you, Conor," said Euan, poking him in the shoulder from behind, "used to flinch and run back into the house."

"I've always been the sensitive kind," said Conor. "Especially when it comes to chickens."

"Was it an earth floor, or is that just a romantic fantasy?"

"I'm not sure, but I don't remember a floor other than hard earth, or was it black flagstones? but as you say . . ." said Euan, trailing off. "Yeah, I think about Ireland a lot. But mostly because of Mum and Dad. It's always going to be a special place because of that, I suppose."

And, coincidentally, they both looked at Conor.

"Yes, OK. What do you want me to say? I think about it a lot too, though the last few years haven't been fond memories. You never get your parents out of your genes. Sometimes I look at both of you – a look, a glance, a mannerism, a laugh and I could swear it was Dad if I closed my eyes. Sometimes there's Mum in you too, Ronan. More than us, I think. Words and their magic. She was good at that, like you. You even speak like a novel! And she had a gentle humour that's got mischief in it."

"God! You can talk!" said Euan. "Except skip the 'gentle'! It's true though, isn't it? Sometimes when we're all laughing . . ."

"At one of your stupid quips!" said Ronan, massaging the 'gentle' and looking at Conor.

"I hear Dad too – very clearly. But there's more of Mum in all of us than we think. She did such a good job with the family budget and we had huge meals. Nutritionists these days would frown, but there was always a fried egg on top of the mountain of potato and sausages and beans and peas and we loved it. And we ran so much and played outside even in the snow and ran to catch buses. There was not time to get fat. I think we remember those things about her: how busy she was and slim and how, when she could least afford it, we always got the best she could manage. She was a very proud lady."

"Yeah, I remember she always tried to keep the peace between us three – not an easy task. I remember lots of fights," said Conor: "always you two on to me."

"Oh, you poor thing," said Ronan. "You obviously deserved it even then." And he laughed.

They settled back after that, lost in more memories, reversing their film, slowing down the good bits, using 'pause' indiscriminately to get a better look at the scenery and the faces, seeing some in black and white deliberately to mark their passage and then fast-forwarding back to the present and, secretly glancing at each other, realizing how much had changed and how little. All independently wondered what the others were thinking, not realizing how close and happy their thoughts were.

Euan and Ronan, deep in their own thoughts, stared out through the car windows at the scenery passing by and watched the few cars approaching and the grey sulky clouds passing overhead.

The scenery was as they remembered: lush and green and soggy and puddled with recent rain, sectioned off with wild-grown hedges in some places and grey stone walls that wandered up the gentle hills while the car did the same. There were wild grasses, trees and cottages in abundance, gates and cattle – heads down at the industry of eating. It seemed to be largely grazing land they were driving through, hay piled up like badly brushed hair and everywhere churches and 'For Sale' signs and seemingly empty houses.

"What do you think if we stop at the next town coming up just ahead? It's called Mullingar," said Ronan. "From what I can see it seems like a big enough place to grab a bit of lunch. There's bound to be a café somewhere where we can grab a bite and a cuppa."

"Good idea," agreed Euan. "We have to come off this main road slightly and head over to the left. There's a sign," he said. "Yep! That's it! Mullingar! I'm starved. Could eat a bear."

"Looks like you already did," said Ronan, and Euan leaned forward threateningly.

"No! No! No! Can't touch the driver! Too dangerous!"

Just in case, Ronan leaned a little to the side to avoid a possible clip.

"I remember that name being used around the house quite often," said Conor as the sign flashed by on his left and he checked it on his map. "Looks a reasonable size. We might as well. It won't take that long to get to Longford. We're not far from a place called Edgeworthstown. It's a short drive to Longford and a reasonably straight-looking road on to Strokestown. The rest of today's journey won't take long at all."

He tapped the map, folded it badly (like you do with maps) and put it in the glovebox.

"OK. Well, you two look for somewhere. I'm keeping my eyes on the road and the traffic. There's a bit more here to keep me occupied now."

Chapter 19

It wasn't long before they saw a good collection of shops on the outskirts of Mullingar and guessed that they would find what they wanted there or down one of the many narrow, interesting-looking side streets that they were passing.

There always seemed to be a square or a monument in the towns, or at least a gathering place, which probably made it easier to organize rendezvous points – unless some places had more than one, which was likely as many of the small towns were growing and the new centre was moving away from the old. In fact these former landmarks, and their locations, were like social and geographical commentaries on the changing face and size of village life in Ireland.

They couldn't find any distinguishing feature, but were not keen to go too far into the town for fear of getting locked in some busy traffic queues in which they might get squeezed down some unwanted roads that would be hard to get out of. They found a good-sized car park down a side street, locked up the car, put their jackets on again – it was starting to rain – and headed back towards a wider street that beckoned with signs and activity. They soon found what they were looking for and went in for coffee, a few savouries and sandwiches. They took their time, listening to the conversations around them and the lilt and velvet of the speech.

"No rush," said Conor, and he nodded to the outside.

He was right. It was bucketing down, the colour of a clear plastic sheet so that you could barely see through to the objects running and fumbling with umbrellas on the other side.

"Don't fancy going out in that," he said, "so I'll just enjoy this coffee. Suggest you do the same."

They agreed.

It pelted down for nearly fifteen minutes before it became possible to get back to the car without being drenched, and even then, when they finally fell inside, they were three drops off being soaked. Euan and Conor swapped places.

"Bloody hell! It's a while since I've seen a downfall of rain like that," said Euan.

"That's because yours is all frozen and white," said Conor.

"And so is your rain," said Ronan, and the chortling laughter started again.

They were soon on the road to Edgeworthstown after being taken around and around by navigator Conor, who commented at every opportunity about the lack of road signs making it impossible for all but those who had lived for sixty or more years in the town to find their way out.

"I don't ever remember this next place being talked about in the house when we were kids. Do you?" asked Euan. "And yet it's not that far from Longford and I'm sure one or both of Mum and Dad would have driven through it a few times."

"Might be a good reason to miss it out, then," said Conor.

They got back on the road and had a reasonably good run before they reached the signs for Edgeworthstown, after about a fifty-minute drive, and they were able to miss the township by using an underpass. Before they knew it, they were headed for Longford, probably about eighteen kilometres away, and into familiarly named territory that held a vault of memories for them all.

Euan wanted to take a detour if they could and go to the right, off the main road, and make their way back on to the N4 by going left somewhere once they had seen and driven down some country roads.

"It's one of the things I remember and liked," he said defensively.

"Ever thought of becoming an Arctic explorer?" asked Conor. "With directional accuracy like that, you couldn't go wrong. Just go left at this polar bear and we'll head back to the right once we've experienced a bit of polar bear, angry and hungry for a Canadian moose!"

"I agree with you, Euan." And Ronan turned right at a sign saying 'Corbay'. "The sun's out again and it'll be great to see the countryside."

Sure enough, the sun was shining down quite brilliantly, and the road was starting to steam very lightly as they pinched down to narrow roads and sudden corners almost too tight to slip sideways through.

They took in the countryside and the smell of freshly wet grass, warmed by the sun and amazed at the amount of wild fuchsia that spattered the hedges with a purple, pink and red mosaic of colour. They recognized the wild angelica, burdock and hedge parsley everywhere they looked among the hedgerows and along the roadsides – a riot of flowering.

They drove in this Edenic scene before coming across cow shit all over the road, moistened by the rain and slurrying under the car as Ronan took it at pace around a corner and came up suddenly behind a large tractor in front of them, taking up three-quarters of the width of the road.

He came up close and quickly, hoping the farmer would see him and find a way to let him pass. It was a mistake, and it's doubtful the tractor driver even noticed him – there were no wing mirrors on the tractor. They were travelling quite quickly, so Ronan was hopeful the farmer would get the message, as he sounded the car horn, and let them get by, but he received a wave. The tractor driver never even looked round, and it was just then that thick gouts of cow shit flicked off the back wheels of the tractor and slathered the front of the car, windscreen, roof, backs of rear-view mirrors, and sides, where it slid along graciously before getting the moisture whipped out of it.

"Holy shit!" said Euan.

"There's nothing holy about this," said Ronan.

"It stinks to high heaven though," smiled Conor.

"It's as thick and wet as it comes." Ronan was clearly unimpressed.

He slowed down and dropped back to give the windscreen washer and wipers a fighting chance. As he did so the tractor pulled into a field on the left, where the cows were casually ambling in, in that moody hip-swinging way that only cows can do well with innocence, on the way from an overgrazed field to lush pasture.

Conor used the window control to just let down the window a small amount and shouted out, "Pity we're not in Cork! Your cows could use some!"

If he was hoping to get a response he didn't, and it's probable the farmer never heard him anyway. However, he turned and smiled and gave a friendly wave as he roared in through the gate and on to the field.

"I think he was laughing," said Conor.

"I'm sure he was!" said Euan.

"Another great idea of yours, Euan. A reminiscence of childhood with a romantic trip down the narrow memory lanes of Ireland. Pity that Pooh Bear arses and friends were out in full force!" smirked Ronan.

"Yeah," agreed Conor. "Back to nature and our earth mother. Little did we know that our earth mother would be recycled through the collective large intestines and oversized ring pieces of about sixty cows with diarrhoea and then chucked all over our rental car with the assistance of one of the sons of the earth!"

"I don't know about a son of the earth," replied Euan. "More like a bit of a sod! So, OK, OK, we're covered in enough of it. There's no need for you two to start talking a pile of it. Let's move on." And Euan chuckled quietly to himself.

The sun shone brightly with a surprising heat in it and they made their way to Longford via Moatfarrell, left to Corbay Crossroads, back on to the N4 for a very short journey, and into the outskirts of Longford. Just what Dr Euan had ordered, but without the dessert.

"Longford," said Ronan. "This is a pretty memorable place for you, isn't it, Conor?"

"Mm," said Conor. "Yes, it is."

He was silent for a while and Ronan and Euan thought he

wasn't going to say any more, so Ronan prompted him: "I remember you sent us an email . . ."

"Yes, I did," he started, and paused briefly before adding, "I told you that Mum and Dad had returned to Ireland and, for some reason, had come to Longford and bought a house there. I don't think Mum liked it that much and I never even asked, 'Why Longford?' Why not somewhere more romantic or just different? Dad was obviously not keen to live too near family because he had become a bit disillusioned with some of the goings-on and he was unpopular with Mum's family after spiriting her away to England in the 1940s to get married. I don't think Mum had any family left to visit in Ireland anyway, so anywhere would do, maybe. Certainly there was no one left in Kilteevan that she knew. They had all long gone. But Longford was still close enough to both of their birthplaces.

"It was as if they could and couldn't quite leave it all behind. Mum was already sick then, and you and Maria came over for a visit, Euan. It wasn't long after you'd left that she deteriorated rapidly and died the following April. Dad was devastated and I came out to support him with the funeral."

Both Euan and Ronan unconsciously looked downwards, but had to look up again to give him support.

"When Mum died we drove away from the house in Longford. I remember Dad said he didn't want to come and see us leave; I think it was the day after the funeral. Just before we left, reasonably early in the morning, he came upstairs to the bedroom where Tessa and I were and he looked out of the window and he crumpled. I apologise if I've told you some of this before," said Conor. "It gets easier the more I talk about it. Like massaging an injury. He said to me, 'What am I going to do now?' and I couldn't answer his question. I worry about it sometimes. Why did he ask that question? Did I fail to understand what he was really asking? I was really stressed and I've never forgotten it. Eventually he sold the house, moved into a cottage, bought a dog and moved to Galway. Why Galway? Same as 'Why Longford?' And I don't have an answer for that either. The rest I think you know. It's still hard to talk about it."

Ronan looked surreptitiously in the rear-view mirror and saw Conor's eyes and furrowed brow and knew he was upset. Euan reached his right arm over the back of his seat and patted Conor on the shoulder.

"You did a great job, fella," he said. "For all of us. Thanks, Buddy."

Conor continued to stare out of the window as they drove further into Longford. The sun continued to shine and the day grew warmer as the hours ticked by.

"Whoa! Whoa!" shouted Euan. "There's a car wash there! One of those brushless ones that just use jets of water and stuff."

"A car wash?" asked Conor. "Why do we want a car wash? You mean all this?" he asked, pointing at the congealing cow crap on the windows and bonnet. "You don't wash rental cars," he said in astonishment. "It's part and parcel of what you pay for."

"Aw, get off! You can't take it back in this state. If this weather continues like this it will be baked on hard by the time we leave Galway and return the car, and it will probably damage the paint. Anyway, we still have a fair bit of travelling to do and I for one would rather not look as if I'm a poor country cousin out for the day in the city."

"It smells too," agreed Ronan, using a compelling argument they could all agree with. "It's coming in through the vents even though I haven't got the air con on. We've got one of these brushless car washes just down the road from us back home. It's great."

Euan opened his window a fraction and sniffed the air.

"It is pretty ripe," he said. "It may be drying out, but the smell lingers. In fact it's worse in here than outside," he said, taking another nose-ful of fresher air coming through the open window.

"I agree," said Ronan, and he turned around a roundabout and headed back towards where they had seen the car wash.

"Waste of bloody money," Conor muttered complainingly to himself.

They pulled on to the forecourt and parked the car while

Ronan got out and went inside to pay for a car wash. He was quickly out again with his piece of paper and his code number. He got back into the car waving the ticket.

"Nine bloody euros! I could get a full vehicle service for that in New Zealand."

"In your dreams," said Conor. "Anyway, I told you not to bother, but . . . you can't be told," he said in his best condescending voice and with his nose in the air in mock derision.

Ronan drove the car around to the car wash, and fortunately there was no one else there apart from a car getting the last stages of the drying treatment, so they were next.

Ronan opened his window, put in the number on the pad, wound up his window and drove in, watching carefully for the green light to go off and the red light to come on, signalling him to stop. It was always nerve-wracking, he thought, using car washes in another country as if it was a new language that you might not understand and you worried that you might be left looking foolish; but it all seemed to be working as expected.

The water drummed on the windscreen as the swivel bar moved along the front and over to the left.

"It's not coming through the windscreen, is it?" asked Conor. "Because I can feel it spraying in the back here. In fact, it's pissing in!" he yelled, ducking his head down.

Ronan turned to look and noticed that Conor's window and Euan's window were both open – only slightly, but open.

"Hurry up! Close your bastard windows! Your damn windows are open!" he yelled urgently as the swivel reached the left corner, spun, and moved down the side of the car.

They both scrambled for the window catches, fingers feeling like frankfurters with the urgency and panic, which made them clumsy.

"Mine's not working!" screamed Conor exaggeratedly, tugging at the window switch as he was engulfed in jets of water that stung his face and pelted past him to stick like needles on Ronan's arm, raised to protect himself from the stabbing water.

"Hurry up!" screamed Euan as he tried to bend himself down in the back seat and hide from the water that was now jetting in through his window. "Aw, c'mon. Aw, fuck! What's wrong with this? Mine won't work either!"

They could hardly hear themselves above the noise of the thundering, drumming water and the explosive tattoo as it hit the inside car lining and windows.

"You must have the engine turned off!" yelled Conor. "Turn the fucking keys round until the lights come on. Fucking hell! Quickly! Hurry up! Shit!"

Suddenly the windscreen wipers were arching back and forth across the windscreen.

"Not the bastard windscreen wipers, you tosser! They're about as useful as a soluble fire hose! The ignition! Turn the ignition on!" screamed Conor in frustration.

As Ronan turned the key, both windows came up with a 'thunk', but the swivel was already at the back corner and heading around to wash the back of the car. Ronan checked that the two on his side were closed before the washing jets got around to him and came in through his windows.

They all leaned back in their seats, expelling the air they didn't know they had been holding in, and relief showed on their faces as they looked at each other, all soaked and looking absolutely forlorn and miserable. It wasn't even a clean wash, as some of the cow shit had been collected on the ends of the water jets and carried in through the windows and on to the three of them struggling helplessly in the car.

Afterwards it was hard to remember who started laughing first, but they were helpless within seconds as the wash continued and they just tried to get their breath and stop. But every time they looked at each other it all started up again, and they were soon aching and breathless and forced into whimpering silence.

They drove out when the drier had finished and the green light came back on, and they parked in a parking space to the side of the garage.

"OK, who's going in?" asked Ronan.

"For what?" asked Conor.

"For what? For some rags and a bucket of water! Have a look around in here," suggested Ronan.

They did all look and realized that water was dripping from the ceiling of the car and most of the driver's side panelling and the inside of the windows was spattered with water.

"We need to wipe it all down and some of it isn't quite fresh water either, now that it became mixed with the shit on its way in."

"You go, Conor," said Euan. "You look the wettest and you'll get the most sympathy."

"And the most piss taken too. Look – they're queuing to look out through the window in there, staring at these bloody stupid people who can't even wash a car safely. I can't believe that!"

He got out of the car, slamming the door firmly behind him, and went inside.

"Good afternoon again, sir. Have you been for a wash too now? Sure you didn't dry yurself too well."

The other attendant smirked and looked away when Conor eyeballed him.

"I tought ye asked for a car wash. Did ye tink 'twas a bath house?"

As he talked he took the card of another customer, whom he shared a wink with, then he swiped it and gave him back his card and his docket.

The customer walked away, too embarrassed to be in the vicinity, but clearly enjoying the ribbing that was going on.

The cashier was relentless: "You're supposed to stay in da car, not go roamin' around in the car wash. Sure dat's a silly ting to do, so 'tis." His shoulders sagged and he hunched and held himself in while his crumpled bundle of eyebrows hid his laughing eyes. He then feigned seriousness: "How can I help you, sir? Do you want another car wash?" He obviously couldn't help himself.

"I would like some dry cloths – three if you could – and a bucket of clean, warm water if you wouldn't mind tearing yourself away from your solo comedy performance," said

Conor, struggling with his patience and wiping away the water which was running from his hair and down the sides of his nose. "Do you have those things?"

"Are ya going to wash it be hand now, sir?" he asked, smiling.

"No. No, I'm not. You're a born comedian, aren't you? Look – just answer the question and then I can get on with drying the inside of the car out."

Conor was losing his patience, but he soon subsided when he thought about it and realized he would be doing just the same if he was on the other side of the counter and was not the butt of the joke.

"I'll get some for ya. It's the least I can do to thank you for the entertainment. I haven't laughed so much since the mother-in-law died."

He went out the back of the garage and quickly returned with all the gear that Conor had asked for.

"Do ya want me to give ya a demonsthration of how to use them?" he asked, and Conor swung a cloth in a mock gesture as if to hit him with it.

The attendant ducked playfully out of the way.

Once outside they took a cloth each, and, opening all the doors, washed all the panels and the dashboard and put the floor mats outside to dry. It wasn't as bad as they expected because they had been very thin needle jets of water. At the time it had felt like more than it was, but it took them a good fifty minutes before they felt satisfied with their efforts.

"That'll do, guys," said Euan. "Don't want it looking better than new."

They both agreed and threw out the water and dropped the cloths in the bucket. Conor went in to give the gear back to the attendant.

"Don't start!" warned Conor as the attendant went to open his mouth, but he tried one last comment anyway. Conor played fall guy to the attendant. Again he'd picked the humour of the man and let him orchestrate it. He was good at that too.

"You three are a right pair if ever I saw one," he said, and his face split open with a smile.

They both laughed as Conor left through the sliding door, and the sound died away as the door hushed shut.

"Bit of a jokester, was he?" asked Euan.

"Yes, he was. He was that. I was going to give him a nasty look, but he already had one."

"I'll bet you were well matched," laughed Ronan.

Conor smiled, but didn't answer.

They were soon on the road again, tamed by the incident but realizing it would be good in the telling a few years from then.

"Don't suppose we want to spend too long in Longford?" asked Conor. "Would that be right?"

"I don't mind," replied Euan, "but I'm just as happy to keep going. We know they lived at Ardnacassa Lawn and we—"

"I'd rather keep going," interrupted Conor.

Beforehand, they knew in fairness that his would be the casting vote, and so they found the N5 and headed on the fairly straight road to Strokestown, where their mum and dad had met and where their mum was buried. It was about twenty-four kilometres away and they were soon coming down the hill from the east and heading into the small town full of memories.

"Wait! Wait!" shouted Euan from the back seat. "This is the hill where Grandma and Grandad – Dad's mum and dad – had their cottage. Can we stop here and have a look?"

"You're right," said Conor. "I didn't think you'd recognize it. I wondered if you would. I just about missed it myself."

"Well, I wasn't sure," answered Euan excitedly. "It seems such a small hill looking down there now, and in my mind it was very long and very steep. Do you remember when we had to walk to the church at the bottom of the hill? It seemed like miles."

"God!" That was all Ronan could say. His surprise was the same and he just stared as he steered the car in to the kerbside. "Things are never the same when you come back as an adult to a kid's playground, are they? Everything is smaller, shorter, less scary, and you don't always recognize some parts which you thought were carved into your memory."

They all got out of the car and looked back behind them to the top of the hill, just a few metres away. They stared at what was the site of their grandparents' cottage, but it now had a modern bungalow on it which their auntie, their dad's sister, had built there when both her parents had died.

It was small with a grey-tiled roof. The walls were plaster and fawn/yellow with vertical and horizontal inlays of coloured bricks around and under the windows at both ends of the house and down the outside end of the single garage. It was on the rise of the hill with trees at the back and sides and the beginnings of some sort of development at the front. The earthworks going on there now were in front of the cottage, on a lower piece of land, but they didn't bother to look; it wasn't what they remembered.

Their auntie had also died and there was no longer anything tangible there to draw their interest, only happy memories of a previous home away from home for short periods of their lives.

"It was somewhere around here that we had to take a bucket or two and get some water from the spring for the cooking and the tea. It was over the road here somewhere, wasn't it?"

Conor started across while Ronan took the keys out of the ignition and stood staring down at the town a very short distance away.

'No suburbs,' he thought. 'No real separation between town and country.'

Chapter 20

The accident had happened on a country road, and as he got older Ronan found himself thinking more and more about it and what it had done to the family. How had things been different and for how long afterwards?

How long before they stop raking over the memories and understand the consequences and disinterestedness of fate?

How long before the strident echoes fade?

What faceless anger buried itself in their hearts to tear away at love and God for years afterwards?

Having a family of his own now, he often thought about how he would have felt if one of his sons had been killed in a road accident. Even though he was only trying to get a sense of the feelings that would tear a family apart, trying to understand the pain that his parents would have had to grapple with, he found himself almost tearful with the sheer terror of it as, each time, it came to life in his imagination.

The images in his mind seemed to be getting stronger rather than weaker, even as time and a headlong future took it further and further away from him in years.

More often than not he found himself in awe of the resilience of his parents to survive something as shattering as that. When he thought of the love they shared, and the closeness they knew, he realized the strength that it must have taken to rebalance a loving life to protect the rest of the children in the family from an anxious and sheltered childhood.

He remembered now that they wandered far from home on

snowy Saturday mornings exploring frozen canals and ponds, sometimes arriving back in the gloom of a late afternoon; they stayed out at night in safe streets playing games with other street kids; they came home late at night in the dark from sports practice at the Catholic grammar school, thirty and more miles away; they were out late on Guy Fawkes Night playing dangerously with bangers and other fireworks round a blazing bonfire of accumulated rubbish on the back field.

How do you let go and grow independent kids after a tragedy like that?

What's to stop you being housebound and smothered with protective, suffocating love?

What if you grew up without confidence and afraid of every experience that was testing?

Could you ever blame them if your life had been changed dramatically by one circumstance?

Would you torture the moments before and dream of how life could have been different?

Chapter 21

Euan followed Conor across and they looked around on the far side of the road. Ronan soon joined them. There were lots more houses on this side than there had ever been before – the one replaced by many.

"Have a look back over there at how close the cottage was to the spring, because I'm sure it was around here somewhere that we used to carry the buckets. Look!" he said, pointing. "We used to complain all the time and do everything we could to avoid having to go for water."

Euan seemed almost disappointed at what a short distance it was because he had fanciful images in his head of struggling up the hill with two buckets weighing him down, stretching his arms, lowering them carefully to the floor and looking at Grandma with a martyred uplifted face, whereas she had bent down to lift them and she carried them to the pots over the open fire as easily as if she was carrying two dead turkeys.

"It could just have dried up," said Conor, "or else the changes around here – the McGreeveys' house has gone too . . . and there are two new places here – might just have covered it over. What a shame!"

"You wouldn't have said that fifty-odd years ago," laughed Ronan. "You would have looked for anything to cover it over!"

"Do you remember when we used to come across the road and watch the McGreeveys milking their one or two cows? They would tell us to come close and look carefully, and then they would turn up the teat and squirt it in our faces. Do you remember that?" asked Euan.

"She would ask us to try and milk, and I remember the strange feel of the udder. The loose skin of it," laughed Conor.

"Aye, and we all know why you enjoyed it so much. It was twice the size of anything you'd had in your hand before," agreed Ronan, and they laughed till they ached. "Let's go on into the town, do you think?"

They were all beginning to feel like it was holy ground that they had entered, that they were moving closer to the fire and that their nervousness was overheating. This was the den of their memories and they approached cautiously and uneasily, afraid of their feelings and what was lurking there.

They got into the car and drove the short distance to Strokestown, where they found a parking place in the middle of the main street. They had been expecting to take their pick of accommodation, but there was only one hotel in the town close enough to where they wanted to be. It was a long building edging its way along the main street, and there were several dormer windows in the roof. They parked the car in the car park at the left and round the back and booked in at the Percy French Hotel, with a friendly receptionist, and took their gear up to their rooms.

They could have had their choice of rooms. It was a tough time for rural Ireland and there were not many travellers on the road – national or international. Ireland was now an expensive place to come to and to travel in. It was a curious paradox because it was becoming poor again in terms of contraction of manufacturing and rising unemployment. There was growing poverty.

The rooms were comfortable and the service very friendly. Their booking was for two nights.

The day hung between early and mid afternoon; so they decided to have a look around the town, and walked out on to the main street. The walk didn't take as long as they thought it would. Again their childhood imaginings and wide-eyed memories of the large town they had visited infrequently shrank in the clench of their comparative adult experiences since those years.

They also had memories of a very busy little town, full of

country folk, sheepdogs and market stalls, old cars parked randomly anywhere there was a space (and there were plenty in those days), thriving shops and huddles of conversations – every one of them a swirling cloud of smoke from pipes and a few cigarettes.

"Do you remember", said Euan, interrupting their thoughts, "those days when there were small herds of cattle and flocks of sheep being driven through the main street and not a care for the slopped messes they left behind? We used to giggle watching their bums and the ooze coming out and nobody even caring – least of all the farmer."

"You would remember that, wouldn't you, being a lad from the wild north?" teased Conor. "Being more cerebral, I remember the weathered-faced farmer – oblivious, as you said – walking behind in his collarless shirt and tweed jacket, baggy trousers tucked down his wellingtons, and his flat cap, and his stick in the air threatening a smack on the rump for a dawdling cow or used as a temporary shepherding rod for his wandering sheep. I got the impression that old Farmer John was pleased when it happened; even in those days there was probably a social separation between the 'country bumpkins' and the 'snobby townies'."

They walked quietly along. There was no sign of Mannion's General Store and pub, which they had visited with their mum and dad. Their parents would wander down the hill and into Mannion's pub, attached to the store, to catch up with friends while holidaying in the home country, and the boys were allowed to sit quietly at a table with a glass of lemonade each. Womenfolk would cast admiring glances at them and they would smile at the serious look on their faces as they stared through the smoke around them in bewilderment at the crowds and the noise.

They sat quietly and watched their parents laughing and joking with people they never even knew. There were some embarrassing moments when people came over to say, "Are you Danny and Margaret's boys, then? Now, what are your names? Fine-looking lads!" And they would wander back to their group of adults with an occasional glance across at them; they knew they were being talked about. They didn't have much to say for themselves and didn't know what to say, but people just seemed to be happy coming for a look.

The store part had been a crystal cave of things that they had never seen in the small corner shops of home. Even the Co-op, their giant store around the corner from their third home in England, had seemed dull and adult, whereas this had been a treasure house too big and crowded to take in. It had gone.

"Was the store gone last time you came here, a few years ago, Conor?" asked Euan.

"Yes. I'd say it went a long time ago. I wanted you just to have your own impressions rather than get them second-hand from me. You'll notice other things too, but I won't tell you what they are."

"Well, I see the pubs are only just opening," observed Ronan, "which is very unusual. I thought they were open at sunrise and then stayed open until the next sunrise, when it was time to open again."

The doors were opening at two pubs as they walked past and the familiar waft of ale filled their nostrils as they strolled by.

"There are still plenty of them though. I've counted at least five places where you can get a drink, and that's just in the one street here."

"There are not many people around to enjoy them, then," said Euan. "I have pictures of lots of what seemed like modern cars (well, for the times), horses and carts with various loads (none of which I can remember), happy, red-faced men and women and lots of laughter and noise and smells – funnily enough, of cigarette smoke and stale ale. Probably nostalgic imaginings again. But look at this! There's no one else out except for two drivers. Tumbleweeds will be coming through here soon," he joked.

They went back to the hotel to get the car because they realized that they could get around quicker and there might not be a lot to see; there was no need to pretend there was enough to occupy a good walk.

They went back up the main street again, came to a roundabout and went straight across and on over.

"There's a familiar name," said Ronan, and he pointed at a sign with gold and white lettering on a black background displayed over a shop frontage.

The sign said, 'Farrell's Property Sales: Auctioneers–Valuers, Estate Agents–Mortgage Brokers. Letting Agents'.

"That's one of our cousins, isn't it?" he asked.

"That's right. But I for one don't want to go visiting, so just look and don't touch," said Conor.

"It's a real shame that the extended family ties have become so weak, and yet the closer family ties are getting stronger," said Euan. "Dad and Mum were really the only ones who settled in the north of England. Everyone else from the Strokestown diaspora went London way, and I suppose it just got too tough to keep calling around to keep in touch," decided Euan.

Conor disagreed: "I'm not convinced it was as simple as that," he said. "There seems to have been an independence about Dad. I never knew whether it was just a hard-wired personality trait or whether something had happened that made him want to be away from it all. I know about his marriage to Mum and how much damage that did to her family and his own at the time, but in the end it was a match made in heaven."

"Yeah, remember too that we didn't have a phone at that stage, so I suppose keeping in touch was pretty difficult. It used to be a lot of fun though at Christmas times, didn't it? But it didn't last long. I think there are many things that happened that we don't know anything about, maybe, and we never asked to find out. Chances not taken again," concluded Ronan.

Euan was perplexed, and in a way they all were. Intimacies of family were never discussed and, in the busy days of boyhood, they never asked. And now they regretted that they had not found out more of their family history in detail. It was a tragedy of lost connections and untold stories, and yet they all realized that the days of living two doors down from your parents, or five doors down from your uncles and aunties, were over. It was true of all families that the ties broke over time, and in their case it caused disintegration that would never be mended.

Conor too was a little annoyed with himself and disappointed that they knew so little about their family history. He knew more than the others though, especially of their parents' later lives. Not the come and go of small-time life, but the fate and the choices, the chance and the destiny and the purposes behind the big decisions that shaped who their parents were – and now, who they all were. It wasn't enough, but in a sense he knew that in reality it was as much as you got these days if your family changed from nuclear to global.

"Perhaps we're being too tough on ourselves," Euan said. "Those big decisions that people make are sometimes not that easily talked about or explained. Sometimes it's a notion, an impulse, and the timing is when everything just feels right and they shift your life on to another pathway."

"But we missed those opportunities of conversation. Mum and Dad worked so hard and such unsociable hours and we always seemed to be travelling and working," Conor reminded them, "so it was inevitable in my view."

"You're right, Conor. We had our long hike to grammar school for seven years – up at 6.30 a.m. every weekday morning." Ronan sighed. "And then homework when we got in after five, and then we had tea, then bed and up in the morning, and on we went. Not much time for philosophical discussion, was there?" he said.

He was in two minds about the need for more information about their lives and whether or not it might ruin some of the bliss of ignorance.

"You used to help me with my maths and physics, Euan. Do you remember?" he asked. "I was hopeless at both. In fact you were quite good at all that sort of stuff. He was, wasn't he, Conor?"

Conor didn't let him enjoy the limelight for long: "I don't remember," he said. "I was pretty good on my own."

"And I used to help you both with your English, but I clearly wasted my time," Ronan said, trying to even the score.

Euan smiled, but ignored Ronan and carried on from Conor as if there had been no interruption: "All we have to cling to here now", he said, "are vague distorted memories of a small town in the middle of Ireland where we spent many happy holidays.

But we never really learned or remembered anything more than we already knew about our family. We knew that Mum and Dad had their mum and dad – no surprises there – and they lived a completely different life from their son and daughter-in-law. Sadly, I doubt now that we will ever get to know any more – certainly not in any helpful way."

"It's better that way," said Conor. "What would it do other than provide a history of relationships? It seems to me you would still not be getting the interesting stories of their lives. It won't tell us how they felt; it will only tell us who they knew and what they did – the sketchy outline of their lives. We'll only ever be able to guess at the emotional highs and lows of their lives, and we can assume from what we do know that there were plenty. Those things are the most important part. At least for me, anyway."

"I think we're silly to beat ourselves up over this," said Ronan in an impatient tone. "This place here and then Oranmore are for us the two most important places on this particular trip, though I suspect that's all they will ever be. Places that don't really help us to fully understand and know the two people we love. Let's enjoy the fact that there are images and ghosts. Yes, I can see the look on your faces – I meant *ghosts*. There are images and ghosts of our parents all around these places because the landscape and the life here shaped them and made them what they were. It's who we knew. After that they impacted back on to everyone they came across in their lives here, and – who knows? – everyone's lives here may be different in some tiny absolutely undiscoverable way because our parents lived here as youngsters and fell in love here. We don't need to know every detail of their lives to confirm how special they were to us. I think I can be happy with what I have and not spoil it with clutter or rob it of its mystery or imagine we can find comfort in a couple of cold graves. We – us three – are the emotional content of their lives; and just as much so, if not more . . ."

By this time they had done a circuit of the town's few shops and, unnoticed by them, there had been many looks from locals who saw these three strangers step out of their car, look around and get back in. They wondered who they were – were they somehow connected to someone in the district? – but they couldn't put their questions; it was not their way any more. Strangers didn't come to this town much now, so everyone new was stared at.

They were ready now to take the plunge and seek out Mum's grave in the one cemetery in town. It was starting to rain again, the sky a mixture, like them, of sun and cloud, and so they thought it would be best to go now before it set in too steadily.

"Here!" pointed Conor to a sign on a lamp post on the main street as they seemed to be heading into the country. "It's up this road – Elphin Street – and I seem to remember that it's not very far. We can park the car just here and walk it," he said, pointing to a place where the kerb ended in loose stones and there was plenty of room to park.

They walked together at a mixed pace of quick and slow, keeping it a natural dawdle in the quiet village, not wanting to rush, but unable to wait – particularly Euan and Ronan, who would be seeing it for the first time. Conor knew what to expect, but it didn't make it any easier. Elphin Street sloped gently upwards, and in a short while they arrived at the cemetery, which was at the end of the street on a small rise.

'OK,' thought Ronan, stretching and bracing himself. 'How hard can this be? Bloody hard!' came the quick answer back from within.

It was still raining, but it wasn't getting any heavier. Just the fine, gentle rain that soaks you. Euan was blinking hard as it blew gently into his face in a fine and delicate spray.

"This stuff catches you everywhere, doesn't it?" he observed. "At least when it comes down vertically you can keep some parts of yourself dry before it seeps down to your feet, but this stuff eventually gets through the pinprick holes in the fabric."

They stared to the south from just outside the double gates across at the landscape greening off into the distance. It was an expansive view almost uninterrupted to the south-east and south-west. The landscape was of smoothly mounded hills and sparsely treed clumps of settlements consisting of several black-roofed white-plaster cottages, one with a startling bright-red front door. Hedges and stone walls embraced fields pierced by a narrow wet-striped roadway as thin as a waved black ribbon. There were cattle and sheep in the fields, meagre and still, pastoral and irrelevant, and the beauty of it all escaped them in their misery.

"It's over here somewhere to the right," indicated Conor. "It's been well kept, so it's easy to see."

They had just walked through the two-metre-high wrough-iron gates of the cemetery, supported on both sides by a great stone flat-topped pillar, square and staunch. There was a pedestrian stock-protection gate to the left, but the big gates were open.

It was a strange feeling, like a homecoming of sorts, but an empty one. The drizzling rain added to the feeling of discovery and loss. The blue sky, dappled now with darker grey and white clouds, and in other parts by weak sunshine, was as contradictory as the weather and their mood.

"Who looks after it?" asked Euan.

"I presume that they have someone whose job it is to look after the whole graveyard," answered Conor. "I've never really thought about it."

"I wonder who pays?" asked Ronan.

"I don't know that either. She's buried in a grave beside Grandma and Grandad – our dad's mum and dad – and I suspect someone from the family takes care of it. Maybe one of Dad's cousins. I really don't know," Conor admitted impatiently.

Every time he had visited the graves he found himself swallowing hard to calm his feelings and control his rapid heartbeat.

For a considerable time they idly looked around the graveyard, pretending interest in the other gravestones and calling out to each other interesting comments for the dead and staring at the houses massed behind tall trees at the back of the graveyard. They were playing for time, delaying the moment, gathering their thoughts and looking for courage, and it was only a matter of time before they found what they had and hadn't been looking for.

And it wasn't hard to find. They gathered together in front of the grave to stare at a headstone (two of them for the first time) which said so little and meant so much.

MARGARET FARRELL
Died 25 April 1981
ENDLESS LOVE

And there was a long silence as the sympathetic fine rain ran down their faces.

Ronan broke the silence with a whisper: "Endless love? Is that for her or from her?"

"Both," said Conor.

"I lingered under the malign sky and wondered how anyone could ever imagine unquiet slumber for the sleeper in this quiet earth."

"What did you say?" asked Conor.

"Just a quote I changed to suit because the wind and the elements and my feelings forced the comparison. It's hard to imagine her there," he said, waving dismissively in the direction of the grave. His voice started to break. "It's just so cold-looking and bleak on a day like this, and she always seemed to feel the cold so. I hope heaven is warm." He stopped, unable to trust his voice any further.

Euan came close and put his arm around Ronan's shoulder. Then, to his surprise, Conor came to his other side and put his arm across his shoulder too; and he could tell by the feel and movements behind his head that they had reached across to place their hand on each other's shoulders as well, and they all felt it was the best of moments – a moment that they had not planned or expected of all the plans and expectations that had accumulated around them over the last few years, and yet, now, this was the one that counted most. They felt stronger together and able to get through their collective grief a little easier . . . and the rain was easing.

They stood there for a long time just looking at the grave, taking photographs and trying, unsuccessfully, to get a sense of what lay beneath, but instead remembering, successfully, her liveliness and care and getting comfort from all the warmth of their memories and the support of each other. They chose not to look at each other, protecting their own and each other's private grief, and in the end it was Ronan who broke the spell.

"That's it for me," he said. "I don't know I can ever be back here. This is too tough." And he sighed unevenly and slipped away from his brothers. "The grave is well looked after, but Mum's not here." He stopped and turned to look back at them. "At least not for me. I don't think I want to come back. There's no real need. It's the one missing piece I needed to complete my memories of them both once we have visited Dad's grave, and that will get me through the remaining years. I can't believe that all that warmth is cold now in the ground." The other two just looked at him and he felt the need to explain himself: "I'm glad I came. I had to come." He was crying now. "But I don't get a sense of her here. Cemeteries, they're such sterile places of stone and fucking fading flowers" – he pointed to a weary-looking posy as he spoke – "and airy words that just don't give me peace; only emptiness and a silence that doesn't speak to me. It feels so empty. She's here," he said, touching his heart, "and here," and he tapped his forehead softly with the tips of his fingers. "These speak to me of her . . . more than this." And he drew a tired arc with his hand across the sky above and round the edge of the cemetery.

"We agree with that, but—" began Euan, but he was interrupted as Ronan carried on. He seemed to feel the need to get his thoughts out to unscramble them.

"I know, I know. Sometimes you feel you have to come to a place – a memorial spot – that is a physical reminder, and we all had to do it at least once. More times for you, Conor, but that will get more and more unlikely for all of us as we get older. I have to have my own way to remember her and Dad, and so do you. So we're gathering more memories and photos to finish the picture that will give us peace, of a kind."

"I'm not sure I agree with all that," said Conor, "but I understand how you're feeling. I felt the same when I first came here. The gravestone revived, for me, some of my memories of Mum, so I'm not really sure what you're saying."

"Neither am I," agreed Ronan wearily. "Revived or just focused?"

He looked at Conor and Conor looked back.

"So you wouldn't come back here if you were in Ireland again? Would you stay away?" asked Euan.

"Yes, if I was in this area I suspect I wouldn't come back, but I can't say for sure. It wouldn't add anything to what I have now. But I know it gets us closer to her than we have been for years, but I think I can do that in my mind better than by coming here," replied Ronan. "And I wouldn't want them to think I didn't care just because I didn't visit their graves."

"They know well enough how you feel, Ronan. I'm just glad I came with you two," said Euan.

The other two smiled at his disarming honesty.

"He's right. It's just nice to be here together, Ronan, because in fact it's highly unlikely we will ever be here together again. Euan is right," Conor emphasized again. "It's just good to be here and I'm glad we came."

Ronan nodded slowly, and carefully took in air through his nose. "I'm glad I'm here with you two. I've said goodbye to Mum and Dad so many times, but it's now as a family. And I feel better. But there's one thing that really pisses me off!"

"And what's that?" asked Conor, hoping that opening it up would get it closed.

Ronan had a couple of mis-starts before he said, "They never got to see Declan grow up. They never really got to see two of their other sons grow up because of the distance between; and, apart from a few brief glimpses, they never got to see their grandchildren growing up. What a terrible lot they have missed for two people who believed so much in family! And we can't tell them all the things that have happened to us all in that time. They never saw it all. That hurts more than anything."

He bowed his head, wiped the rain from his face with both hands and made his way to the main gates. He stood there waiting for his brothers, staring out across the road to the fields.

They stayed where they were for a few moments, arms around each other's shoulders, and then they too made their way to the gates to join Ronan. The struggling sun was edging through the clouds; they hadn't even noticed that the rain had stopped.

"Ronan, they've seen everything," said Conor. "They have seen everything."

Ronan looked at Conor and smiled and gave him a thin nod of agreement.

As they looked across the hills beyond the gates so that they could carve the scene into their memories, the sun finally broke through a gap in the clouds and poured gold on the fields and hedges, and the roads shone like ebony.

A kestrel hovered over the fields, telescopic eyes peering into the hedges and into the long grasses near the stone walls, before it glanced down the wind on a fickle gust and began quivering once more on another stilled shelf of wind.

For the first time they saw the buttercups and clover scattered everywhere, and even the attentive thistles were regal, bright heads of colour. Along the roadside walls, chickweed and white dead nettle flowered and swayed. Mixed groups of hard fern and hart's tongue were jostling in among the hedgerow areas just inside the gated walls.

Nearby, to the left of the main gate, the bramble was ripe with red, purple and black fruit; pale yellow, orange, white and blue flowers nestled close to the walls that bordered the roads and, with the grass, pushed through the thin line of soil and grit blown up against the walls to offer the willing seeds a passing chance for life.

As they looked off to further colour, they noticed for the first time that gorse was everywhere among the hedges, past its best but bravely yellow. Other yellow and white flowers and wild fuchsias, a riotous crowd of colour, littered their view like bright lights. Their seeds, scattered by careless breezes and moody winds alike, had bumped up against the walls or had been scattered in the hedgerows and fields. They landed a long, long way away from where they had grown and, in spite of or because of that (it was hard to tell), they endured all and flourished and bloomed in adversity, no matter what the soil. It was a glorious scene they hadn't noticed till now, but they were slowly and finally drifting away from guilt, uncertainty, and even longing, and their mood swelled and burst and bloomed.

There were almost simultaneously loud and deep breaths taken, and they turned and smiled at one another. It was a beautiful place to have been laid to rest, but perhaps they no longer needed to look for their mum in this place or any other place as they carried her with them everywhere they went.

"I need a good stiff drink or twelve," said Conor. "Let's go!"

Without another word he led the way back down to the main part of the town, leaving the car parked where they had left it; and he stopped at the first pub he came to, expecting the other two to have followed.

It was more crowded inside than they had anticipated, and, though it wasn't particularly lively, they were pleasantly surprised. They got the usual curious glances from the locals, who watched the three strangers who had blown in while continuing to talk as if they hadn't noticed.

Chapter 22

Euan was first to the bar with his hand in his pocket, and he ordered three pints of Guinness and three whiskey chasers. His accent attracted further interest from the rest of the patrons round the bar, but after a final casual glance, uninterrupted from their talking, they carried on with their own muffled conversations.

Conor and Ronan had found seats, and within a few minutes Euan brought across the drinks and put the glasses in front of them, on a table with beer mats and drink rings. He was always taking the part of family minder, playing big brother in his serious way.

"Take hold of the whiskey," Euan insisted; and they did. "I'd like to propose a toast to Margaret Farrell, to Mum, to a life well lived and a mother deeply loved."

They clinked glasses. "To Mum!" they said in unison, and downed the whiskey and dropped the shot glasses on the table with a significant crack.

Down-headed sideways glances panned their way, but revolved back to the front while the muffled chatter rolled on around them.

"Well done, buddy," said Conor in a mock Canadian accent.

"Are you taking the piss?" asked Euan.

"Yes, I am. But thanks," replied Conor, picking up his glass, raising it to Euan and then putting it down softly on the table and smiling gratefully at Euan.

"She was one smart lady, wasn't she?" said Ronan. "D'you remember how good she was at crosswords? She invariably got them out once she started. And yet neither of them had much schooling. Dad was the mathematician and Mum was the English-language scholar. Not a bad combination for three young kids sitting exams to go to grammar school."

"Yeah," agreed Euan, "she was the soft touch and Dad was the hard man. If you were in trouble you would always try to get around her. It wasn't worth even trying with Dad."

"That's right," said Conor. "Remember when we were on the building site playing around the half-built brick houses that were springing up everywhere and we were with Pat Moroney and you said to her, 'I'll show you mine if you show me yours,' and you pulled your little pecker out?"

"It's still the same," interrupted Ronan, and they broke up with laughter.

They paused to drink and to gather their wits and thoughts together.

"She told her mum," continued Ronan, "and her mum told our mum, and Mum said she would tell our dad when he got in from work after the morning shift. Fortunately for you, it was her birthday and we had picked some wild flowers down over the brook at the bottom of the road and gave them to her that morning for her birthday. They were weeds, but she said they were so beautiful and she had that way and that smile that made you feel ten feet tall with your generosity."

"I know!" laughed Euan. "I pleaded with her not to tell Dad because it was her birthday and it would spoil the day for her as well, and in the end she didn't tell. Well, we don't think she did."

He didn't sound convinced and he drank thoughtfully from his glass.

Ronan took up the story: "Yeah, because we were lying in bed that night – we shared the double bed, and you", he said to Conor, "had the small box room. They always sat together at night in the living room talking, and if we were really quiet we could slip out of bed and go and sit on the stairs and watch the door to the lounge in case we saw the handle move. We could usually catch bits of the conversations drifting up the stairs. If she was going to tell on us it would be then. And suddenly Dad burst out laughing and it bubbled up and out, racing faster and faster in that infectious way of his."

Euan was nodding, smiling. "We were sure Mum had told him, but he never said a word. She would have pleaded for us anyway. She always did – well, nearly always."

"Not always successfully though!" laughed Ronan.

In the time of their conversation many of the locals had left the pub, and it was now quite empty; a couple of weather-beaten older men, on stools, were still leaning against the bar as though to keep it from falling.

"Shall we try somewhere else?" suggested Conor. "There are other pubs just a few doors away. We might as well do the rounds. What d'ya think?"

"Yep, let's go," agreed Euan.

"I'm with you two," said Ronan.

"Don't remind us," quipped Conor. "We'd almost forgotten."

He got a clip over the ear from Ronan for his cheek, and exaggeratedly pulled away from the swinging hand.

The next pub was only a few doors away, and they went inside to a slightly bigger space and a bigger crowd than the last pub; but when they looked around they noticed that three-quarters of the clients were the same drinkers who had been in the previous pub and who had left just before they did. They still had the flat caps, jackets and snugly worn boots on that the three of them remembered from years ago. In spite of the passing of years, it was as if time stood still in this small part of Ireland.

"They must just do the rounds of the pubs each evening just to keep all the owners happy. The money – what little there is – is being shared around evenly. Would you believe that?" asked Euan.

"Always be prepared to be surprised in this country," answered Conor.

There was a new group of people in one of the corners of the lounge, away from the rest, and close to them was a rostrum which looked like it was a place for bands or performers to entertain; but it was not in use and was not likely to have been for some time. The group (four men and one woman) were deep in conversation and ignored the rest of the people in the bar.

Euan, for one, was curious – especially as they had cases with them which clearly suggested they had musical instruments and were a group of musicians.

They decided on one more shot of whiskey. Euan went to buy them and soon returned.

He raised his glass and said, "To family!"

"I'm not drinking to that," objected Conor. "I hardly even know you."

"You will before the end of this trip," suggested Ronan. "All right, then: to us!"

"I'll drink to that," agreed Conor, and he drank it in one.

Three glasses hit the table at the same time.

"Do you remember the way Dad used to talk about potcheen?" asked Euan. "He used to refer to it as moonshine. Do you remember?"

"Yeah, I do," smiled Ronan as he remembered. "It was illegal-still whiskey, wasn't it? Powerful stuff, from what he used to say. They were always trying to brew it without being caught by the police."

"Caught by the police?" asked Conor.

"Yeah, it was illegal and you could be arrested for brewing it. They used to brew it out in their barns or have a hiding place out in the woods somewhere," explained Euan.

"Didn't they used to make it with potatoes?" asked Conor, and Euan nodded. "No wonder they all left the country when the potato crop failed. The whiskey supply dried up."

"The best stuff was made with barley though, and it was hugely alcoholic." Euan seemed almost in awe – or was it sadness at the loss?

"You can't buy it now though—" began Ronan.

"Oh, but you can!" interrupted Euan. "You can buy it in Canada from specialist stores. I don't think it retails in New Zealand."

"So, you've tried it, then?" asked Conor.

"No," admitted Euan. "It goes from 60% to 120%! There are other ways to numb my brain."

"So what did you use instead, then?" asked Ronan.

Euan laughed and carried on: "I will buy some one day, just to see what all the talk and legend is about, but I suspect it will be drunk in thimblefuls at our place. You can't just buy it anywhere. There are specialist outlets and very, very few of them. I think the brewers are very careful who they allow to sell it."

"You seem to know a lot about it," said Conor suspiciously.

"Just an extension of my interest in chemistry," said Euan, and he winked.

"I find talking about drink doesn't quench the thirst," said Conor, fondling his empty shot glass suggestively.

"OK – got this one," said Ronan.

He went up and collected three glasses of Guinness from the bar. While he was there he asked the barman if the group was going to play.

"Unfortunately, no," sighed the barman. "I tink dey're on the road ta somewhere else, where there's a bit more money in the pockets of the locals ta be able to afford thum. The young lass is a local girl, so dey're probably here for a fleetin' family visit."

Ronan carried the glasses to the table and passed them out.

"Ah, look at that!" said Conor, holding up his glass with the thick creamy head on it. "The parish priest! What a fine-lookin' fella!"

"That's a band over there," said Ronan, pointing in the direction of the small group sitting away from them with what looked like instrument cases stacked in the corner. "The barman says they're not playing here, but he says the girl comes from here. Sounds like it's a money thing. No crowd here, so the barman won't pay. Would have been good to hear some real Irish music, wouldn't it?"

Euan got out of his seat.

"Perhaps we can."

He headed over to the group, where he was soon buried in earnest conversation. The next thing his brothers knew, the group of musicians were unpacking the instruments from their cases and Euan came back across to resume his seat.

"They're going to give us a few numbers." He spoke in such a matter-of-fact casual way that, for the briefest of moments, his brothers didn't believe him, and couldn't be bothered to find the words to tell him so. But the group was taking out their instruments and were clearly intending to play.

"How did you pull that off?" asked Conor in genuine admiration, realizing now that they were getting ready to perform.

"I told them that I was from Canada and holidaying in Ireland with two of my friends. I said that you two never stopped talking about the music and how good it was, and yet I hadn't heard live Irish music since I landed in the country several days ago – just a little lie," he explained. "I talked about the wonderful tales, even in Canada, of Irish musicianship and said how great a story it would be to take home with me about the group we met in a pub in the middle of Ireland, who unpacked their gear and did an impromptu concert for me and my buddies. They were sold. Though it's going to cost us a few drinks," he added guiltily.

The sound of instruments being tuned and the mournful sound of the uillean pipes drifted across the floor. The band assembled on the rostrum for a final tuning.

"They're travelling the country performing in various small and larger towns, working the pub scene. They're honing their skills in a two-week trip to various centres. They finished last night in Charlestown, Mayo – the next county across. They rattled off a whole lot of other places before that, but I can't remember them. A quick stop here, because Clare, the girl, wanted to catch up with family. Didn't think they would get a big enough crowd here to perform in the home town. Stopped here for a drink first. She hasn't seen her family yet. And tomorrow night they're performing in Longford, making their way to Dublin for their last concert before heading for England. They're called 'The Hobnails', and we'll soon see if they have the magic."

"You found all that out in five minutes?" asked Conor in astonishment. "You must have been talking faster than that fiddler can play." He pointed to the big man swishing the bow across the strings at lightning speed.

Euan sat there smiling and looking very pleased with himself.

The bar had gone quiet and the girl spoke out into the silence: "We've been asked if we will play for this Canadian gentleman over here" – and she nodded at Euan – "because he has never heard live Irish music before. Can you believe that? He's here with a couple of friends, who I'd have to say look remarkably like him, and they've been telling him how good Irish music is. I hope we don't disappoint you, sir." And she bowed. "We'll be playing five numbers for you; one jig, one reel and three romantic songs I'm sure you'll all know. Please sing along with us if you feel the urge. One, two, three, four."

The locked-up sound crashed out, and within seconds feet were tapping and fingers were drumming, heads were nodding, shoulders were rolling and reddening faces were grinning all around the bouncing pub as the music drifted through the windows and spread like gossip all over the town and beyond. They weren't sure when it happened, but, as the jig flounced out, the bar started slowly filling as first individuals looked in and decided to stay, and then couples. Before long, groups of keen and jostling customers came looking for rapidly disappearing seats, but were happy enough to prop up the bar or pressure the floor, and there were tables being moved aside and impromptu dances occurring everywhere.

It was as if the music seeped out of every opening in the bar, and the sound waves, like a fragrant scent, drifted around the town and then out into the country and drew them all in to what was essentially the music of their souls.

The three of them had to stand up now to watch the band as all around, in front of them and to the sides, people were jigging frantically, arms twisting and turning and bodies reeling and jigging; and, in among it all, ale was being carried and spilt and passed around by the armful. Heads were thrown back in joy and laughter, and everything else was set aside for the ceilidh. No one was allowed to sit for long before being dragged on to the floor and twirled around in a desperate lurch, picked up by the next body to come near them and spun round again in a movement that closely resembled a stumble but turned into a swaggering jig of delight, surprise and clumsy grace.

"Good man yourself!" shouted a young country-looking lad, red-faced and laughing at Euan. "Your doin', I heard. Well done for asking!"

And he skirled away and sank beneath the crowd.

"I didn't know there were this many people in the town!"

yelled Ronan above the music and the shouts and the laughter. "Where'd they all come from?"

"Beats me," cried Conor, and he shrugged his shoulders carefully.

He carried a round of drinks over to the band and placed them on a table already full with drinks. Everyone was buying rounds for them, and there was also a mounting pile of money on the table, from those hoping they would forget the time and keep on performing. So far, it seemed to be working.

At last the jigs and reels came to an end, and Clare, who seemed to be the spokesperson for the band, picked up the fiddle of one of her band mates and then began to speak into the silence that settled: "Now we have a couple—"

She was interrupted by a shrieking voice: "Clare, me lovely, ah, I knew you was comin'!"

"Ma!" shouted Clare as she stepped off the little stage and moved towards the speaker, who had just come in through the door.

A man also entered and crossed towards the standing mother with his hat in his hands.

"And Pa!" cried Clare delightedly, and the small group hugged while everyone else looked on, abuzz with speculation. "I meant to be with you sooner, only I got waylaid by these three young men, who asked me to play." She pointed at the three of them standing with smiles as wide as the floor, trying to look youthful.

"Carry on, then, my love," said the mother, and the father nodded in agreement. "We'll join the fun and catch up with you later!" And they moved away as Clare rejoined the band.

However the word had gone around, it had travelled far into and out of the town, and it was apparent that many of the folk in the pub did not see each other often or had not seen each other for a while, for there were hands being shaken, shoulders being thumped and slapped gently, words of welcome and stories of absence being passed around from table to table across the room. They even saw the owner of the hotel they were staying at, and her husband, come in, tip them a wink and join the crowd queuing at the bar. Before long, Seamus was behind the bar, helping to serve the tide of customers wanting a drink. And still the people came.

"Ah, Jesus, Mary and Joseph, look who's here!"

"Will you look at that! I haven't seen ya in an age, Mick."

"Where da feck have you bin hoidin'?"

"You've become even prettier since I last saw ya, Francie. Now, how long ago was dat, da ya tink?"

"There's the man himself, and look at herself sittin' on his arm!"

Clare was back on the stage and a couple of loud notes were enough to silence the crowd in dwindles.

"We're going to play a popular ballad for you now and if you know the words, or when you remember the words," – she laughed – "join us. It's called 'Maggie'. We had a request for this one."

The pipes and violin struck out while Ronan and Conor both looked at Euan and watched his face concentrate and his eyes shift away from them quickly. It was a song that their dad used to sing often to their mum.

It couldn't have been a better choice, and they both looked gratefully at Euan, who avoided their stares in a studied way, but with a knowing grin on his face.

Many of the crowd were now in nostalgic mood, knowing this was a special night. Such a night had not been seen for a time and might not come again for a while, and so they joined in where they could and the three brothers lent their voices to the massed crowd as they remembered, faultlessly, the part that had always endeared them to the song.

And they lifted their voices high to the sky as they realized, at last, that they had found a real place of rest for all of them, and especially for their mum and dad.

"You sentimental old bastard, Euan," said Conor. "Well done though." And he nodded his head gratefully.

The night was ended all too quickly and folk started to drift away as the band packed up their gear and loaded it into their van outside. They were happy to put the gear away now because the van had no locks and they were leaving. They had brought their instruments into the pub for safety, and no one could have known how much that decision, unnecessary as it probably was and based on previous bad experiences in larger towns, changed the mood of the small town for a few memory-filled hours, and, for the three brothers, their feelings towards the town forever. It was now holy ground, with sacred scattered memories.

They were thanked by just about everyone who was leaving, almost as if they had given the concert, and in return they thanked everyone for coming and wished them well.

Euan, generous as always and feeling the responsibility of making them work, gave them a donation that lit up their faces and made it all worthwhile for both parties.

It was after 11.30 p.m. before they finally left themselves, after the barman filled their glasses with another pint of Guinness to thank them with "one for the road and for the grandest night of the year".

There were still people outside standing around in groups or talking and laughing with people sitting in cars with their windows down or in farm trucks with the younger people in the back. They didn't want to let go of an evening that was like a dear friend departing for overseas.

The three of them waved their farewells and trod carefully across the road and down to their hotel as the voices and loafing echoes died away behind them. As they were heading up the stairs Seamus called them into the lounge and handed them three large shots of whiskey.

"'Twas a great night, lads. This one's on me. I'm off to bed now. Early start for me in the mornin'. If you want any more, just help yourselves." And he left the bottle on the table. "Don't forget to turn the lights off in here when you go. Leave the glasses in the sink. Maureen'll clean them up tomorrow. Thanks, now, and goodnight to yous."

"Thanks, Seamus!" they called in unison as he headed out the back to the living quarters.

In fact they didn't help themselves. It had been a turning point in the trip in many ways, and they had drunk enough to enjoy it and to be sure to remember it, and one more would be fine.

Euan raised his glass: "To family!" he said, and he looked pointedly at Conor.

"To family!" echoed Ronan, and he too looked at Conor, and waited.

"Aye, to family!" yelled Conor, and it was like a barrier was finally swept aside as they touched glasses and drank.

They sat though for a long time talking things over. About what a comic and romantic their dad was, and yet hard as nails when it came to discipline in the home (there were several sides to that complex man). About where a person's roots really are and how anyone could ever know. Could a person have more than one place or country that they felt incredibly drawn to? Would they ever feel at peace if that was the case? If someone emigrates and leaves behind family, alive and dead, where does he or she really belong? Where can they call home? Do they even have a home? What defines home?

Tonight they had just experienced the Ireland they all liked to think they remembered. It had been the stereotypical evening of story and legend, and they had lived it for a brief few hours, and it was again a reconnection with the land and life of their parents, a symbol of what their mum's and dad's lives may have been like in the best of times – maybe frequently as kids; maybe in snatches as they grew older.

Their parents' stories of their early lives had always been funny ones, though both sets of grandparents had clearly been strict, and they had been childhood and teenage rascals – or certainly their dad had been, by all accounts.

They wished they had heard more stories and asked more questions. But in the lounge, sitting together and teasing out their thought and beliefs, the prevailing sense, for the time being, was of peace and contentment and a certain fragile sense of home and a much stronger sense of family.

"Tomorrow we look for Kilteevan," said Conor. "Last time I was here I couldn't find it and nobody could tell me where it was with any certainty. Mind you, I didn't have a lot of time and I wasn't in a great mood for looking. You guys OK with that?" he asked.

"Fine with me," Euan said.

"Me too," answered Ronan. "I'm off, then. Goodnight. Great evening. Best company. Thanks. See you in the morning."

"I'm off too." And Euan moved to the stairs.

"I'll look after the glasses, guys. Don't worry about me. I'm used to being skivvy for you two."

Conor minced like a seductive barmaid, one arm exaggeratedly held out to the side with a drooping hand trailing a lingering teacloth. He pursed his lips and looked out from lowered eyes to resemble an alluring siren, dropped one hip lower and placed his hand on it. The other two laughed and carried on up the stairs. He put the glasses in the sink, turned off the lights and was soon behind them as they disappeared into their own rooms. They didn't worry too much about the noise of their passing; there seemed to be no one else around.

They lay down with their own thoughts and mulled over the conversations and the whole transformation of the evening, and thought of the trick of chance that had made it happen.

'Was it chance or fate?' wondered Ronan. 'And what's the difference anyway?' He lay there for some time thinking, and as he drifted off to sleep he thought he had found the answer. Fate was your map laid out for you, destination known by someone, but chance was the episodes that you made happen along the way by who and what you were and the choices you made. One tip of your world could roll you in a different direction on your way to your fate.

As he drifted off to sleep he heard the evening closing down with a squeal of tyres outside as one of the truckloads of revellers headed back out to the country.

Chapter 23

She sat on the floor, legs tucked to the side, broken-hearted and unable to stand with grief, and the tears rolled down her face and the sobs shook her uncontrollably. They had been talking for what seemed hours, trying to shake loose the guilt and the sense of a random world that they didn't understand.

"It was my fault!" she cried. "I should have held his hand! I should have held him tighter! I always did before! Because that was a dangerous road out there! How could I be so careless!" *And she covered her face with her hands and almost burst with grief.*

"Oh, my darling, it wasn't your fault. We can't keep kneading this over and over. It wasn't anyone's fault. I can find myself to blame as well if I look at it. I usually got off my bike a couple of hundred yards from the house, crossed the road and walked to the house, just to be safe. No – let me finish," *he said, putting his hand to her mouth as she went to interrupt.* "But this day I didn't because I was late and couldn't wait to get home to see you all! As soon as I saw you come to the road, I had this awful sense of a fatal decision and I wanted to shout – a shout so loud it would wake the slumbering heavens – but it was already too late. If you want to find blame, it's my fault."

He too was tearful, but trying to be strong for them both to get through this.

"But I usually kept the gate closed and only opened it once you had come over the road and lifted the gate latch, but this time I didn't and I don't know why! I don't know why!" She was almost screaming and she buried her face in her hands. "Our lovely boy! Our firstborn, and now he's gone! I keep wanting to wake up out of this nightmare and hold him close, and I'll promise him never to let him go ever again and I'll kiss him until he's smothered in kisses!" And she sobbed a sob that tore at Danny's heart. "But I can't! I can't and I never will! And it's my fault! Even if I could have held him for one moment and looked into his eyes so he would know I was with him for all time . . . but he was already gone and he must have felt so alone and so confused and shocked in that moment of impact when the pain struck and everything just blew apart. He expected to be protected by the adults in his life and I let him down. My darling son deserved an explanation of the random cruelties of life and I couldn't give it to him. He died thinking life was not his to have by right, and he died because of my neglect. I'm terrified sometimes when I think of that blinding second when he died. I'm terrified that for that millisecond he thought, 'Why have they let this happen to me?' I can't bear to think that he might have felt so betrayed and unloved. When I picked him up I couldn't say his name, Danny. I couldn't say his name. I thought if I didn't say it, it would stop it being real and he would still be alive. I was clutching the air looking for something to hold on to and it was the only hope I had. I can't remember how many times I have woken up over the last few years and just for a millionth of a second, as I wake, I have thought and then hoped it was a dream. But it isn't. It was my fault and I can't escape that."

Danny couldn't count the times they had had this conversation, over and over again, looking for meaning. He always left her to talk the pain through, hoping it would at least cauterize the wound.

"It's not your fault, love! If there's any fault it's mine, but in a sense it was no one's fault. It was a time that we could never have expected and a gathering of circumstances that we could never have foreseen." He was desperate now to haul his wife back from the edge of a breakdown. "God decided it was time to—"

"Don't talk to me about God!" she yelled at him. "God! What right has He to take my child? There is no God if He's so cruel and thoughtless! I thought God was love! Where was the love when He ripped me apart from my son? I don't believe a loving God would let this happen! My son has been sacrificed by an indifferent God! All my life I've tried to live as a good Christian woman should, and this is how I'm repaid!"

"It doesn't work like that. You know that. It's a chance thing, and you can't expect special favours."

"I didn't want any special favours! And I don't need your quiet reasonableness! I just wanted my boy to grow up into a big, strong, lovely young man. Was that too much to ask?"

Danny shook his head.

"It's a simple dream. It's a mother's dream. Why can't I have it? Tell me why I can't have it!"

"I can't," he answered quietly and despairingly. "I can't."

He broke down. He dropped to the floor beside her and they held each other tightly to stop the world from overwhelming them like a drowning wave, as it had almost overwhelmed them several times in the past few years.

He soon recovered. He had to and he knew it.

"We have to get through this for the sake of Euan and Ronan and now Conor. And for ourselves too. If we can't, we're finished. Or I am. And the whole family might be. I can't do this without you. We have to get through this together. I need you to help me and this will be the biggest challenge we have ever faced. Please help me, love."

"Help? There is no help! We didn't get much from Father Ratray, did we? He comes out here on his bike, huffing and puffing his big fat arse off, because the neighbours phoned to tell him our son's been run over; and what does he say when he gets here? 'Why did you bring me all the way out here when the boy's already dead?'"

Her anger was redirected now, so he let it run.

"That's a man of God! Those words came from a man of God who stands there every Sunday and tells me how to live my life with compassion and concern for others! What compassion and concern did he have for me, or us, or for my son? God's not coming out of this very well at all, is He? Him or His bloody *labourers! You were right about the dreaming heavens, or whatever it was you said before. God slept. And while He slept, and because He slept,* my son died! Our first son, Declan, died!" *And her voice and emotion and grief were as shrill as nails and as bitter as gall.*

Ronan woke with a start. He blinked and turned his head quickly both ways to hear what had woken him, but it was silent. He stared around the darkness of his room, looking for clues and waiting for something to sound again; but it didn't, and he was soon fitfully asleep again.

Chapter 24

They were up and about early the next morning, gathering for breakfast in the hotel restaurant, entering in dribs and drabs for a full cooked breakfast that was cooked individually for them because of the small number of people booked in. They couldn't manage all the toast, but the cups of tea were lifesaving and they had at least two cups each.

There was still a feeling in the restaurant like the morning after a wedding. Everyone in the kitchen and the one waitress on tables seemed caught in an afterglow, as if they had been warming themselves in front of a blazing fire or just stepped off a dance floor. Everyone in the kitchen seemed to be humming a tune and they all seemed to have smiles on their faces. There wasn't much talk between the brothers in case it stopped them remembering, and there was a comfortableness now that didn't require silences to be filled.

Conor was the first one to break the spell: "What if we just walk round the town and call into a few shops and see if we can get a fix on where Kilteevan is? What do you reckon?"

"I'm OK with that," replied Ronan.

They both looked at Euan for his agreement, but he seemed in his own world.

"Look," said Conor, "just because you think you're now a band's road manager doesn't mean you're too famous to talk to us, you know! What do you think about the idea?"

"That's OK. Two's a majority, so you don't need me to say anything," said Euan.

The others just looked at him.

"I was just reliving some parts of last night. I'm allowed to, aren't I?"

They both decided to ignore his casualness.

"I'm ready," said Ronan enthusiastically. "Let's go, then!"

"I'm sorry," said Euan. "I didn't mean to ignore you both."

And they were off.

There weren't that many places open because it was still only just after 8.15 a.m. and there weren't any people around on the streets as far as they could see. Euan, making amends for his grumpiness, headed into the open door of a beauty shop while the other two waited outside. There was an elderly lady in there whom he took to be the owner, and she was talking to an old grey-haired man, tweed-jacketed. He was wearing a trilby, and his trousers were tucked into thick woollen socks. A sturdy pair of brown brogues finished off what seemed the archetypal country gentleman. He had a gnarled-looking but beautifully crafted walking stick. He appeared to be quite deaf and the shopkeeper was talking loudly.

"Bit of a ceilidh in the town last night, Sean, from what I heard! Over at Manannan's Bar! Right hooley going on there, so there was!"

Euan stood around, interested in the conversation. He was looking idle, waiting for attention but getting none.

"Too noisy for me, Margery!" shouted Sean. "Can't hear yourself talk, so you can't!"

"Town was hoppin', so I'm told!" yelled Margery as she cast a disapproving look at the intruder interrupting her morning conversation with his presence.

"No, I haven't done me shoppin' yet!" bellowed Sean. "Was just goin'—"

"Hush now for a minute, will you, Sean," she interrupted impatiently, "while I see what this gentleman wants?"

The curl of her lip and the line of sight down her long nose left Euan in no doubt that in her eyes he was not a gentleman.

"Can I help you, sir?"

"Do you have any idea which road I would take to get to

Kilteevan, please?" Euan was almost sarcastically polite.

"You're an American?" she said disapprovingly.

"A Canadian, actually, ma'am," corrected Euan as pleasantly as he could.

"Oh, that's all right, then," she said enigmatically. "Now, where was it ye was lookin' for?"

"Kilteevan."

"Kilteevan, ya say? Now I've heard of dat place, so I have. Small place somewhere round these parts. But I'm not sure where 'tis. I reckon Sean will know though. Lived in this area for years, he has. Older than the hills themselves. Still got his wife livin' wit' him, though her health is failin' now. How's your wife keepin', Sean?" she asked.

"As good as can be expected!" replied Sean. "Not lookin' forward to the winter though, she isn't. Makes her old bones ache somethin' terrible!"

"Is she takin' anything for it?" asked Margery.

"Nothin' that's any use at all. Costs, but does nothin'," he complained.

"Sure they're a fearful price those tablet things. They are too. You're right – a shameful waste of good money! How are the daughters, then? Still living and working in England? Sure, there's nothin' for them here any more, is there, now?"

"Not a bit of it," answered Sean. "In fact it's getting—"

"Excuse me!" interrupted Euan loudly. "Hi!" And he waved his hand mockingly for attention. "Kilteevan, remember? Do you know where it is?" he asked quietly.

"Oh, you're still here, then? Kilteevan, Sean? Do you know where it is?"

"Kilteevan?" cried Sean. "Out the door, turn right down to the main street, right again and first right at the bottom of the hill and keep driving. Ye can't miss it!" answered Sean.

"Aye, that's right," agreed Margery, sour-faced, peeved and looking quizzically at Sean, surprised by his miraculous hearing recovery.

She distracted herself by fussily and noisily tidying things on the shelves in her beauty shop.

Euan couldn't wait to get out as the conversation trailed off behind him.

"You never said a truer word." It was Sean's voice. "Those tablets are a fearful price, so they are. What was dat? Can ya speak up?"

As Euan got outside he was attacked by both brothers.

"Where have you been?"

"How long does it take to ask the way to Kilteevan?"

"Is there a bar out the back? Is that where you've been?"

"We've been around the town three times!"

"We could have been to Kilteevan and back by now."

When Euan told them what had happened, they teased him and laughed till their sides were sore.

"You obviously weren't important enough to interrupt a conversation for. They would have taken more notice of fly shit on the shop window. At least she would have rubbed you off instead of snubbed you off!"

They headed back to the car park at the rear of the hotel, piled into the car and pointed themselves in the direction of Kilteevan.

It was a very pleasant drive along country lanes – overgrown grass-lined lanes with narrow verges, stacked to the sides with hedgerows, shoulders hunched, holding back the fields and trees. The sun shone with selective grace in the narrow strip as the car, like an arrow, whisked along the dappled roads. The road signs disappeared with alarming speed, and when they came to a Y junction there was nothing to say which branch to take. It became all guesswork and random stupidity. The air in the car was filled with quarrel.

They slowed and stopped alongside a young guy driving a small delivery van, and he slowed down to pull alongside.

"Can you tell us where to go for Kilteevan?" asked Ronan as they came level.

"Kilteevan? Aye. Small place. Why are ya after goin' there?"

"Our mum was born there," answered Conor, "and we'd like to see the place."

"It's important to us," said Ronan.

He was a friendly-looking guy, with a ruddy face and handsome features. His eyes showed he understood the importance of their journey.

"Keep goin' along dis road and take da next right. Carry along dat road. Turn left at the first turning and you'll see da road sign saying 'Kilteevan'. And you're dere! Dere's not much to see though. Not even a pub," he concluded sadly.

"Thanks," said Ronan. "You're a grand fellow."

And he pushed the pedal and they headed off towards Kilteevan.

It wasn't long before they realized they were lost again. They travelled down a few dead-end, mute country lanes before they pulled up suddenly outside a large field with a new house being built on its ample land. What had really drawn them to it was the van parked outside on the muddy beginnings of a drive which had the sign 'Naughton Builders' written along the side – royal-blue letters on a white van bearing their mother's maiden name.

It was Euan who first drew it to their attention: "Hey, stop!" he yelled. "There's someone who might know."

As Ronan reversed slightly to get a better view, he pointed to the van in the field next to a largely completed family cottage: "If he doesn't, I don't know who will," he concluded. "So, who's going?" asked Ronan.

No one moved.

"OK, it's me, I suppose."

He turned the engine off, climbed out of the car and walked across the muddy tread of the ground towards the cottage.

"Don't stay all day in there talking either!" called Euan from the back of the car.

Ronan just looked at him, wide-eyed, pointed a finger at him and blew a breath at him dismissively.

They sat and waited.

Ronan got to the new front door and knocked.

"Hello! Anyone here?" he called into the empty house. He knew there was because he could hear somebody slamming with an electric nail drill somewhere inside in some other part of the building. He decided to walk in towards the sound, but hadn't got far before the source of the noise appeared with a safety helmet on, drill in hand and questioning smile on his face.

Ronan decided to speak up first: "Ronan," he said, extending his hand in friendship.

"Kerry," he said, and shook Ronan's hand strongly.

"I'm looking for the village of Kilteevan," said Ronan, "and I keep getting lost. Been driving around your narrow country lanes, but can't seem to find signs after a while. What's the quickest way to get there?"

"Are you walking or driving?" asked Kerry.

"Driving," said Ronan, a little confused by the question.

"Ah, sure that's the quickest way, then," said Kerry.

Ronan looked long and hard at him, but got no signal of his real meaning.

"OK, now, Kilteevan," he replied. "Divil of a place ta find. It's not very big. There's nuttin' dere, ya know. Not even a pub!" He said that as if it was a clear indication of a lack of civilization.

"I know. I mean *we* know. My brothers are out in the car." And he waved his arm in the direction of the door. "We were here as kids and all we remember was the cottage where our mum's parents lived – the Naughtons. Same as the name on your van outside."

"Really! Now dat was a touch of good luck, but there's no Naughtons around here that I know of. This place has been cleaned out and everyone has gone elsewhere to look for work or different shores. What was your mum's name?"

"Margaret – Margaret Naughton," replied Ronan.

"And what were the married names of your mum and dad?" asked Kerry.

"Margaret and Danny Farrell."

'Farrell? No – no, I've never heard of either of them. More's the pity." He looked up at the ceiling with one eye closed against the paint glare, but found no obvious inspiration. "But I know just the man you should be talking to. He knows everything about the country round here, and the Kilteevan you're looking for is only just around the corner."

Ronan looked sceptical. He had never known corners as long as the ones in Ireland.

"So I'll show you where to go to get to Kilteevan, and I'll give you this fella's contact number."

He put his drill down, looked in his pockets for something to write with and found a fat leaded pencil. He looked at Ronan as much as to say, "I've found the pencil; where's the paper?"

Ronan patted his pockets and held his hands out to indicate he had no paper. "I'll get something from the car," he said, and turned to go outside.

"No, no, no. Wait now. I'll get somethin' from the garage. Give me a minute."

He went off to the far end of the building. Ronan could hear him banging about and timber being dropped. The next minute he appeared with an off-cut piece of timber about sixty centimetres long and about ten centimetres wide and thick enough to make it heavy. He walked to his lunch table, placed the piece of timber on top and wrote a name and a phone number on it.

"There you go," he said, looking pleased with himself and clearly not seeing anything unusual about what he had done. "He's your man. Give Ryan a call and he'll tell ya everything ya need to know. I'll bet he knows your family. He's got a ton of information. Now. Kilteevan – you're practically there." He walked Ronan to the door. "I see the way you're goin'. Stay on that road now and go to the end. You'll get to one of those T junctions – only a left and a right; no straight ahead. Turn right and drive down there for about two miles and you'll see the sign on the left side of the road as you're comin' into the village. Can't miss it."

"Have done several times," replied Ronan.

"Ah, you're a card!" said Kerry, slapping him on the back and rattling his ribs. "Good luck, now."

They shook hands.

Ronan thanked him and he lumbered back inside after waving to the two men in the car.

Ronan tucked the phone number and name under his arm

and went out to the car, knowing exactly what was coming. He arrived at the car and Conor was at the wheel.

"My turn," he said. "You've got us lost often enough, so I thought it can't be any worse with me being at the wheel."

"We debated that for a long time while you were inside," added Euan.

"Cheeky bastard, isn't he?" said Conor, and he waited for Ronan to go round to the passenger side and get in.

"I know this isn't going to be easy to answer," said Conor, "but what have you got there?"

"It's a name and a telephone number," explained Ronan.

'So obvious,' he thought.

"Irish text message. What else would it be?"

"Indeed," observed Euan. "So did Moses in there give you the other tablet, or just the one?" he asked.

"Ha ha! Good one, Euan!" cried Conor.

"Just the one," answered Ronan in a matter-of-fact tone.

"And whose phone number and name is it?" asked Conor. "No, don't tell me. I don't think it will matter."

"Tell *me* then," begged Euan, hands joined together in mock prayer.

"It's a guy who lives round these parts who does a lot of genealogy stuff in his mind. He knows everyone who was ever born or lived in these parts. He said to give this guy a ring. He reckoned he has a memory like an antique collector. Anyway, he had nothing else to write it on," said Ronan, holding it up as if it was all explained that simply.

"Of course, so he wrote it on a plank of wood," stated Conor, nodding understandingly.

"There'll probably be a piece missing from one of the door jambs in there when the house is finished, because he gave it to you. Staggering, these people, aren't they? They're just so eccentric, but they don't see it." Euan was bemused and delighted at the same time.

"Are you going to contact him, then?" asked Conor.

"Not at all. Make you laugh though, don't they? We don't have the time to get involved in all this – I just want to see where Mum was born, have a look around and then leave quietly. What about you guys?"

"I'm the same as you," said Euan. "In, breathe it in and then we're away; breathe it out and keep the memories. I'm happy with that."

"OK, let's go, then. Which way?"

Conor started up the car and moved away from the edge of the road while Ronan gave him the same directions as Kerry had given to him.

"Let's hope not," said Conor when Ronan explained how he had been told they couldn't miss it.

This time it was exactly as explained to them, and Ronan spotted the white-rimmed blue sign with the white writing almost hidden in the long seeding grasses at the side of the road on their left: 'Kilteevan' in English and its Gaelic equivalent in capitals above it, 'CILL TAOBHAIN'.

"Right! We've made it!"

Conor carried on to the centre of what he could only assume would be a very small settlement somewhere soon. It came more quickly than any of them expected.

Immediately noticeable was a shrine with a statue of the Virgin Mary in a blue dress and with a white veil covering her head. She stood on a high concrete block in characteristic pose, hands to her breast and with her head tilted ever so slightly to the right, as if listening. The statue itself was in an arch, closed in at the back and set against a wall which was an edge to the field behind. The arch had pillars down both sides and looked like a very small part of an ancient Greek monument. The statue's coloured robes were bright and fresh, and at her feet was a stone-walled semicircular space for planting; and growing in there in profusion were pink and white flowers, their splashed beauty emphasized by the bright sunlight.

Surrounding the whole thing was a pure, well-kept lawn on both sides of a pathway leading, invitingly, to the statue, and the whole was protected by posts and chains on the boundaries of an area just on the corner of a crossroads to their left as they drove, more slowly than in the town itself, taking it all in. It was a pivotal spot – all things led to the statue, where the blue and white tugged the eye.

To their right, and directly across from the shrine, there were two very tidy, newish, pebble-dashed cottages, one surrounded by a concrete wall with brick pillars and the other bordered by a fastidious drystone wall of amazing fit and perfection. This cottage had ivy tendrils groping up most of the wall, but the ivy was not yet in full smothering glory. The rest was free-growing, grass borders running along outside the unkempt hedges bordering the surrounding fields, which seemed untended and neglected. The whole scene was wild and constrained in equal measure.

They soon noticed that all the buildings they could see – and one swinging glance could take them all in – were made of pebble-dashed walls and slate roofs; and they were upstanding and sturdy-looking, but blankly closed.

They cruised slowly over the crossroads and Conor eased up outside another pebble-dashed public building to their left. Conor nestled into the side of the road and parked. They all decided to have a brief walk around to see if there was any more to this little place that had occupied such a big place in their minds.

An old hand-operated water pump, across the road from where they were parked, immediately caught their attention, and there was a young man with a long-handled weed eater keeping the grass down around it. They couldn't tell if the water pump worked; there were no telltale water marks on the concrete surround. The pump itself was on a dry concrete base inside a metre-high white-painted brick wall with a small entrance to enable people to get to the pump, place their bucket and operate the handle. The wall was topped all around with grey capping stones. It was only waist-high. The caretaker (or whatever he was) never looked up to see them, but carried on as if visitors were a distraction from the work in hand and one visitor was much the same as the next. They stood there for a while just taking it in and wondering where was the place where their grandparents – Mum's mum and dad – had lived?

And then they looked around at the long fawn pebble-dashed building behind them, admiring the apparent durable neatness and warmth of the walls, the flawless state of the roof and the tall several-paned windows on the front wall with small flower boxes on each of the sills and they wondered when it had last been attended to, to make it so impressive. There were two flagpoles with flags fluttering gently in the breeze. One of them was the Irish flag; the other they didn't recognize.

There was a sign on the wall which read 'KILTEEVAN NATIONAL SCHOOL, 1897', and as three sets of lips mimed in unison, they just stared.

"This must have been where Mum went to school," said Euan with quiet awe.

"Here or one of the many other schools around here," said Conor with gentle sarcasm.

"It has to be," said Ronan, affirming what they all knew.

"This is it, isn't it?" asked Euan.

"Yes, this is it," answered Conor. "Don't know what a National School is though. This will be the biggest place around here for miles. This is it. This is where our mum was born. Somewhere round here."

And they all stood in silent tribute, unaware of what a strange picture they made to the young man across the road, taking furtive glances from under his brows when he thought they were looking another way. He continued to cut through the fresh, wounded heads of grass, the motor and circling blade roaring into their silence while, with his steel wheel flying wild, he occasionally sliced deep into the very heart of the earth banked behind the pump wall.

It was like a small prayer gathering as the three of them blinked against the sun, blanked their ears against the noise deafening their thoughts, and looked around at what must have been their mother's playground as a girl. The memories of her and imaginings of where she walked and which direction she would come from, and whom she would be with and what friends she played with in the schoolyard, all gathered around to make them feel as if they too were home for this brief moment and nothing else around them mattered at all. But she wasn't here, though somehow their imaginings of her presence added another layer to memory.

Another piece in the picture puzzle of her that they had somehow not been able to get from stories, but were able to see now in their minds, fell into place. In a distant kind of way they felt she was here and always would be, even as memory, factual history and the invisible traces that everyone leaves on the social and physical landscapes are forever part of the life of every place you've been. They each stood quietly, just moving around on the spot and absorbing all that they could see and feel and imagine.

Chapter 25

"We have our three lovely boys now and we have each other and we are starting to get through this," said Danny.

"But our three boys will never meet Declan. Only our eldest will have vague memories of him," complained Margaret.

"It's our family, Maggie. It's all we have, but we are a family."

"That's all we have," said Margaret. "We left all our other family behind in Ireland to come here to England. Is this home, Danny? Do you feel this is home?"

"Home is where your family is, Maggie. I mean this family of ours, here, now, with us. We had to leave. There was no future and no work for us over there – you know that. I want more for my family. I want them to get a good education and to be happy and successful. You want the same, don't you?"

"Of course I do. You know I do," she said, sounding slightly offended. "But it would have been perfect if we had still got Declan with us."

And Danny could feel the shudder again.

"He was part of the dream too. There's not a day I don't wake up and, just as I'm thinking of a bright day, I remember what we've lost and I fill with anger and sadness again. I wait for the boys to come running into our bedroom in the morning, and they are the light of my life, but I still see my one missing little darling and so I cuddle them harder and I see them look at me, mystified and surprised by how intense it is. I think they are bewildered by what they see as sadness mixed with the joy I get from holding them."

"Don't you think I feel the same?" asked Danny. "I loved Declan too and I'll never get over it, but we have to move away from the guilt and concentrate on the family and the life we have here. You don't ever forget, but we have to go on. This is our home now."

Margaret sighed. She knew he was right, but it was so hard. "Sometimes I know with absolute certainty that this is my home, and at other times . . . I just don't know where my home is."

"We will make this our home, and if, later on, when the boys are grown-up and independent, you want to go back again to Ireland, I'll take you back."

"I think that will make it worse," said Margaret with a troubled voice. "Then I'll never know where to call home. We are getting through all this, Danny, thanks to your strength. I don't know how you do it sometimes. You're a marvel to me and I love you so much." And she reached out and held him tightly.

"We will never forget Declan. He'll always be here with us. He's one of the family forever," said Danny, "but our three young rascals will keep our minds occupied and will give us joy and, no doubt, a measure of pain as well. We're coming right, Maggie. We're coming right."

Chapter 26

Ronan, with hands in pockets and a troubled look on his face, spoke for them all first: "It's taken me a while to realize that places are only milestones on a long journey, like songs we hear that take us back to a time and a place. This takes me back to an earlier place and time than this.

"You know, Conor, we were really lucky to grow up when we did, in sixties and seventies England. It was one of those rare golden ages. Sorry, Euan, but you missed out on the later bits, and they only got better. It was an amazing time – not least in terms of the music. Of course, when I think of the music of that time it's mostly the Beatles I go back to. Do you?"

"Yes, to some extent," agreed Conor, "but there were other good groups around. But no – you're right – nothing as timeless as they are. We were training to be teachers in Liverpool at the time."

"That's right," said Ronan, taking it up again. "They were like close friends singing the soundtrack to our lives. So many of their songs when I hear them, even now, take me back to a person I was with, a place I was in, or something that we were doing or something that was happening to us at the time. Crazy days, but great days indeed! All those songs are like pointers to an episode – a time in the life of—"

"The song without the memories wouldn't be quite the same, would it?" asked Euan.

"That's right," agreed Ronan. "It's the people you were with and the things that you were doing together that made the song what it was, but not entirely. The music fixes the time and place; in a funny kind of way we were singing our own songs to life then, and the Beatles were writing the lyrics for us; they expressed perfectly everything that was happening to us at that stage in life. It was us in those adolescent situations. 'I Wanna Hold Your Hand', 'If I Fell in Love with You', 'Yesterday' – they captured in their words our own lives and the loves, the losses and the failures of life as a teenager. The songs themselves were enough then, but now it's the memories they revive that seem to make them so important and vital. Their songs were about the feelings of a generation, even down to the end with 'Give Peace a Chance'. I know what you're going to say, Conor, so—"

"No, I won't say anything for once, 'cause I agree with you. I often find myself thinking, 'What was I doing at the time?' when I hear a song, and, if it was a really good song, I can usually get a picture of what I was doing when I first heard it and who I was with. And yes, sometimes it's hard to decide what creates such powerful feelings."

"But sometimes there doesn't need to be any music for me – only incidents or places I remember or people and places that I just loved," interrupted Euan. "OK, so we missed out to some extent in Canada, but in the end it's the people or the person we remember. And a place like this," said Euan, indicating with the turning of his head the breadth of the village, "isn't really important except as a place where some of our memories are kept. This could be Paris or Afghanistan or Clapham Junction, and it wouldn't make a scrap of difference, but the one constant in all those places, even if she had been born in any other one of them, would be that it's the place where our mum lived; it's the person we're here for and the place, now I've seen it, will help me to remember. It won't be a song that will remind me of where Mum is buried or where she lived; it will be the places I've just visited with you two. Not every part of your life can have a soundtrack to it. Songs, places, incidents. You know sometimes it's a smell or a taste that I haven't experienced for a long time that triggers nostalgia for me, but I do remember

'In My Life' by the Beatles, so we didn't miss out completely and I think that song says it all, Ronan."

Ronan agreed: "Yep, dead right! It can be ordinary things which are just as likely to set you dreaming. In the end though, isn't it the people who you're with that make your experiences what they are? Your heart sings in harmony when you're with people like that. Maybe we were just lucky that music and song was such a huge part of our younger lives. For me, it's definitely the songs."

Conor picked it up: "It's a lovely place and, like you said, it's a milestone that puts us in touch, in a funny, distant kind of way, with Mum's life. In the end though, because we have nothing else to go on, they're just invented memories or wild imaginings. But it's the person, not her resting place. In the final analysis it's whatever does it for you – songs, places, events, tastes, smells, people. They're all different, but they're all part of the same and for this moment they're all about Mum."

"I can still see why we needed to do this," insisted Euan, "but we won't get to do it again – at least, not together. Or I don't think I will. I think you're right, Ronan. I have it all inside me now to get me through, and, I have to admit, every time I hear 'Maggie' from now on I will remember all of this, and more." And he smiled.

"I may visit again because I'm closer than you two," said Conor. "But, as you said, Ronan, at Mum's grave, she's not fully here even though we imagine her traces linger – and perhaps they do. We even imagine her in the playground shouting and running like a little girl. You almost see it, don't you? You half expect some magical touch or experience will happen to tell you she's watching, but it doesn't and there's a kind of foolish disappointment; but you knew there wouldn't be. Where do all the people go to when they die? I can't answer that. I'm not even sure they go anywhere except in the ground or up in smoke." He smiled as if he was nervous. "But this place gets me closer than I have been for some time because this is where it began for her and a part of her must be here, mustn't it? Whatever part of her that is." He sighed.

"God, Ronan, I'm beginning to talk like you!"

"Sense, you mean?" asked Ronan.

Conor sniggered. "Let's just have a wander down the road and feel her come up through our soles." He winked at Ronan and moved off down the small lane just past the shrine. Within a few seconds he called out, "Guys! Come and have a look at this!"

Euan and Ronan walked a few paces down the lane after Conor and saw he had pulled himself up the grass bank and was holding the post of a wire fence and looking into a field, a huge grin on his face. They clambered up the bank and looked at the three donkeys in the field. The three donkeys looked back at the three of them outside the field and then headed over towards them.

"There's you, Euan!" said Conor, pointing at the largest, and silently they all knew that if they were going to compare the three donkeys to each other then the one Conor pointed out was a spitting image, in donkey-kind anyway, of Euan.

It was brindled and not just tawny, but almost orange-brown in places, mixed with grey and white and even a remnant of black in abrupt and rough patches. It was almost a salt and pepper with other coloured spices thrown in, and it was true that Euan's hair, when he was younger, was much fairer and, in the summer, much blonder than either of the other two. The donkey had the grey patches and single strands of white instead of the black. It was the first to lumber casually over – no fuss, no bother. It had an air of calm indifference and yet a slight, protective mistrust; probably it was the eldest of the donkeys.

"And there's you, Ronan!" shouted Euan, pointing to the small, squat donkey with its head in the air, nostrils flaring for a scent and looking around along the fence line to see what else was going on. "He's getting ready for a reflection," he laughed, and, sure enough, the donkey trotted quickly to the fence line, noisily unravelling a braying to break the sky open.

They all laughed then.

"And look what's left," said Euan: "a flea-infested, spindly-legged, shoulder-hunching bag of bones and flying hair with an idiot grin fixed permanently across its sagging jaw. I wonder who that could be. Who d'ya reckon, Conor?"

The last donkey hobbled and stumbled its way across to them as if on strings, with bobbing, sharp, clumsy trips across the uneven ground. Its movements seemed to be excessive in view of the short distance it had to cover to get to the fence.

And for a few moments it started up again as they pulled clumps of luscious grass from the bank and handed it across the fence.

"C'mon, Euan! We're not going to do anything! Get some more food inside you. Fresh vegetables here. Mum always said to eat your greens. Get your laughing gear round this."

"Conor, y'old clumsy bone-bagged bastard! This might strengthen those drinking-straw legs of yours. Come here, Ronan! What are you waiting for? Are we going to get a treatise on eating first? Get your nose out of the air and your gob down here."

And the grass was swished against the donkey's nose and then tugged from the hand.

Donkeys were almost as big an icon for the three of them as the shamrock. Their granddad – Dad's dad – had owned a donkey and a flat-decked cart to go with it, and they had gone off to somewhere (a place they couldn't remember) and had spent several hours digging turf to stock up for the cooking fire. Ronan and Euan had been taken into the field to try a dig. It wasn't only digging with a special slicing spade; it was also collecting turf that had been cut and stacked some weeks earlier, and while that was going on there were other parts of the field being cut in readiness for another collection on another day. Neither of them was old enough to fully work out what was going on, but everyone in the family seemed to have his own job to do, the final one being to put the previously cut pieces into large bags to carry to the cart before heading for home.

All this time Conor had been left to hold the reins of the donkey. He had only told them in later years, when they were in their teens, how he was 'scared shitless' in case the donkey took off and he couldn't control it. He realized in later years that there was as much energy in the donkey as in a piece of driftwood, but all he could think of at the time were the stories that his granddad and uncles told of the intractable stubbornness and determination of donkeys. He was so relieved when it was time to go home and Granddad took control and grabbed the reins telling him he was 'a broth of a boy' and a natural horseman and to clamber up on the tail of the cart, 'there's a good gossoon'. Conor remembered he could barely control the prideful smile as his chest puffed out and he grew three inches in a second, sitting on top of the coarse, stained turf sacks on the back of the cart with his brothers.

They stayed long enough to remind themselves of the attractiveness and idiosyncrasies of the donkeys before heading back to the car. They had seen all they could see and were resigned to the fact that the house where Mum lived – the house they had visited on some of their many trips back to Ireland – was not possible to find. They doubted they would recognize it anyway and had no idea which direction it was in, never having seen this school and this area before, but in a funny kind of way it didn't matter. The sense of their mum was as much on the edges as in the centre, and they took it all in.

Conor beamed. "Now for some real driving!"

He turned the key and the engine fired up, and, as they had come to expect of him when the serious part of him took over, he drove back the way they had come, flawlessly, back to the car park outside the hotel in Strokestown.

Chapter 27

They washed quickly in their rooms to freshen up, had a quick lunch of chicken-and-mushroom filo, hot chocolates and mochaccinos in the hotel restaurant and then decided on a 'family' afternoon.

Ronan wanted to phone Catherine later in the afternoon, and Euan was able to phone Maria a little later in the day; Conor had no way of getting hold of Tessa, so he said he would have a 'family rest' for the three of them and have a snooze on his bed. They arranged to meet up again at 5 p.m. in the hotel lobby.

So it was a restful afternoon and they were left to themselves.

Conor, after a few snores more than a snooze, read for a while and got most of their things packed ready to leave early in the morning of the following day, then all three of them headed down to the lobby as near to five o'clock as their characters would allow.

"How long have you been here?" Conor asked Euan.

"Since five o'clock," answered Euan. "That was the time we agreed to, wasn't it? Is your watch broken?"

"No, it's been stolen," replied Conor.

"I was here four minutes later," said Ronan. "Took me that long to creep into your bedroom while you snored, and pinch your watch." And he showed Conor his missing watch firmly attached to his wrist.

"That's why I was late. I didn't know the time," Conor smiled.

"OK, I'm outta here! The convoluted crap is starting again!"

Euan headed out through the door closely followed by Ronan, and a bemused Conor brought up the rear. As they hit the street, Conor leaned his forehead against Ronan's back and swung his arms and legs wide as he marched, and Ronan leaned his forehead against Euan's back and swung his arms and legs in time with Conor's. Euan got it straight away and swung arms and legs in time with his brothers and the three of them moved off down the street in a coordinated caterpillar of exaggerated marching linked by their heads against each other's backs.

A few people stared and the three of them couldn't have cared less. It broke up in a shambles when Euan tried to turn himself around full circle and lean his forehead against Conor's back, but the circle was too tight and they separated, laughing like children.

"The three of you, grow up!" shouted Conor.

"You and the other two!" yelled Euan, pointing at Conor.

"Both of the three of you!" chuckled Ronan.

They decided that they really only wanted fish and chips, and there was a chippie not far along the road from the hotel where they were staying. It was run by a very pleasant couple, brown and crispy like their batter, and they ordered six fish and three scoops of chips all in the one packet. There were plenty of other items on the whiteboards in the shop, but they really just wanted to sample Irish fish and chips.

"Pity they didn't have any mushy peas," said Ronan. "You can't beat them on fish and chips," he said. "In the old days every chippie had a pot of them boiling on the stove and they were scooped out in a fishnet ladle and drizzled all over your fish and chips just before wrapping. Even the newspaper wrapping tasted nice. You have to buy mushy peas in tins in New Zealand and make your own."

"I do remember that," agreed Euan. "The newspaper did taste nice. If you couldn't separate it from the fish you just ate it."

"Me too," said Conor. "Much overrated by fading memory and passing time."

"Like everything," said Ronan.

They couldn't believe the amount they got. It was like the

whole Irish catch that day, and the potatoes from every field of spuds around the town had found their way into their order. And they had to admit it was superb. They sat on a seat in the sun and ate them, feeling young and casual and unconcerned about passers-by or amused glances – temporary escapees from the prison of age.

But they couldn't finish it all and they had to parcel the leftovers up tightly and cram the warm grease-blotched bundle down into an overfull street bin. Ronan was overruled when he suggested they save them for breakfast in the morning before they got on the road to Galway. With very little discussion, they decided to go back into Manannan's Bar and have a few 'quiets' and maybe an early night before the next part of their journey. All was peaceful in the bar and they knew not to expect a repeat of the previous evening; nor did they want one. A few faces drifted their way and smiled in welcome. The peaks of caps were touched, but the silence settled again like a thick mountain mist and the conversations were muffled and seemed spiritless. They found a corner table and sat down. Ronan went to get the first round in.

"Well, that was a good day," began Euan. "We got to see all the things we wanted to and revived a few memories."

"And created some more," put in Conor.

"Aye, we did that too," replied Euan thoughtfully.

"What's the matter with you?" asked Conor, noticing his brother's quiet mood.

"Oh, just reflecting on Mum again and— Thanks, my friend."

Ronan had returned with three pints of Guinness and was placing them on the table in front of them.

"I'm just feeling a bit guilty again about how we left you to do all the funeral arrangements for Mum and Dad."

"I agree with you, Euan. I don't feel good about it either," agreed Ronan as he sat down. "It was all—"

"Look!" interrupted Conor firmly. "I think enough has been said about this already. I think it's time it was buried. I don't want to keep hearing about this every step of this bloody pilgrimage around Ireland! Don't fucking interrupt me, Ronan! It's my turn! I was Johnny on the Spot and so it was my job. You two were miles away and would never have made it back for either funeral, so what would have been the point? I knew this was coming, so we might as well get it out of our systems now! Yes, if I was honest, I would have loved you both to be there just for the support and to talk it through with someone, but in both cases I knew no one at either funeral apart from the obvious ones: Dad at Mum's funeral, and so on. Skinny congregations. It was a lonely time and I'm not going to pretend it wasn't, but I didn't blame either of you for not being there and I don't hold any anger or resentment towards either of you. Do you understand that?"

"Not really, fella," said Euan, "but I'm grateful that you feel that way because I've thought about it lots of times over the years. While I live a long way from where I was born I don't want to lose touch emotionally with what, for me, is still the place where my heart and soul will always have a place. You chose to stay here and I sometimes envy you having yourself firmly rooted in one place instead of always feelings stuck halfway between two."

"He's right, Conor. You can say that you don't blame us or have any resentment towards us, but it doesn't keep the guilt at bay. No, you let me finish this time! The feelings for people you love don't weaken when you are further away; if anything, the feelings get stronger. Catherine and I made it home twice to the UK – once before we had kids and the second time with young Paul and John – and a lot of the motivation behind that was to try to reconnect on a physical, tactile level and give our kids grandparents. You know well enough it didn't work out. Parting both times was the hardest thing we had to do. We didn't know it then, but Mum and Dad would never have seen our boys if we hadn't made that second trip. But it was heartbreaking leaving both times. I think for all of us it would have been better if we had stayed away and just kept in touch from a distance. It's an awful position to be in and it hurt. You don't ever really get over things like that. It happens to millions of people each year, and it happened for you, Euan, and for me and for Catherine. People set adrift, not knowing where the tide will carry them or where they want to go or, in the end, where they belong. But it's the way of the world."

"The way of the world is to buy your long-suffering brother a drink when he's thirsty! Must be your round, Euan." It was said wearily and not playfully – unusual for Conor.

Euan got up straight away and went to the bar.

When he was gone, Conor continued: "I'm glad we are having this conversation now," he said. "This has been like a lump in our throats ever since we met at the airport, and we need to clear it so that we can all breathe easily. It's a damn sight easier to do face-to-face than by emails or phone calls, though in some ways it's also harder."

"I just don't want it to break up the family friendship we've rediscovered though," replied Ronan. "Yes, I know," he conceded, holding up his hand. "It needs to be dealt with."

"It won't break the friendship or the family. It was never strained and it will never break. Believe me," said Conor.

And they both smiled with relief.

"You know, I sometimes wonder if I should have been a little more adventurous, but I believe I was, by staying in England. And I don't regret it at all."

Euan arrived with the drinks and they took a drink to ease their throats.

Conor picked up the conversation again: "I'm speaking about this for the last time. I don't ever want to hear another word about it after this, so you'd both better listen. Do you hear me?"

Ronan and Euan nodded in unison. They both knew that he was the only one of them that could really say what needed to be said and allow them all to fully relax with each other with no barriers, real or imagined, between them.

Conor took a deep, quiet breath and then began: "You both have or had every right to pursue a life wherever you thought you wanted to be for whatever reasons – a better lifestyle or a good place to bring up kids. I'm sure you've both been homesick at times too. Well, sometimes I regret not moving away. You talk about envying my simplicity of choice, Euan, but I envied you two your daring and courage. I've envied you your lifestyles when I've seen postcards or photos or programmes about New Zealand or Canada on the television, though I don't envy the wrench it must have been for you both – and two times for you, Ronan. But I made my choice to stay here. I have moments of 'what if?' – and I know you do as well – but I can't live my life like that and neither can you two. What's done is done. I stayed and I was the only son here to bury Mum and Dad."

Conor was clearly distressed and Ronan and Euan willed him to keep going.

"As you can clearly see, Tessa and I live in a beautiful part of the UK, in a country that has a richer history than any other place on the globe, including your two countries. Its architecture, literature and arts generally have dominated the Western world for centuries. We had the Beatles, remember – not New Zealand or Canada. We're happy here. We have two wonderful daughters, as you know, and we wouldn't leave for quids. We're all lucky to have made great and happy lives for ourselves and our families and we're all still together. Now that retirement has arrived, or looms, for all of us, there will be lots more opportunity to see each other (God help me!) and each other's places, and so we'll have the best of all three worlds. That's my eulogy on guilt, guys, and I want it to end here. Now it has to be cremated and there is to be no more raking over of the ashes – no more. I never want to hear it mentioned again. Can we do that?"

He held out his hands and they reached out too and held fast across the table.

"Now let's drink," he concluded, "and stop wasting a fecking good night. Let go of my hands, Ronan, or I can't hold my glass!"

Ronan jumped as if frightened out of a dream, and let go. The other two laughed.

The night passed quickly and well. Talk, invariably, was close-ups of their times as kids together and the holidays they had with their parents and stories of their new lives while raising their own kids; they spoke of the ways they found themselves behaving, talking and dreaming about their kids' futures like their mum and dad had done with them and even becoming like them in many of their habits and characteristics.

"Only four certainties in life," said Conor: "death, taxes, change and we all get like our parents."

After several more pints that slipped smoothly down, they decided to call it a night and get some zeds in for the journey to Galway, and then Oranmore, the next morning.

They crossed over the road and walked down to the hotel. Then, with a solemn shake of each other's hands or a pat on the back (or both) in the lobby, they retired to the welcome of their rooms and untroubled sleep.

Chapter 28

The next morning was casually busy. They came down for breakfast and coffee, went back to finish packing and agreed to be back down again at reception by 10.30 a.m. or thereabouts. The hotel wasn't busy, and they were told they could have a departure time of 10 a.m. or later if they wished. So they took full advantage of the friendly invitation and decided to meet in the reception lounge at 10.30 a.m.

"Nothing's changed since the cathartic conversation of last night," commented Euan wryly as Conor arrived ten minutes late.

"I've settled the bill," said Ronan, "so let's be on our way."

The other two protested, but to no purpose. Ronan would not take any money.

"OK, but as a way of punishing you I'm driving."

And Euan grabbed the keys from Conor.

"Oh, God!" cried Conor, holding his head in anguish. "Just remember it's not a dog sled."

Yeah," agreed Ronan, "or everything could turn to mush!"

His wit was rewarded with a thumping crack from Euan on the upper arm, and he rolled away in feigned agony.

"Let's go!" urged Conor. "You two can play games when we get there. I'm in the front!" he shouted, and he grabbed his bag and ran out through the door.

Euan grabbed his and ran out after him, Ronan close behind. Seamus was round the back, and he came across to say goodbye as they were putting their things into the boot and getting jackets off ready for the journey.

"Take care, now, boys," he said. "Thanks for a grand night the other night. Gave the town a real lift, it did. Best craic we could all remember in a long time."

"Pleasure, Seamus," said Euan, and they all shook his hand before getting into the car.

As they drove off Euan sounded the horn and they all waved. Seamus waved back wildly as he disappeared into the background behind them and they headed out for Galway.

After giving Euan plenty of ribbing about his driving, they settled down again to enjoy the Irish countryside on a cloudy, cool but pleasant enough day threatening sunshine. There was a slightly subdued mood anyway as they realized that there was a strong chance, at least for Euan and Ronan, that they would not be here again. For Conor it might be different, but even then there was no real reason to return; the grave was well looked after by someone and he felt no need to pursue it any further. Visiting her grave together had somehow made it more significant and appropriate – a final family farewell.

They headed west on 'Highway 5' as Conor, reading the map in the front passenger seat, explained it.

"Highway?" mocked Euan. "We'd only call something this narrow a driveway. I've see wider and longer roads than this leading to someone's house from the road!"

"Just drive," said Ronan from the back. "We don't need a 'supersize me' lesson from behind the wheel."

The country reeled by and the mood lightened.

"How far does it look on the map?" Euan asked.

Conor looked for the scale and then did a quick calculation.

"It wouldn't be far off 100 kilometres," replied Conor, "but not as the raven flies. It's got a few bends and sometimes we have to go west to get to the south. It looks like a very pleasant piece of country and it's nice to relax."

"And where are we staying in Galway, revered tour leader?" Ronan was trying to find out if Conor had paid for anything else without telling them. "Are we just going on spec?"

"No," replied Conor. "It's approaching the quiet season at this time of the year, so there was no need to make a booking. At least that's what the lady at reception advised. Galway and the surrounding towns are popular spots to visit, but it's tapering off at this time of the year."

"So you've booked or you haven't?"

"No, I haven't. I took her advice. No, I haven't booked anything and we pay when we get there or, more likely, when we leave."

"No, we settle the bill when we leave," said Euan, pointing at himself and then hitching his thumb in Ronan's direction in the back seat.

"Please yourself. No big deal," muttered Conor, and the other two knew him well enough now not to say any more about it; just to do it.

"You still haven't told us where we're staying," insisted Euan, leaping for the safe ground.

"Oh, right. You distracted me. It's a place called the Oranmore Bay Lodge, and if you look on the website it says it's ten minutes east of Galway City on the Dublin road, which would have got us here a lot quicker if we hadn't had to go north to Strokestown and other places. I've stayed before and it's very good – good service and very friendly and accommodating."

"Wouldn't have missed Strokestown for the world, all the same," said Euan, echoing Ronan's thoughts exactly.

"Shannon Airport is just sixty to seventy kilometres from Galway town centre, slightly closer to Oranmore Bay; maybe it's three to four kilometres shorter. That's good for when we get ready to head back to England before we catch our flights home or catch up with our families who are on the road again," said Conor without conviction.

They all felt that voicing it made it seem too real, so they kept quiet about it, like kids afraid of the dark. Instead they settled to enjoy Galway, the next couple of days and each other's company.

"Now," said Ronan, the back-seat navigator, "you'll come to a fork in the road after about ten kilometres and you should take the left fork at a little place called Tulsk – doesn't sound very

Irish, does it? And then you're on Route 61 to Roscommon. I'll tell you where to go once you get there. OK, driver?"

"Whatever you say, buddy," answered Euan.

It was only a short time before they were at the fork. Euan dutifully took the left fork as directed, following the sign, and at last they were heading south to Galway on Route 61. They had to admit the roads were good quality and quite wide on the main road system – not as endearing or as challenging as the country lanes. Because of the clearance around them they were able to admire the gently rolling, lush green of the hillsides with their patches of woodland; the whole landscape was divided by hedges interspersed by an occasional tree. The drystone walls they loved so much lined the roadsides, as resilient and enduring as the people who populated the land.

They chatted and laughed, telling stories of their times as kids beginning with "Do you remember when . . . ?" or "You got me into trouble, you bugger!" or "Talk about stupid!" Every one brought back memories of a happy childhood, not rich and not poor, made possible by sacrifice and driven by ambition for better, guaranteed by a good if not expensive grammar-school education.

They were all three surprised by how much came back to them when one of them remembered an event which the other two had never thought of during the years since it happened. Now memories bounced and jiggled around like lollies shaken in a jar, vying for position at the top, and each one was unique and full of promise. Some were scary at the time, but had now passed into happy thoughts, providing good conversation. Many of their tales had an air of innocence and naivety, heightened by the inevitability of more complicated times over the passing years. Sometimes one spoke of a memory the other two couldn't remember anything about.

Everything frightening or worrying in the past became as nothing with the passing of time.

The accumulation of memories gave them pause to consider the fullness of their lives in a simpler age, where the challenge was to fit in everything that a day held for them before falling into bed exhausted every night. Mum tucking them in with hot-water bottles on a cold winter's night, taking them downstairs to refill them on a really cold night; Dad arriving home late from the club and putting his big heavy overcoats over their feet before creeping out of the bedrooms. The lights would go off and they would hear their mum and dad quietly talking away in their bedroom next door. On wintry mornings they used their nails to scratch the ice off the inside of the windows to make tiny peepholes so they could look out on to the white world which had magically appeared overnight.

Their ribs were sore with laughing, and they slowly but pleasurably ran out of steam. They settled back again and gazed off into their own distances, smiled and nudged closer together without realizing it, tucked up together in their waking dreams.

Euan's driving, for all the teasing, was safe and smooth and the miles rolled by. The day had made something of itself, and its confident sun was burning away the clouds to make way for a fine day.

"I wish I knew more about the flora and fauna of Ireland," said Ronan. "I see lots, but I don't know what they are. The bird life seems to be the same as in England, but I'm sure Ireland has its own special birds. Probably some are more familiar here than in England. You're the birdwatcher, Conor – do you know what they have here? All I hear is birdsong coming from the trees and the hedges, but I've no idea what they are."

"Just the usual," replied Conor, seemingly uninterested: "sparrows, blackbirds, song thrushes, finches, fieldfares and lapwings seem to be everywhere. And a wagtail or two. Remember Dad used to call them Willie wagtails?"

They both nodded.

"I know they have robins here, but I've never seen one, lots of goldfinches, blue tits, chaffinches – same as England. I'm sure some of those will be in your countries too."

As he was speaking he pointed to a field in front of them to the right where a few swallows were darting and dipping like miniature black kites.

"I'm sure you've got those in both your countries. There

are some migratory waders and geese in some of the inland waterways, but I don't really know much about that side of things."

"I wonder why some birds, like sparrows, have been so successful, travelling and settling throughout the world?" Ronan persisted.

"I think sparrows migrate accidentally," said Euan, "or 'travel', as you call it, crossing from one country to another in places like Europe without even knowing it. I suspect many of those that end up in faraway places across large oceans were introduced by homesick Poms or other immigrants to foreign countries."

"I remember that Catherine and I saw them in India when we were there. India sticks in my mind, but I'm fairly sure they are in many other parts of Asia too."

"I think they spread rather than migrate. They've obviously been very successful. Wherever humans are, then you'll usually find sparrows. Symbiosis," concluded Conor.

"Do you get them in Canada?" asked Ronan.

"Yup, and all over the States as well. What about you? Australia and New Zealand?" asked Euan.

"Yeah, everywhere." Ronan looked at the other two. "There you go! Just what we thought. The world's first internationalists. They settle all over the world, adapting to life in a foreign land, then they never look back and never come back except maybe being driven by a freak of weather into neighbouring countries. They settle in with the natives, far from home, and they seem as if they have always been there."

"Right, that's the sparrows and the rest of the world's bird life sorted. Does anyone know where we are?" interrupted Conor.

"Yes," replied Euan smugly, "we're about ten kilometres from Roscommon. If we stay on Route 61 and follow the signs through the centre of town, it will show Highway 63 off to our right. We need to take that. We are then well on the way to Galway. Unless you want to stop in Roscommon?"

"I don't," said Ronan. "We've only just left Strokestown, so

I'd rather move on. It's up to the rest of you as well."

"Perhaps another time," said Conor. "If we ever do come back we should come back with our wives and do the whole country together and spend a lot more time here."

"Nice idea, Conor, but . . . I suppose you never know," said Ronan more brightly. "You never really know where you'll end up or what's in store, do ya?"

He got no response.

"OK, we're driving through and on we go."

The conversation consisted of pointing out features of the landscape or cottages. Some harvesting was taking place, but they weren't sure what crops they were. It looked like some fields were of barley and maize. In a couple of large areas potatoes were almost ready for harvesting, and a large combine harvester was thrashing its way through a field of wheat. Euan argued that Ireland imported most of its wheat from Canada anyway – the other two couldn't argue about that because they didn't know.

There were small gatherings of familiar trees like oak, ash and beech. Silver birches could often be seen in the few gardens they passed. On a hill in a field a solitary liquidambar was already starting to faintly turn into autumnal hues, though hawthorn bushes were still flowerless but with freshly green leaves and daring thorns.

The time passed quickly, and soon the outskirts of Roscommon were running past them on both sides. Again they felt that strange sense of familiarity because the name was so commonly spoken in their home, but they knew nothing of the town itself outside their romantic connection. They moved through its centre with little time or need for regret. They knew they couldn't do and see everything – what they *needed* to see was more important. Maybe some other time.

"It looks like a lovely place," suggested Ronan.

"I'm sure it is. Last time I was here I never really had time to look around." Conor was matter-of-fact about it. "Let's keep moving, unless someone really wants to stop for coffee or something."

"Only just had a big breakfast!" commented Ronan.

"And your point is what?" asked Euan.

Then he just hummed a tune quietly to himself and looked carefully for signs to get him out on to Highway 63.

"There's a major road sign just down here," said Conor, pointing to a large sign on the left, straddling the footpath.

It pointed to the left for An Longfort, straight ahead for Baile Atha Luain and right for the N63 and Galway, or Gaillimh. None of the distances seemed far that they were driving and Conor reckoned that with any luck it would be just over an hour before they reached Galway. They turned, and so did the weather as the rain poured down again.

"God," said Conor, after taking hold of the map, "I'm not surprised it rains so heavily round here. You should see the number of lakes in the area we're going to, and we're very close to the Atlantic Ocean as well. We're hemmed in by water, and we're driving closer to it. I never picked this up last time. There's one massive one, several medium ones and a lot that look like puddles. Some of the islands off the coast are quite large too. There's one called Inishturk, and others are called Inishbofin, Lettermore Island and Gorumna Island. There are some at least I've heard of and always wondered where they were, such as the Aran Islands. God, there's a heap of them! Everywhere you step there's a small lake to fall into. County Galway seems to be huge!"

"I wonder if anyone lives there – on those islands, I mean," said Euan. "How would anyone know? Does anyone ever go there to see if anyone is still alive? What do the people who live there do?"

"It wouldn't include stage shows, would it?" agreed Ronan. "I wonder how long they've lived there for? Will they live there all their lives and never know what else is out here. Or do they care?"

"Are you sure that it isn't just that the area is flooded with all the rain, and when it stops the submerged land will all surface again and join up and the people will all just drive around like us?" asked Euan.

"Wouldn't it be great if the whole world was just one landmass and we could just drive everywhere and live anywhere?" concluded Ronan.

"I'd hate that," said Conor. "That would ruin all the possibilities and excitement of travel."

The other two thought about the comment, but needed more time to think about it and decided not to.

The journey continued in the pouring rain. It spoiled the view, but they saw plenty of rolling gentle hills, and fields very, very green spotted with small clumps of trees. There were occasional whitewashed houses looking clean and spectral in the rain and mist. Small villages were everywhere. That's hardly the right word for them as they are more like random settlements – nothing large enough to warrant inspection or a soaking. They decided to drive on to Galway and have some lunch there. They were already more than halfway, and apart from the sluicing wipers and the occasional misting of edges of windows it was a relaxing time in the silence that sometimes says enough.

Chapter 29

In less than thirty more minutes they were on the edges of Galway and were looking, first of all, for signs for Oranmore. They looked to get to the town centre for a brief look around and a bite to eat. The map they had was not detailed enough, so it became a matter of driving until they saw a parking space and then getting out and walking, choosing their own directions and stopping places. In the meantime they were shepherded along by vehicles which clearly had a better idea of where they were going than they did.

They were not prepared to be as impressed as they were, because the conditions put a dampener on their spirits and made everything that much more difficult. They parked 'somewhere', which was trial enough in itself as the city was packed and splashed with people, very busy with vehicles. Visibility was poor with the torrential rain.

Where they parked was near to a building looking like a large church or a cathedral, close to a raging torrent of a river (they guessed it was the River Corrib they had seen on the map) and what looked like a city centre in terms of the quantity and quality of shops. They memorized the surroundings, picking out landmarks to help them get back to the car when they had finished looking around. They decided that, given the weather, it was better to park and just do the looking on foot rather than hesitantly driving round in nose-to-tail traffic in a place they didn't know, infuriating everyone – not least themselves.

They put on their hooded parkas (though they couldn't even

agree about what they were called because of the different names used in their respective countries), and took an umbrella with them and began to explore, tentatively, the town of Galway, near the resting place of their dad. It was far from comfortable as the rain was drenching, and yet they were quite warm once they had their jackets on. It felt quite humid, but they never felt the same urge to stroll and relax as they would have done had it been warm sunshine. They guessed it to be between thirteen and fifteen degrees – uncomfortably warm in the heavy raincoats they were wearing.

   They remembered seeing Williams Street and Shop Street, among others, and were delighted with the beauty of the streets, which no amount of rain could dampen. Many of them were cobbled and narrow, and most shops were pastel-coloured plaster buildings; others were bright orange, plum and green. Above the pavements outside shops there were hanging baskets of flowers. The shops had old-fashioned frontages and seemed cosy and brightly lit, while the flowers, all in bloom, bravely provided splashes of brightness to a deep-grey and cloudy day. The old-style signs, swinging on arms above the doorways and under the eaves, added to the sense that they were in a nineteenth-century township, and at any moment they expected to see horse-drawn carriages go past on the streaming roads. They wandered aimlessly but happily into and out of shops, charmed by the feel of the place. They had no particular wish on their minds, and were not even in search of anything in particular, but they had that sense you sometimes get in foreign places that there are hundreds of people moving around you. Some caught their eye and smiled or nodded; others were engrossed in their busyness and abstract thoughts. They concentrated on their own lives and their own dreams, ambitions and anxieties. The brothers had no idea who they were or anything about them, but people are alike even though they are different: a kind of anonymous relationship that binds all of humanity in a common desire for success, whatever that is, and happiness, whatever that is. So although they were strangers they still felt distantly welcome.

What was really appealing to them was the bilingual signage around the streets.

"I think that's something that we should have expected as we moved further west," said Euan. "We're moving further away from the centre of Westminster, and, much like in England, the further you move north and west from the centre the more you get the 'auld' languages preserved or emerging again. Dublin is no different."

"You're right," agreed Conor. "Very clever observation for a Canadian who studied chemistry, physics and maths and knew nothing about English. I suspect they're very protective of the Gaelic language over here on the western side of Ireland. I don't know how we find out in the short amount of time we are here, but I bet we would find lots of native Gaelic speakers and perhaps even a movement to preserve and teach the Gaelic language somewhere in this area."

"I think that's great though. It's so easy to lose all the lovely flavours of dialect and other languages once we get a stir of the pot to make everything look and taste the same. Good on them for fighting to keep it alive," said Ronan. "Not unlike the Maori in New Zealand, they are trying to revive their language, and that's really important. Or at least *I* think it is."

Some shops they stayed longer in, trying to compare the prices of shirts and shoes, jerseys and electrical goods and books, DVDs and CDs. They helped each other work out the equivalent prices in their own currencies and, as usual, agreed that in the end prices were probably about the same when you realized some prices were dearer and other prices were cheaper than those at home. Though the shopkeepers realized they were merely looking, they were met with kindness, friendship and humour. In conversation with some of the shop assistants, they were told to go and have a look at the heart of the town, Eyre Square, but the locals seemed unwilling to give them too much information, hoping instead that they would go and look for themselves.

"Forget about the shower of rain, and enjoy the surprise!" they were told, referring to the sculptures and other interesting features of the square.

After more time of wonder and fascination they were directed to a nice pub and got themselves a lunch of a half-pint of Guinness and some good hot food at The Way Inn. It warmed them up and got them out of the drenching rain for a good while before they headed up the street in the direction that had been indicated. Conor seemed content and smug and never said a word, though they knew it was not that long since he had been back in Galway. It was clear from the expression on his face that this was a place that appealed to him.

"Bloody heavy shower!" complained Euan.

"This isn't a shower." replied Ronan. "It feels like everyone is emptying their baths out of their upstairs windows all at the same time—"

"Over us!" interrupted Conor.

"Wow!" exclaimed Euan, who had been first to breast the small rise, turn the corner of the street and stare out across the square.

"Wow! You said it," agreed Ronan, reaching his side.

Conor, who had seen it just on two and a half years ago, when he had come across alone to place a more permanent headstone on Dad's grave, couldn't help but smile. It was just as impressive as it had been on his other two visits, and he stared through the rain at the town square that no amount of rain could spoil.

They moved across the small side road to get a better view. All thoughts and concerns about the rain had gone. The square was a mixture of slabs and grassed areas, young trees and standing plant boxes, also full of blooms, as well as benches all around, understandably empty just at this time. There were a number of aluminium flagpoles in a long line across the front of the park facing a main road.

"Probably the one we should have come in on," commented Euan ruefully.

On each of the poles was a flag with a crest, all brightly and differently coloured. It was like a burst of defiant spring at the end of a winter. They decided to remain where they were rather than go and explore fully. One of the local store owners had cheerfully told them that the forecast for the late afternoon was reasonably good, with the odd shower; the following morning would be better, though rain was due to come in again in the late afternoon and get worse in the early evening.

"Sure, it's never far away in Galway. Always lurking somewhere just around the corner, so it is. But 'tis a soft old day today and she'll be a better day tomorrow."

He had the look about him of someone who had enjoyed the sun when it came, laughed a lot even when it didn't, had read the skies for years and was very well read.

"Look," said Conor, cutting into their thoughts, "why don't we head out for Oranmore and get settled and dry? We can come out again in the morning and look around when the weather is better. There's plenty to see, and you need to see it without the rain. Maybe this afternoon we could go and look at Dad's grave and see what needs to be done. Maybe even a little look around Oranmore if we feel like it. What do you want to do?"

"I agree," said Ronan. "Even if it's only a chance of a small break in the weather, I'd like to be able to spend time wandering comfortably around in the morning and have a really good look around. He talked about the 'odd shower', but I think this is what they call an 'odd shower'. There's probably a few other things to see as well. And yeah, maybe a look at the grave this afternoon, briefly, and then a proper tidy-up tomorrow afternoon once we've had some time in town here in the morning."

"I'm fine with that," agreed Euan. "I want to get a more lasting impression of Galway. There's no chance I won't, but without the rain it would be real magic. Let's go."

They headed off in the direction of the parked car, easily able to pick out the landmarks they'd identified, and soon arrived back where they had started. They took off their wet jackets as quickly as they could, gave them a good shake and squeezed them into the boot, making sure they touched only bags and not other clothing. In spite of their speed they still received a mild soaking by the time they threw themselves into the car.

"Now you may not believe this, but I'm still not sure if I can remember how to get to Oranmore from here." Conor was staring at the map and moving a forefinger across the paper, an uncertain frown lining his brow.

"I believe it," said Euan.

"Me too," said Ronan.

"As I expected," replied Conor. "Look for signs for the airport and maybe even Dublin and then hang a right really, get on to Route 18 if you can find it, look for Breanloughaun and then Garraun, and shortly after that a right turn on to a lesser road, R338, and into Oranmore township and the Oranmore Bay Lodge. We're heading south-east. OK?" he concluded.

"Should be easy with directions as good as that," quipped Euan.

Surprisingly it was, and within a short space of time the signs were all located, the roads travelled and they were heading along the coast road for Oranmore with the sea already beckoning.

Chapter 30

"Right, that's got it all done and booked," said the receptionist. "Do you mind if I just go through it with you once more, Mrs Doherty, because we need to get it right, don't we, if it's going to be a proper surprise?"

"No, no, me darlin', I don't mind a jot. That's just fine, isn't it, Rory?"

"I think—" began Rory.

"You go ahead," interrupted Mrs Doherty. "Tell me what you've got written there in that grand book of yours."

The receptionist worked her index finger along the relevant page as she began to recite the details of the 'surprise' event.

"You've booked eight double rooms for guests for tomorrow night and you'll all be arriving at about 8 p.m. Some other friends of your son will be arriving at about 9 p.m. You don't want dinner – only a supper a little after 9 p.m. Right so far?"

"Aye, perfect, me darlin'," replied Mrs Doherty. "She's got it right so far, hasn't she, Rory?"

"I think—" said Rory.

Mrs Doherty hammered on: "Sure, everybody'll have their dinner before they come out because the guest of honour, my son Kieran, is going out for a quiet romantic dinner anyway with his lovely wife, Bridget. There'll be lots of young people comin' a little bit later. I told you that, didn't I?"

"Yes, to be sure you did," said the receptionist. "It was a good job you booked like this, even though we haven't been that busy so far this season, because I've only got one room left now – mind you, it's quite a large one."

"But none of their younger friends will be staying the night. You know what the young folk are like. After the bit of a shindig here they'll be back off into Galway and pick up a bit of nightlife at one of the pubs. No doubt Kieran and Bridget will go with them. The rooms I've booked are for the oldies, like Rory and meself, who need somewhere to fall down." Mrs Doherty winked at Rory and laughed like a horse that snorts first before breaking into full-blown whinnying.

"Right, no, that's good. As I said, I've only got one other room left anyway," continued the receptionist, smiling. "If you don't mind, I'll let that room if someone arrives looking for a place to stay. It shouldn't be a problem, should it?"

"Goodness me, no!" exclaimed Mrs Doherty. "As long as they are quiet people and stay out of the way. I don't want anyone to know what's going on though tomorrow night. Just a casual word dropped here and there and the whole secret could be ruined. So lips sealed, if you don't mind," said Mrs Doherty, winking conspiratorially

"I understand," sighed the receptionist, thinking it highly unlikely that details about the night's surprise could get spread around any other possible visitors to the Lodge, "So how many places do you want for the supper?"

"I'd round it off to twenty, me love. Aye, twenty will be plenty. Oh, did you hear that little rhyme?" And she snickered with pleasure. "Now, can we do without the places and just have a buffet-style instead, because Kieran and Bridget will clearly have eaten and the youngsters will have had dinner too, I would imagine? I've told Niall Barry, who's organizing Kieran and Bridget's friends, to be here just before 8.30 p.m. for supper soon after 9 p.m. Sure, they eat like horses, the youngsters today. He's a good lad that Niall. He's kept it a great secret from Kieran, so he has, and he's asked all of them to park in a couple of side streets around off the main road so as not to be noticed. Bridget's in on the whole thing. She'll be coaxing Kieran in even though the lights will be off and it will look like there's no receptionist here to greet them. She's a good lass that lass, isn't she, Rory?"

Rory opened his mouth to speak, but never got that far.

"Kieran thinks they are just coming here for a romantic stay," she continued.

"OK," agreed the receptionist, who, after a sympathetic smile at Rory, was keen to move on. "And the cake is to have twenty-eight candles?"

Mrs Doherty nodded.

"And we'll put that on one of the tables in the foyer ready to light the candles soon after they come in."

Again Mrs Doherty nodded. "Still my little boy, though he's twenty-eight tomorrow."

"Now, you're sure you want all this in the foyer here and not in our dining hall?" And the receptionist's hand performed a sweep of what was a substantial foyer with a grand timber staircase just to the right of the dining room, on the far side of the foyer from the double-door entrance. The staircase, elegant with a sturdy banister, turned its way upwards to the left and around to the hotel accommodation. In the far-right corner area as you came in through the main doors was a selection of leather armchairs and sofas, interspersed with coffee tables and, at the softly lit end of the room, a bar.

"That's what we want, indeed. Just the lobby is all we need. An immediate effect, ya see. As soon as they come in the door, they'll be right a-facing us all. And anyway, to make it a proper surprise we'll have to have all the lights off. We can turn the lights on once they come in those lovely big entrance doors over there. Oh, it'll be such a surprise for him. I can't wait to see his face!" And there was another tremendous snort followed by the now anticipated whinny.

"That's good," concluded the receptionist. "We'll set everything up in here for 8 p.m. and we'll expect the staying guests shortly after that. The younger group will arrive at 8.30 p.m. and the birthday boy and his wife will be here at . . . ?"

"Just after 9 p.m. dear," nodded Mrs Doherty. "Bridget's going to ring me when they are fifteen minutes away, pretending she's ringing a friend about a job at work the next day. We've got a little code, we have." And she snickered and snorted, enjoying the joke and the secret.

"I'll put the table with the cake on it just over here," said the receptionist, walking a few places across to the side of the doors leading into the dining room. Just on the wall above the table, which will be placed here, are six switches. Once they are on, all three large chandeliers in the foyer here and the wall lights will come on like the sun. The other tables with food will be across in front of these dining-room doors and the table with drinks on will be just by the stairs here," she said, walking back across. "You sure you don't want the bar open?"

"Oh, 'like the sun'! I like the thought of that! We'll be able to see everything, including their smiles," snorted Mrs Doherty as Rory's eyes rolled and the thunder of a horse galloped through his mind. "No bar, thanks, dear. It's a very brief gathering and we don't want to cause a great fuss – sure, we don't, do we, Rory?"

"No, we cert—" began Rory, but that's as far as he got.

"Is that everything, do ya think, my lovely?" Mrs Doherty asked the receptionist.

"I think so. Now, where do you want the CD player?" enquired the receptionist.

"Oh, mother of God!" exclaimed Mrs Doherty. "I nearly forgot all about it. Bless you, bless you," she said gripping the receptionist's hand in a fever of gratitude. "The music, Rory! Why didn't you remind me?" she asked accusingly.

"I never get—" began Rory.

"Just by the table with the cake, if you wouldn't mind," replied Mrs Doherty.

"Do you know how to work it? I'll have the disc already in – The Three Tenors – and the track you want is 'Danny Boy', which is track number five. If you put it on pause just before—"

"That's fine, me darlin'," interrupted Mrs Doherty. "It's not a favourite of mine – I think it's a bit of a maudlin song meself. I think he only likes it because it has his second name in it, but . . . it'll be a lovely touch."

"It's a great favourite of mine," said Rory. "I love a good mournful song like that with a whole—"

Mrs Doherty pulled a face to freeze the beer.

"Don't interrupt me like that, Rory!" And she carried on with her instructions.

"Niall is a whiz on this sort of stuff. He's doing all that for me. Just the player and the CD inside it will be just grand. On to track 5, push 'pause' and then 'play' as they come in the door. Sure, he has it all in his head. Thank you, now."

"It will all be ready for you, I assure you." There was a grim edge to the receptionist's voice – she was beginning to like the long-suffering Rory.

"Thank you, me darlin'. I'll leave it in your very capable hands. See you at 8 p.m. tomorrow."

"That's great, thank you," replied the receptionist. "See you then."

'That'll be soon enough,' she thought to herself.

"C'mon, Rory, and don't forget to turn those light switches on as soon as the song begins! Like the sun – I like that, so I do," said Mrs Doherty.

She linked her arm with Rory's, taking hold like a set of reins, and led him out through the door.

The receptionist stood for a second watching the chattering and nodding – Mrs Doherty tormenting Rory with a torrent of words, as heavy as the rain, while he was dumbly dragged along. She smiled in sympathy and went off to the kitchen to explain the arrangements for the following evening to the cook before returning to the reception desk to finalize some lists and other details.

Chapter 31

The drive was quicker than any of them expected, including Conor. Before too long he remembered where the Lodge was and guided Euan to the car park at the rear of the grand building. It turned out to be about eight kilometres from Galway to Oranmore – 'The Gateway to the West of Ireland' it was called. While they were thinking about it and imagining it, they arrived. Not a sign of life, apart from a couple crossing the car park to get into their car, the woman's jaw working up and down like a piston and the man looking shambled and concussed.

Euan parked the car in a marked area and turned off the engine; it was as if he had turned off the rain. By coincidence it stopped almost as suddenly as the car.

"Wow! I bet you can't do that again!" said Ronan, quite delighted with the timing as he stared out through the window in disbelief.

"Don't want to," said Euan. "I'm getting out now and I don't want to get wet."

"Me neither," said Conor. "Leave the engine off, for goodness' sake."

Euan and Ronan were immediately impressed by the grandeur of the Lodge. It wasn't large, but it was located in very well-kept grounds of neatly trimmed hedges, lawns, roses and an assortment of flower beds. At a distance, to presumably prevent the occasional sun being blocked from brightening up the Lodge, there were small lines of oak trees and elms. Beyond, on one side, there were rolling hills; and the rolling, dark sea was in front, close enough to be clearly audible.

They collected their bags from the boot, shut it, locked it with the remote key and headed for the rounded entrance to the Lodge. It was a medium-sized building, brick with two plaster columns on either side of the wide entrance, which had four very wide, half-rounded concrete steps leading up to it. Above the main entrance and supported by the two columns was what appeared to be a medium-sized balcony with large windows, or they could have been glass doors leading on to the balcony. Brass and glass were in abundance.

When they got through the main double doors, wiping their feet on a large 'welcome' mat, they were greeted by a very large lobby with a curved reception desk over to their left. A set of double doors almost straight across from them led to what was clearly a dining room, flanked by a grand wooden staircase to the right. There was a relaxing area to the right of that again, with a TV and a small but well-stocked bar. The carpet was a plain dark-fawn colour, plush and full of bounce. The armchairs and settees in the small lounge to the far left were upholstered with dark chocolate-brown leather and looked very comfortable, though they were all unoccupied. It was warm and inviting inside as they looked around.

"Can I help you, gentlemen?" asked the lady behind the reception desk.

"I hope so," answered Conor, and they all moved to reception. "Do you have three rooms for two nights?" he asked the young lady behind the desk.

"Now, isn't that typical," said the receptionist, looking up at the three of them with a suitably disappointed look on her face. "I just gave them all away, except one."

"Bugger!" said Ronan. "That's no good."

Conor chimed in: "I phoned you a few weeks ago and you said it was very quiet, so I didn't bother to book. It's Kathleen, is it?"

She nodded. "It was you I spoke to on the phone, then."

Much as Conor would have liked to be righteously annoyed, he realized it was his fault for not booking; but the person he had contacted at reception was relaxed, and she convinced him that the time of their trip was going to be a very quiet time for them.

"Ah," she said. "I remember the call. It was me you spoke to. You're from London? You've stayed with us a couple of times before, haven't you? Conor, is it?" she asked.

Conor smiled. "Well done. Good memory."

"Well, it was very quiet then, and I expected the same for this time too. But . . . a sudden booking, I'm afraid. Look – I'm really sorry about that. It's a big room, the one I have left," explained the receptionist, looking wide-eyed and hopeful, "and we have had as many as four people in there before. There are already two king-single beds in there, and we have a settee/divan that we can move in there from the storage area, so you'll be quite comfortable." She saw the doubtful looks on their faces and hastened to redeem a seemingly lost situation: "I can give you separate rooms for one night – that's tonight – because the other rooms aren't booked until tomorrow night, but you'd have to have the large room for your second night. It's a lovely room, really, and well appointed with a small lounge, tea- and coffee-making facilities and a small under-bench fridge. It has its own bathroom and toilet and a small balcony. It's also very warm and cosy. And you wouldn't need to be swapping rooms after one night. Or I don't think you would. There's a heater in there you can use to dry your clothes – you look wet!"

"Very observant," said Conor, blowing an imaginary raindrop off the end of his nose.

"There's also a clothes horse in the wardrobe to hang your wet gear on. I wouldn't give a loyal customer a bad room." She was looking at Conor, ignoring his jibes, and being as persuasive as she could be.

They closed up to discuss it among themselves.

"I don't know about you guys, but I don't really want to be changing rooms when we're only here two nights. Shall we go and look at this room and see what we think?" Euan was edging towards just the one room for both nights.

Conor, seeing Ronan nodding faintly in agreement, stepped in, guessing what the end result might be: "Can we have a look at the room, please?"

"Certainly, sir. Leave your bags here just in case and I'll give you the key to the room. Are these your brothers?" she asked.

Conor nodded. "Unfortunately," he said.

"God, don't you look alike?" she said.

"Don't push your luck," said Conor, pretending to be insulted. "Do you want to sell this last room or not?"

The receptionist smiled knowingly. "I can organize three keys if you wish?"

"Let's just look at the room first," said Ronan politely. "Then we can make all those decisions. Is that all right?"

"Sure, that's grand," replied the receptionist. "Here's a key, then." And she handed the swipe card to Conor. "Up the stairs, turn directly left at the landing, straight to the end of the corridor and Room 7. It's pretty well above us here." And she pointed to the ceiling.

"Bags OK just here?" asked Euan. "Or do you want us to move them away from reception?"

"Just there is fine." And she smiled at Euan for his consideration.

They headed up the stairs and along the well-lit corridor to their left. It was long and quite broad and there was only one door off it to the right – Room 8. They arrived outside Room 7.

"She's a pleasant lass," said Euan.

"Yeah, she's good fun and enjoys a bit of banter," replied Conor.

"They don't get a choice with you anyway," said Ronan.

"Why don't we give the key to you?" suggested Conor. "You're good with these swipe keys."

"Ho ho! Genuinely funny, Conor!" sneered Ronan. "Get on with it, smart-arse!"

Smiling to himself, Conor pushed the card into the slot, watched the light turn green and turned the handle. It was as if they had walked into a room full of treasure, judging by the amazed looks on their faces. The room was stunning.

There was a huge wardrobe over to the right, with mirrors for doors, giving the illusion of even greater space. There was a small sink and workbench with a small fridge underneath along the wall just around behind the door, and they could see that there was plenty of tea and coffee. No doubt there would be some milk in the fridge and some cutlery and cups in the drawers and cupboards surrounding the sink.

One of the two king-single beds was against the left-hand wall and the door near to it could only lead to the en-suite. The other king-single bed was against the same wall as the door, but just inside to their left as they came in. The small lounge referred to, containing two comfortable-looking armchairs and a good-sized coffee table, was filling the rest of the room, with most of the seats turned towards what turned out to be huge double doors leading to the balcony they had seen from outside as they arrived. There were equally large side windows and a half-arched window at the top.

It was clear why the furniture was arranged this way: the view was spectacular even on a gloomy day like this. They looked across gardens, lawns and hedges to the sea and the shadowy islands beyond, barely distinguishable and more a suggestion of the eye than a reality.

They could see at a glance that a divan/settee would easily fit and still leave plenty of room for everything else. The large-screen TV was in the small alcove between the wardrobe and the curtains on the right, which would close off the large glass doors and window space. They were converted in an instant. They didn't even need to discuss it. Almost as one they turned and headed down to reception, chattering away excitedly.

"Can't believe that view."

"The room is tremendous."

"Do you think we'll see the sun go down?"

"Room with a view – and a half!"

They arrived at the desk, excited and animated.

"We'll take it!" Conor said urgently, almost afraid that someone else might have booked it while they were upstairs looking at the room. "For the two nights!"

The other two nodded, with smiles as wide as the bay.

"That's great!" The receptionist was delighted, but not totally surprised. "Here's another card key," she said, holding one out to Euan, who took it from her. "Here's a key to the double-door entrance as well, just in case. Would you like a third room key?"

"Your call, Ronan," quipped Euan mischievously.

Ronan looked at him and shook his head. "No, thanks. Three are easier to lose than two," he told the receptionist, a resigned smile fixed on his face.

She returned the smile and shrugged her shoulders, dipped her head ever so slightly, and indicated the stairs in a welcoming gesture. "You can fix the account up when you leave, if that's OK?"

"Great!" agreed Euan.

"What time does the bar open?" asked Ronan.

"At 4 p.m. – in about fifty minutes actually," she answered.

The three of them picked up their bags and headed across to the stairs and up to their room, chattering away excitedly and choosing beds.

"Wow!" shouted Euan. "To think we almost gave this away!" He stared in disbelief at the room and, more especially, at the view. "Wow!"

"This is amazing!" said Ronan, putting down his bag and jumping backwards on to the single bed nearest the big glass doors.

"There's only one drawback," said Euan: "I have to sleep in the same room as you two!"

"Does anyone snore?" asked Conor.

"I don't know," answered Ronan. "I'm always asleep if I do."

"I don't. I just walk and talk in my sleep. Don't you remember?" asked Euan.

"That's right," said Ronan. "Mum and Dad watched you come down the stairs one night when we lived at Lilac Crescent. You were heading for the door and they asked you where you were going."

"Did he say anything?" asked Conor, who couldn't remember the incident at all.

"Yeah," continued Ronan, "he said he was off to school. And evidently he was dead serious. Mum and Dad often talked about it. I don't know if there were any other incidents."

"Always a keen scholar, eh, Euan?" jibed Conor.

"Absolutely," said Euan. "Couldn't wait to get there. Even prepared to go in the middle of the night. That's how keen I was."

"Well, if you leave the room tonight, mate, you're on your own. Anyway, I didn't notice a school round here so there's no reason for you to go walkabout," said Ronan.

"Anyone want a tea or a coffee?" asked Conor.

"Tea, please."

"Coffee, please."

"How do you like your tea, Ronan?"

"One sugar, wet and black with plenty of milk, please!"

"And how do— Oh, right, wise guy, you'll get it how it comes, then."

"Euan?"

"Black, thanks."

Conor soon had the mugs lined up, kettle huffing and the milk top off. Ronan went over to put his own sugar in and, while they waited for the kettle to boil, all three of them started unpacking some of their gear and finding space in the en-suite for their toilet bags.

Euan was happy to have the divan bed, so he did a little bit of furniture rearranging so that there would be space for his bed when it arrived. They all changed their tops and jeans, shoes and socks because everything on the outside had got wet and everything under their raincoats had got sweaty with the warmth and humidity.

They made use of the clothes horse – Euan said he hadn't heard that word for years – and the heater, and their wet clothing was soon draped across it to dry. They opened a window just to stop the room from getting steamy, and the air was refreshing and warm.

The kettle wheezed and boiled.

As they sat there drinking, Conor on the bed nearest to the big glass doors and the other two in the wrap-around armchairs, they stared silently at the view and didn't feel the need to speak. The weather was clearing, as the old store owner in Galway had said it would, but the sea was still in a temper, rolling up on to the shore like a threat. The westerly was blustery and bullied the cringing trees.

"Do you know," said Euan, "if the clouds continue to drift away and the weather stays clear we may actually see the sun go down on Galway Bay tonight – Oranmore Bay really, but it will be something similar."

"Yeah," agreed Conor. "The song 'Galway Bay' didn't sound the same when it used to be 'and watch the sun go down on Oranmore Bay'. It didn't scan so well, so they decided on 'Galway Bay', and it's been like that ever since."

Ronan finished the last of his tea and stood up.

"Either way, it will be a great view if the sky stays reasonably clear."

He went into the bathroom and cleaned his teeth and did his best to convince his hair that it needed to cover his head. Then he came back into the room. The other two hadn't moved.

"Right!" he yelled, a single clap of his hands emphasizing his impatience. "What's the plan?"

"Oh, God," said Conor, drooping his head and putting one hand over his face, "it's Action Man again! Don't you ever slow down?"

"I don't know. I'm always asleep if I do," replied Ronan.

The other two looked at each other, smiled and shook their heads.

"OK, here's the plan," said Conor: "it's five to four, the sun is beginning to shine, we've got a place to stay; do you want to go and have a quick look at Dad's grave and see what work we have for tomorrow afternoon, or do you want to relax here for a while? (I know you didn't understand the word 'relax' in that last question, Ronan.) Then we could go for a walk around the village, find a nice restaurant and pub and have a relaxing end to the day. Tomorrow will be a fairly busy day, and so a bit of relaxation for the rest of the day might be a good idea."

"I think we can combine the best of the ideas," said Euan. "Let's have a brief look at Dad's grave. By the time we've walked and done that it won't be worth coming back here. We might as well stay out and eat and have a couple of drinks and then come back, relax and 'watch the sun go down', etc. The bar will be open here. In fact," he said, looking at his watch, "it's open in a few minutes."

"I'd rather get going as soon as we're ready and have a drink in town after we've seen Dad's grave rather than get a drink here," suggested Conor.

"I can live with that," agreed Ronan.

The other two visibly relaxed.

"Well, let's get going, then," he insisted.

The other two visibly tensed. Conor looked to the skies for assistance.

"He must have been born on one of those fast-moving trolleys that they place expectant mothers on in hospital, to get to delivery at super-speed," he muttered to himself. "Let's take our time," he pleaded. "We'll still get there. Why the rush?"

"We don't have time to muck around," replied Ronan. "Look at us. We've got 'Return to Sender' stamped all over us. We're in the email outbox, the final departure lounge, so there's no time to lose. Every day counts! So c'mon."

"I think he's serious," said Euan, staring at Ronan.

"I know he is," said Conor.

Ronan smiled and they were less certain.

"Well, if it's OK with you, Action Man, I'd like to just freshen up for a few minutes."

"Me too," said Conor. "So if you can just give us ten minutes we'll be right with you. All right?"

"Sure. I've done my ablutions so I'll go down to the lobby and wait for you there."

And he headed off almost at a trot.

"Hey, Ronan!" Euan called out.

"Yeah?" said Ronan, having to quickly about-turn just as he was going through the door.

"Don't have your wallet in your back pocket, will you?" said Euan.

"Oh, funny guy!" said Ronan, giving Euan the one-fingered salute.

And he was gone.

Chapter 32

Ronan headed out through the door and right down the stairs. At the bottom he headed left towards the bar, which was, as they had previously been told, just opened. He spent several minutes at the bar talking to the bartender and sorting out a surprise for his brothers, and then sat in a seat which enabled him to watch the stairs for Euan and Conor coming down.

There was a middle-aged couple there, sitting next to one another on a settee having a drink, and Ronan took a seat that meant their backs were towards him. They were obviously very much still a couple, and he could tell by the gentle touches and the secretive glances and closeness, and the sides of their faces creased with smiles and lined with old familiarity, that their intimacy was strong and had survived for a good many years.

Ronan thought that they were like the mum and dad he remembered from photographs they had sent – in their late fifties and approaching sixty and still full of the dreams that had made them exiles from Ireland and, for a time, exiles from contentment. They too were unafraid of being lovers in public no matter the passing years – affectionate and attentive, but not embarrassing, just snug in each other's company.

He wondered what they were talking about while his thoughts drifted again through the imaginary conversations that would have dominated his parents' lives and made them so driven – driven enough to overcome all of the worst things of life. His mind slipped sideways into a familiar world.

"They're great lads," said Danny. "I'm so proud of them and what they've achieved."

"I know," said Margaret. "It's all been worth it, hasn't it? It hasn't always been easy, but it's mostly been a great time. The time we lost Declan was the deepest and darkest part of our lives. But we've come through." She cuddled closer to Danny and smiled a smile to stop the moon.

"Yes, we have, and we've been blessed. We couldn't ask for better kids. All of them teachers or principals and fine figures in their communities. The best job in the world – shaping the future and preparing kids to redesign it. That's what they're doing and it's what we've done too, you know. They've hardly given us a moment's anxiety, and in the present age that says something."

"But we don't have them with us, do we?" stated Margaret. "Euan is in Canada and Ronan is in New Zealand. Both are overseas. Conor is in London – that's overseas too from here – and here we are in Roscommon. Not exactly a tight family, are we? It seems, one way or another, we can never keep our family together."

"Maybe not tight in the sense of living close to one another, but more closely knit in terms of our relationships than we could ever have imagined, and in many ways stronger than if we were living closer together. It doesn't always breed happy families, you know, living in one another's pockets. And sometimes you don't get to see each other as often as you think."

"I know. I know you're right, but they have kids – we're grandparents, and there are some of our babies we haven't even seen yet. I want to see them all. Who knows how much time we have left! The sixties is the 'packing your bags' territory, Danny," she said jokingly, "not a time to hesitate and put things off."

"God, that's a bit morbid, Maggie. Look at us. We could live for ever. We've never been better. Tell you what: I just thought of something obvious." His eyes widened with the possibilities. "Why don't we go and see them all? Visit the whole lot of them on a sort of world trip. What do you think?"

"What do you mean?" asked Margaret, her voice edging excitedly. "You mean that we should go and see the three of them and their families? Can we do that?"

"Of course we can. Now that the three 'horses' have left the 'stable' we don't spend anywhere as much as we used to on 'oats and hay', and so we have been saving without meaning to for years. We can afford it if you want to do it. What do you say?" Danny was laughing and excited, and he could imagine the possibilities and the huge joy that it would bring to Margaret and to their scattered sons and their young families.

"Yes! Yes! Let's do it, then! It will be wonderful!"

She laughed and hugged Danny and knew this was a moment in time that they mustn't lose. It would chip away at some of the residual pain of the loss of Declan, though the loss would never be relieved, and she would get to see all the grandchildren. It was such a great idea that she couldn't believe they hadn't thought of it sooner.

"OK, so when do we do it, do you think?" asked Danny.

"Er, um – oh, God, I've been caught out now. I never suspected you would think of doing this. You really want to do this, don't you?" She was scared to ask in case he was joking or, worse, going to change his mind.

But Danny nodded enthusiastically.

"OK; we really will do this. What time is it? Where are we? What planet are we on? What year is it?"

"November 1980, my love, as if you didn't know." And he kissed her again.

"So when do you want to go? Next year? The year after?" She was finding it hard to contain her joy and anticipation.

"I'm thinking! I'm thinking! Give me a minute. From planning to flying in a few seconds. Let me think," pleaded Danny. "What about the end of next year? Too late now to load ourselves on to them, and it would also give us time to save more and plan properly. What if we went to London first to see Conor and Tessa and their family and then fly on to New Zealand to see Ronan and Catherine, and then fly to see Euan and Maria in Canada and, finally, back home? What do you think?"

"Fantastic! Fantastic!"

Margaret was edging forward in her chair, afraid that some of his words would fall to the floor and roll away and be lost forever like unpredictable dice; that if it wasn't planned quickly it would somehow spill away from them both. She jumped out of the chair and clapped her hands together and then to her mouth and bent her knees and hunched her shoulders – a bundle of tightly sprung joy.

Danny got up and pressed her back into her chair.

"Before you get uncontrollable, let's just look at this logically and carefully. There are all sorts of things to do before this can even begin to happen, but I think we could probably be away on the first leg of the journey in a year's time. We could spend Christmas and New Year with Conor and family. They're always asking us to come for a couple of months around Christmas time and I know we'd be made very welcome. So what do you think about Christmas next year? After that, maybe the end of January to mid February we could spend with Ronan and family because that's their summer, isn't it?"

Margaret nodded, catching the fever.

"And by the time we leave there, it will be heading into a Canadian spring, so that will be a good time to be with Euan and family for a few weeks. That sounds like a plan already, yeah? We'll ring them and at least put it to them next week!"

"I can't believe this. Is this really happening? You're not having me on, are you?"

"No, I'm not, my love. We're really going to do this. We'll get in touch with them all and check that the times suit, and then we'll need to get into the planning. They've been individually asking us to come for years, so let's not disappoint them. There's nothing to stop us, so let's just do it!"

"I just need to keep that appointment next week, but I'm feeling fine now. Then we'll be away. Oh, God, this is so exciting! It could be almost the middle of the year before we *get back. Just in time for our summer!"*

They hugged with the excitement and anticipation of it all. Most of the excitement was going to be in the planning and then the meetings and holding their grandchildren for the first time. It was like they had slipped sideways into some magic world where all dreams come true. Even with the cold outside, they weren't in that place any more; they occupied days of brightening summers in their hearts and there wasn't a single cloud on their horizon.

Chapter 33

"Are you dreaming again?" asked Conor, breaking into his reverie. "Are you ready to go?" He had finished his ablutions and collected Euan and headed down the stairs to catch up with Ronan. As they reached the bottom of the stairs they saw him sitting in a comfortable chair in the bar area. Only two other people were there, and he seemed to be almost asleep.

"Hey! Are you ready?" asked Conor more loudly.

Ronan jumped. He had been so preoccupied with his thoughts he hadn't seen them come down, and Conor's voice had been like a soft echo down a long tunnel.

"Yes, I sure am. Where to first? We don't need the car, do we?" he asked Conor.

"No, it's less than half a mile and it's a pleasant walk. We might as well make the most of the reasonable weather. I've got the keys with me anyway, just in case."

And he headed for the main door, Euan behind him and Ronan bringing up the rear, remembering to pick up his backpack from beside his armchair.

Conor paused at reception and asked, "Will the bar be open when we come back in a couple of hours or four?"

"It will, sir, but I'll keep a lookout for you and as soon as I see you coming I'll close it up!" she replied.

"I knew you would. You're an invaluable member of staff here, and I'm sure that in time you'll prove to be a valuable one," he quipped.

"Thank you very much. Enjoy your afternoon. Bar closes at

six o'clock, opens again after dinner at eight." She smiled and nodded knowingly.

He was a hard case and she couldn't always keep up.

The three of them walked out through the heavy double doors. They admired silently the view across the gardens and the foreshore and out to sea, and they walked casually, stopping often, across part of the car park and on to the main road leading to the main commercial area of the small town. The cemetery was along Main Street and in the relatively new St Mary's Church grounds, and Conor told them it could be seen from the street.

The town itself was on the edge of Oranmore Bay. It wasn't large, but it was clearly growing. They guessed it wouldn't take long to look around, but they only glanced at it as they went along, intent on getting their first glimpse – for two of them, anyway – of their dad's grave.

In less than twenty minutes they arrived at the church, which was at the north-eastern end of the village. They glanced at the church sign – white writing edged in blue, with its Saturday-evening and Sunday Mass times and the name of the parish priest. To the left of the sign there was an alcove in the stone wall, on the kerbside, with a long well-maintained bench seat tucked in for the weary traveller. They went through the wrought-iron gate and along the pathway at the side of the church, which was ironically next to a pub, and arrived at the cemetery area at the back feeling like trespassers intruding on the quiet occupants. They relied on Conor to guide them from there.

"It's over there somewhere, close to the back wall." And he pointed to the furthest end. "He always wanted to be buried near the sound of laughter and people having fun, he said, so this spot couldn't be better. Just give me a minute and I'll find it."

He moved confidently down to the end of the graveyard, to the drystone wall, pulled at some tall grass and leaned it away from the headstone to reveal the words.

"Here it is," he said, almost in a whisper. Graveyards respect silence and hushed tones.

Euan and Ronan had seen photographs which Conor had sent to them; and in that sense it was familiar to them; but this was the sight that made it real, and they recognized it in a completely different way. It was very close to the wall, where the less well-tended graves were. In a strange kind of way it lifted their spirits to be near their dad again, and they just relaxed and allowed all the different memories to flood back, imagining his face with those smiling eyes and his infectious laugh. It was almost like a homecoming.

Over the wall was a series of fields and a few nosy cows ambled over to challenge, in their slow bovine way, those who had disturbed their languid afternoon, chewing nonchalantly and staring with those liquid marble eyes while snorting through moist black noses as if annoyed at the intrusion. A couple of those that kept their ground mooed plaintively instead, just so as not to be left out.

They could hear the sounds of planes too, but grey skies ruled out any sightings and they rightly guessed it was airport traffic heading skywards. They imagined that when the pub was full, the airport busy and the cows inquisitive and loud, Dad would have all the noise and company he needed.

There was a patch of bramble encroaching on the wall on the far side of the graveyard, and it had a few ripening fruit on it. It was clearly wild, and unless attended to it might eventually come over the wall and grow over some of the graves closest to it. It didn't matter to any of them, and in a strange way they all felt it would be as good a way as any to shelter and maybe provide some privacy sometime in the future.

All three of them bent down and began pulling the long grass away from the outside edge of the grave, which had a grey flat rectangular wall, about ten centimetres high, surrounding it. There wasn't much room 'to swing a cat', as Dad would have said, and his grave was hemmed in tightly on either side by two other graves.

"He wouldn't care about this, would he?" said Euan. "It would be unnecessary fuss as far as he was concerned."

"He was always too independent to be helped," agreed Conor.

"Well, he's getting it now whether he wants it or not," concluded Ronan.

"It's a bit of a mess, isn't it?" observed Euan. "Maybe not as bad as I expected though."

"It's pretty hard to keep it tidy though, when I live near London!" said Conor defensively.

Euan was startled and upset by Conor's reaction. He had not meant to be critical or for Conor to take it personally, and he rushed to set it right.

"No, I didn't mean it like that, mate," he said. "I can see the difficulties – of course I can. It looks as if whoever looks after the graveyard has given up with these ones along the wall. You can't even get a mower between or around them and the weeds would never sleep. You've done a great job, Conor. I wasn't being critical – honest."

"I know you weren't. I'm sorry I snapped at you. I get a bit angry sometimes when I see it. He was always saying how little he cared what happened to him when he was dead. But even if that was true, I care. We care. It's not just about his feelings. And I know what you're thinking, Ronan, that's it's only a monument, but . . . well, for me it's something more. But I don't know what."

Ronan cast a sympathetic eye in Conor's direction and decided to say nothing.

They continued busily pulling the grass back from the edge of the grave, nobody looking at the others and letting the silence do the mending.

They stood up when they had cleared enough to give them the view they wanted, and took in the simple detail. There was an iron cross, maybe twenty centimetres high, rusting brownly in front of the low plaster headstone, forty-five centimetres high, that Conor had come back a few years ago to erect. Conor said that it had originally had a circular porcelain plaque, which was part of the cross and gave it the shape of a Celtic cross. On the porcelain was Dad's name, dates and a phrase, and that was all. When Conor had come to repair things, he had found bits of the broken porcelain in the long grass at the side of the grave, and he had collected as much as he could find and had sent pieces of what remained to both of his brothers.

The top of the grave was covered in small white pebbles, and there must have been an attempt made, when the grave was first constructed, to put some sort of cloth down to prevent grass and weeds growing. But the persistence of weeds can burst through any good intentions and there were many small and medium weeds growing on the top and grass growing around the rectangular inside edge of the stones.

"Is that the wild fuchsia?" asked Euan, pointing at a gnarled, solid and twisted-looking stump in front of the cross, with a few brown and shrivelled leaves on it.

"Yep, that's it," he replied. "When I first came back here it was about a metre high and thriving, but it was obscuring the headstone. I cut it back to this three-branched stump, which doesn't seem to have grown at all. I tried to pull it up, but I was afraid that—"

"Yes, we know; you've mentioned that before," interrupted Euan, his anxious face giving him away.

Conor took the hint: "Anyway, I cut it right back and, looking at it, I suspect it's not so good now, but I still couldn't get it out of the ground at the time. As immovable and stubborn as Dad could be sometimes. Maybe tomorrow afternoon. Its roots are obviously still alive and it must go right down. There's quite a bit left above the surface, so we can all get a good grip on it."

Euan looked uncomfortable again, and Ronan just looked thoughtful.

They spent a little longer just looking, reading and rereading and taking in the area around them to commit it to memory. It would be all they would have for the future, and so, allowing for fading memory, they wanted a vivid colour print emblazoned in their minds.

"OK, guys," said Ronan, putting down his backpack and opening one of the zips.

He pulled out a small bottle of Tullamore Dew whiskey and three small shot glasses, and he gave Euan the glasses to hold while he unscrewed the bottle top.

"You clever bastard!" said Conor admiringly. "How and when did you manage this?"

Euan just had his mouth open, surprise written in every line.

"I talked to the guy behind the bar before you came downstairs. I told him what I wanted and why, and he was incredibly helpful. The whiskey was the challenge. The shot glasses weren't a problem – he had those for me in no time. He just wasn't sure that he was allowed to give me a full bottle of whiskey from the bar; I'm sure he wasn't, so he worked a way around it. He did give me a full bottle and asked me how much we would be drinking. I said two shots each, maximum, and so he asked if I would bring the bottle back and he would charge me for six drinks when I brought it back. He would then be honestly able to say, if asked, that we had had and been charged for six shots of whiskey.

"When a guy is so obliging like that, then you don't want to let him down, do you? So we'll do as we told him we would. He remembers you from previous times, Conor, and seems to like you. You seem to carry some weight with him."

"I'm carrying some weight because of him," laughed Conor. "He always kept me in fine fettle when I was here before."

"Might have good taste in whiskeys, but not in people," Ronan added.

"He needs me for business," said Conor, ignoring the barb. "I think I keep his bar running for the rest of the tourist season once I've been here."

Ronan broke in: "So let's have a toast to Danny, then."

Euan held two glasses while Ronan poured a shot in each of them and then a shot in Conor's glass.

"To Danny!" they toasted together, and tipped back their drinks in one.

Whether whiskey is good or bad, when a shot or two are swallowed it always cringes the face and spreads the mouth thin and wide, and after a great, hissing intake of breath, and an equally powerful expulsion of air, the taste settles on the palate. They looked at one another and burst out laughing at the unanimity of the response and the sweetness of the whiskey.

The first was quickly followed by the second. Ronan screwed the top back on the bottle, put it back in his bag and took his second glass from Euan. It was a strange and curious sight and would have simultaneously amused and taken the wind out of anybody who had come upon the scene.

"Oh, God!" said Conor. "Oh, dat warms the cockles of me heart!" He used an expression and an accent that they all recognized as Dad's Irish one. And then he coughed.

"Lovely drop, that one," agreed Euan.

Ronan never spoke. He just looked at them with his eyes watering – not from grief, but from the shock of the second shot. The first had been tough enough. He never normally drank as much as he had in the last few days, and he suspected that his brothers might be the same; but it was a chance and a time that might never come again, and they all seemed to agree that it was the best and right thing to do. He personally felt it was a good way to greet and, in a short time, to bid farewell to their dad while they were all together.

They read the simple words on his headstone again, one more time. They knew they would be back tomorrow, but reading the words over and over made them seem less lifeless and empty, and it brought them much closer together as a family to keep saying them to themselves like a mantra.

DANIEL FARRELL
1919–1986
LOVED ALWAYS
Euan, Ronan and Conor

"Right," said Conor, "that's about as much as we can do today, isn't it?"

"Are we going to have enough time to do everything we need to do here if we have a pretty full day of it in Galway tomorrow?" asked Euan.

"There really isn't a huge amount of work to be done," said Conor. "Pull out the dead fuchsia, put the rusted cross down near the bottom end of the grave, so it's out of the way of reading the headstone, lift off the weed mat and the stones and redo the top layer of soil. If we're short we can dig some extra soil from beside the wall – no one will notice. We can put the old mat back on minus the stones – no use wasting it – then put down the new mat on top and tuck down the edges with the pegs. Then we can put the stones back on and we're done. Trust me."

It was like a child reciting poetry off by heart: say it quickly and you won't forget any of it.

"Sounds like a lot to me," said Euan. "Especially getting that bloody fuchsia out." He looked at it with a crimped face. "And I do trust you," he added.

"We'll be fine," said Ronan soothingly.

"We only get one chance. Last day tomorrow; reasonably early flight the next day."

Euan wouldn't be so easily pacified, but he was confident that the three of them would make sure it was done properly.

"Yes, we have, so we're wasting time. We should go for a stroll around the village and retrace some of Dad's footsteps and get cosy with his having been here," said Ronan mischievously.

"You're a mystical bugger, aren't you? You sound like they really mean something to you – the traces. And yet you don't feel they're there, you said back at Mum's graveside. It's just a place, you said, and you almost implied it didn't mean that much."

As he spoke he started to move away, back down the path, past the church and out on to the footpath.

"That's not really what I said," argued Ronan, catching up with Conor and with Euan close behind. "I said that you can't isolate everything that's left, after a life well lived, to a small hole in the ground. It's too big for that. To do that would mean we would all have to come back regularly to stay in touch with our parents, and we can't do that and I don't believe we need to."

"So it's a convenient way of salving the guilt of not being able to come back by saying they are not here in these places?" asked Euan.

They were walking slowly, deep in thought, and trying to get their heads around things that were hard to grasp, with no certainties and no real answers other than the hopes of their own experiences and their own deepest wonderings.

"No, not at all. That's not what I said or meant either. It's getting us closer to what's left of them physically; but if that's all we have, then we have very little. I like to believe in something more permanent for us that will keep them alive, so to speak, forever." Ronan was trying to get his own jumbled thoughts into a coherent statement because it was a good time to air it and the mood seemed right. "I said at Mum's grave that she wasn't there. I didn't get a sense of her, but I did remember and imagine things about her as I stood there. And I agree that there is a point to burials, so there is a focal point to come back to at some time – somewhere to place our thoughts when we think of friends and family who have died. But as spiritual people – and I think that as religion dies, spirituality thrives – we really struggle with the fact that people we loved have died. And we have no idea what that means. Once they're dead, is that it? Is that the end? Can it really just finish like that? When your parents both die you have to believe in heaven; otherwise it's a tragic, comic and inspiring tale with a very sad ending, every time. What was the point? If love matters that much – and we all believe it does [he paused to get confirmation], then where does all that love go?"

"Oh, hell," interrupted Conor. "I'll have to go and borrow a spade if we go much deeper than this!"

"No, let him finish. I'm interested."

Ronan smiled gratefully at Euan and continued: "I'm sorry. I'll probably make a mess of this because I can't always see where I'm heading, and I don't know what to believe. The older I get the more I find myself thinking about these things, but in a peaceful and untroubled way. I bet you two do as well, don't you?" asked Ronan.

Euan was quick to admit that he was the same, though he made it clear that going too far into the maze was not a particular strongpoint of his.

"You're beyond sixty now, so if you're going to reach a conclusion you'd better hurry up before somebody beats you to the answers to all this," concluded Conor.

"I don't feel the need, just yet, to rush to conclusions," continued Ronan. "If my thinking goes astray and in the maze I strike a dead end, I relax, retrace my steps and work my way along a different path. I feel really comfortable doing that – in fact, I really enjoy it – and there's no panic and no sense of frustration. It's as if I have all the time in the world."

"You don't," Conor reminded him again. "And unless you rush to conclusions you'll be trying it yourself, and then we'll never know!"

Ronan smiled, but ignored him. "I sometimes get the feeling that someone is listening and has the good grace not to laugh at my pathetic attempts. At the same time I feel I'm never given any help, though I suspect all the help has been given – I just didn't recognize it when it was given and, if I did, maybe I didn't know how to use it. I know it's my overactive imagination. I think you probably feel exactly the same, but you'll approach it in a different way."

"I think that's fair comment. I'm sure I spend less time on this sort of thing than you do. Maybe it's just a case of there's nothing I can do to stop or change it, so why struggle with it?" said Euan.

"I agree with you on that last bit, Euan, but I still find it fascinating," said Ronan.

"So what were you saying about Mum, then?" prompted Conor, intrigued despite himself.

"I said that Mum was located in my head and in my heart, and that's exactly, for me, where she is at the times when I need to speak quietly to her; but my visions of her are based on lots of memories, some stories, some photos, some songs that remind me of her, and the places I've visited in the last two days. All of them add to the thin tapestry that makes up the life of Mum, for me. Some of it is real – the grave, the town, the country – and some of it my imagination invents to close in the empty spaces."

"Do you ever find yourself having conversations with Mum or Dad just when you're going about your ordinary business, or remembering birthdays or anniversaries or at Christmas time?"

"Yes, I do," admitted Euan immediately.

"Conor?" Ronan addressed Conor directly, putting him on the spot where no joke or glib comment could easily rescue him.

"Yes, I do sometimes," admitted Conor, "though I've never thought about what it might mean. It's just an instinctive internal dialogue or two, expressing the things I would be saying or talking to them about if they were still around. I can't build a theology around that."

They had arrived at the church gate and walked through and sat on the bench seat just along from the sign. They sat down with Ronan in the middle.

"I know you can't, and neither can I, but they are still 'present' for us, aren't they?"

He looked at them both and thought he saw them nod.

"We never take them as blank spaces in our lives that we can't reach, do we? Sometimes when I talk to them I get the feeling they are there with me in the room, but then I think that's just what I would like it to be like. We have songs, conversations, memories, dreams, looks, sayings, habits and values that were theirs and which now echo down through us and, probably, through our kids. And the thing we learnt most from them was the security and love of family and, hopefully, how to be good parents. They're now in our genes and they're our constant companions and mentors. It would be nice to have them still physically with us, but they haven't really left, have they?"

"So is that continuity of values and genes the immortality we talk about? Is that the collective soul?" asked Euan.

"I don't know, Euan. I just don't know. I think it might be a small part of it. I don't know about 'collective' though. As kids in Catholic primary school we were taught that the soul never dies. It seemed to be something inside, separate, like another heart or some separate vital organ, but existing independently and invisible. And it was your own. Funnily enough, we never took it as a religion of love in the early days; we were told to love God, or else we were in trouble."

"I remember that too!" said Euan with some anger.

"Well, same thing. Get offside with any of those 'charitable' staff and there was grief and punishment. Love our neighbours came in there somewhere too, much later on, but we mostly learned about love from our parents. Now I sometimes think that love is in every atom of our being and it can't be destroyed or die. I don't know what each atom of us knows or thinks or is or does, or even if they know of each other's existence, but . . ."

"So many unanswered questions!" said Euan. "Where does it all begin and where does it all end? Why do we make such strong ties with each other if in the end we lose those we care most about and it ends in such sadness? We are created and become part of the creative process, and then we wait for the inevitable end with fear and dread as all Creation dies."

"I don't fear it, Euan. I just expect it. It's the way the seasons turn," put in Conor.

"I agree, Conor. Sometimes I feel closer to answers, and then at other times further away," said Ronan, "and I find I know less now than I used to, but only because then I was made to believe with certainty and feared what I didn't understand. Conor's right. You can't withhold love just because you fear or know you will lose that person. That's being less than human, and, as I said before, do we really 'lose' them?"

Ronan leaned forward, hands clasped on his knees and looking into the distance.

"So where have you arrived at with all this thinking?" asked Conor. "I thought I knew everything, and now I've lost my thread."

"Look – I'll tell you something and you'll think it's really stupid," said Ronan.

"No different from all your other stories, then?" muttered Conor mischievously, and Euan gave him a disapproving look.

Ronan carried on regardless: "I was out jogging one day and I'd been thinking about Mum and Dad and about how Declan had died. It wasn't long after I'd sent you the copies of Declan's death certificate, which I'd got from England. Do you remember?"

They both nodded.

"I stopped to stretch my Achilles because they often cause me grief, and so I leaned against an oak tree and did my usual routine to make sure it didn't stiffen up. My *Achilles*, Conor! And I thought do we ever get any signs that there is someone out there or is everything coincidental or the result of chance? It was autumn and I could hear acorns dropping around me on to the leaves on the ground in a large circle under the tree. So I said to myself, or whoever might have been listening, 'If there is someone, something out there, just let an acorn hit me on the head before I leave and continue my run, and then I might believe.' I think I spent longer than I would normally have done leaning against that tree, but nothing happened. So I pushed myself upright from the tree and was half turned to run when an acorn came down right in front of my nose. If I had stayed where I was, it would have hit me smack on the top of my head."

"And the meaning of all that was . . . ?" asked Conor, his expression a mix of confusion.

Euan spread his hands in a gesture that asked the same question.

"More questions, more doubts and some understandings."

"That's helpful," said Euan.

"Incredibly so," agreed Conor.

"I thought what a ridiculous idea it was in the first place. It was autumn. The chance of being hit on the head by an acorn under an oak tree was quite high given that there were hundreds of them – maybe thousands – up in the tree, ripe for falling. I also thought, 'Why would anyone or anything give away its presence when we have free will, or not, to believe in whatever we wish? It's not free will then, is it, if someone asks you to believe something and gives you the proof of its truth before you can exercise that freedom of belief? And finally I thought, 'If mankind loses freedom of choice and belief then it changes the whole world. People's behaviour would be totally different the moment they knew there was something after death. I suspect the world might be a better and a safer place."

"And what's wrong with that? We'd all be better off."

"Not true, Euan," replied Ronan. "It wouldn't be real. It has now changed from choice to coercion, and that's not how you know real love."

"OK," admitted Euan, "I get that."

"Bloody hell! Does even a jog turn into a theological discourse with you? Can't you just run and get on with it? Where does it all take you, anyway?"

"No destination, Conor. I haven't arrived anywhere. I don't think you ever arrive until whatever, if anything, comes next –

and not even then. I think revelation is eternal for all of us, or I like to think it is, and so we will constantly search, through love, for the heart of the mystery, and never find how deep it goes, even after life."

"That was the most satisfying and unsatisfying explanation of a mystery I have ever heard. Like candyfloss: I thought I had it and then it was gone," sighed Conor.

"I just get on with things and work through them as I go," said Euan.

"Euan, you're such a wise person. I think that's a great way to do it, but we'll all be doing it in the context of everything Mum and Dad meant to us, what they taught us, the love they gifted to us as a family and the love we've taken from them and tried to pass on. You can't help yourself with love. It just spills out from your soul like God molecules." And he laughed.

"So is there any point to a graveyard at all, then?" asked Euan.

"Yes," replied Ronan, "because some people like to visit friends and relatives' graves as frequently as they can if they live close enough. It's a way of honouring the memory of those people. I have to add to that a hope that there is more after this – whatever form that takes. I have to believe; otherwise I see no point to the ebb and flow of humanity."

The conversation moved on hesitantly, covering God and eternity and what they thought they were; about what happened after you died, and how could you ever be sure even if you were told what would happen to you after life, or even that there was an afterlife. Would certainty of the future change anything? Can we ever know for sure what is point of it all? What if there is a God and He loses patience with our bad behaviour? Does the Supreme Being even listen or care? Are we the equivalent of a rat colony, just killing and maiming and bickering and fighting and no one does anything to stop it? Are we simply abandoned in space? They discussed fate and chance, destiny and preordained existence; and finally they considered the question of whether it matters if, at the end, all that is left to us is oblivion. Who would know? The harder they looked for answers the less they felt they knew.

It was a strange and mixed conversation to have on a bench outside the church in the graveyard where their dad was buried, and yet, while Ronan seemed to come from a mystic's point of view, Euan from a humanist point of view and Conor from a very Catholic point of view, none of them could say for certain what he believed. The one thing they had in common, where they found some agreement, was their belief in the indestructible power of love and its continuation through family.

"I suppose you love as much and as many as you can," concluded Euan.

"I find that bloody difficult with some of the twats I've met!" interrupted Conor.

It was perfect timing. They were ready to break it up, and they all laughed with the release of it all and agreed that some people might be just too hard to like, let alone love.

Inwardly they all marvelled at the different paths their beliefs had taken them, though they had started from the same place and been nurtured by the same environments. They understood too that the older they got the more these questions demanded to be addressed and the closer they came to agreement.

They rose from the seat, still laughing quietly to themselves, and headed along Main Street again to look at some of the businesses and shops that made up the township of Oranmore.

Chapter 34

"I can see why Dad liked it here in Galway," said Euan. "It's a lovely part of the country. I'm really taken with it. I wish we had more time to explore further afield."

"Couldn't agree more. But it will have to be another time," said Ronan sadly.

He wasn't sure that it would ever happen again.

"I've only ever come here to sort out Dad's grave, and I've never taken much notice until this trip. I love the area. I'd love to spend more time here too, but exploring the life that's here for a change. I didn't even notice – and I bet you haven't either – that inside the church is a Visitor Information Centre." Conor was uncharacteristically solemn.

"Well, let's take a look, then," suggested Euan.

He headed off through the door and came out moments later with lots of information, which he passed around.

"Right! Well, let's get on with life, then!"

Ronan strode out briskly, his hands full of brochures with information about sights to see and things to do along this wonderful rugged coastline and adjacent areas of Galway and Connacht."

"It's Billy Whizz again. Let's catch up!" shouted Conor.

They settled into an easy lope and took deep breaths of the ocean breeze as they strode along.

"We won't get to see all those places!" shouted Euan.

"I don't care!" Ronan yelled. "I'll be back!" he shouted to the sky, and he continued his brisk walk along Main Street, heading through the town.

It was not as they had expected, and it took a long time to look around the town because it was bigger than they had first imagined. The longer they spent wandering the streets of Oranmore, the more they became attracted to it. It had a good variety of shops.

"Listen!" said Conor. "I'll read to you from this brochure." And he started off as if reciting 'The Court of King Caractacus' or like an auctioneer listing the attractions of the next item up for bids. "There's a pharmacy; a garage and car dealers; boutiques with shoes, bags, clothing and other fashions; a bookshop and newsagent with CDs, DVDs (we'll have to drag Ronan away from there!), cards and toys; a butcher's shop; Tesco's; a hardware store and DIY; a communications and computing centre; a large factory-type building housing blinds, flooring and furniture; hair and beauty and massage salons (we'll have to drag Euan away from there!); a florist; and (a promising sign of young families moving into the area, according to ME) a shop selling prams, pushchairs and baby accessories; a jeweller's selling emeralds; a garden centre which even has shamrocks; a place that provides lessons in Gaelic to give you the gift of the blarney; and a Bank of Ireland." Conor dragged the last word out for as long as he could and finished with a loud flourish. "What am I bid for Oranmore? And if you can afford that, forget about Killarney; Galway is for sale!"

Euan was impressed, and after applauding he said, "It seems to have everything anyone would need."

As they were listed and they counted them off, they realized there was everything here that the locals and visitors would want. No wonder their dad had liked it and had landed here after the heartbreaking loss of his wife.

"Did you notice that some of the streets have no names – no signs?" asked Euan.

"Maybe the place is growing so fast they haven't had time to think of any street names, or put any signs up," said Ronan.

"But this looks like the original part of the town," argued Euan.

"Maybe the signs are all at one end of the street only," suggested Conor helpfully into a growing silence of his own creation.

The other two looked, shook their heads and said nothing.

As they continued their casual ramble, randomly along the streets, they noticed between them a number of attractive-looking hotels, restaurants and some takeaways. And there were even a couple of neat-looking primary schools (they seemed to be called National Schools – like the one Mum went to) and a sign indicating a secondary school, and a special extra-tuition-type school that offered tuition outside of school hours as well. All three of them thought that this was a very enterprising venture and spoke well of the respect in the area for quality education. There also seemed to be a huge amount of building going on, both commercial and domestic. It certainly seemed an optimistic place.

Everywhere they looked, there were brightly coloured frontages – orange, plum, purple and green, all adding vibrancy to the mix.

They knew from road signs and some of the brochures that Ronan had collected from the Visitor Information Centre that there was a golf club, three shopping centres, a cinema and a bowling alley. The more they looked the more they realized they couldn't see, because they didn't have the time. They agreed there and then that this and Galway were places they had to come back to and explore with their wives and spend a lot more time looking around to see all the sights which they had only gently overlooked with their eyes.

The shop they lingered near longest was a vegetable and old-style grocery store, and they wondered if it was where their dad had worked many years ago. No one would likely remember now, so they let it go. But once again the memories were torched by imagination.

"And only seven or so minutes from the centre of Galway town," said Euan. "That's magic!"

"It took you five minutes to get out of the town!" said Ronan.

Conor insisted that they stop at the DIY/hardware/garden centre, and, while there, he bought a three-metre-by-two-metre strip of black plastic weed preventer with needle-sized perforations to replace the piece on Dad's grave, which was letting the weeds through. He also bought twenty inverted U-shaped pegs, almost a foot long, that he said would be used to keep the weed protector in place around the sides and stop the weeds breaking through on the inside concrete edge of the grave. Finally he bought some weedkiller in a plastic spray container. He wouldn't take any money from his brothers, and his look was enough to persuade them to let him pay.

"Are we, you, going to carry all that around all evening?" asked Euan.

"Yep!" answered Conor, unperturbed.

It was now approaching 7 p.m. and there was no chance of them visiting Renville Park, ten minutes' drive from Oranmore, or the fifteenth-century castle of Oranmore, which they couldn't miss anyway in the greying light. It was as if they were only allowed glimpses of some parts of the 'promised land' and were destined, at least this time, not to reach all parts. They accepted it and somehow knew they would be back in spite of some of their earlier resolutions.

"Told you," said Euan.

"I knew," said Ronan.

"Pistols at ten paces?" asked Conor.

Silence.

"OK, let's go and get some food instead."

They found a nicely appointed Italian restaurant and were able to sit down once Conor had persuaded the waiter to allow them to put the roll of plastic and the plastic shopping bag containing the pegs along by the wall, just behind their table; just a small amount of furniture shifting, and it was as tidy as light.

Fortunately the restaurant was not that full yet, so the inconvenience and fuss seemed just bearable to the waiter. It was a lovely atmosphere inside, and spicy, enticing smells wafted in from the kitchen. The wall lighting was subdued; the walls were pale, relaxing, pastel cream, punctuated occasionally by colourful paintings.

They had only to sit for ten minutes in this seductively warm and darkened room before they realized how tired they were. Two bottles of wine, one red and one white, didn't help

– or they did help, depending on which way they looked at the evening?

Conor ordered the grilled fillet of chicken with a selection of vegetables and rich, luscious sauce; Euan had the beef sirloin steak, also lavishly sauced, and Ronan decided on a seafood chowder with ciabatta.

"I can't eat big meals when I'm beginning to feel tired," he explained, responding to the enquiring looks he got from his brothers.

"You're tired?" asked Euan, not really believing it. "In that case I'm rooted," he concluded.

"I don't believe him," said Conor to Euan. "He probably wants to go for a run in the morning."

"I didn't rule that out. I just said I was a bit tired now. I'll be fine until after the sunset on the bay."

"Oh, I forgot about that. Right – well, we might as well take our time, then, and enjoy the food," said Euan.

The meals arrived simultaneously, and Ronan realized that his plan had backfired as a huge bowl of seafood chowder, thick and creamy, and enough ciabatta for all of them arrived on his place mat. They all had very large portions, so they didn't really have a reason to make fun of the size of Ronan's meal; they were too busy eating their meals in their imaginations to see if they could finish them.

Everybody tried a little of everybody else's meal and found something scrumptious in all of them though they were all happy with what they'd ordered. The wine went down well, so they ordered a third bottle. That was the conversational one as opposed to the thirsty others, so they relaxed and talked easily as the restaurant started to fill up. The skies outside darkened and pale strands of dying sun glowed mutely through the gently piled clouds.

The waiter too had relaxed with them once he realized, with growing contentment, that they were enjoying the food they had ordered. The restaurant staff were clearly proud of their food and their preparation skills and warmed to guests who appreciated their efforts.

It just turned out to be a very relaxing evening, and the conversation was easy.

"Do you remember that time when we lived in Lilac Crescent and Mum and Dad had some visitors one Sunday afternoon? They were older people and they'd visited before and it was quite boring for us as we were never part of the conversation."

Already the other two were nodding and smiling, remembering the event and knowing what was coming.

Euan carried on: "Mum told us to go upstairs and occupy ourselves. I seem to remember it was a miserable wet day, and we soon got bored, so we sat on the landing three-quarters of the way up the stairs. D'ya remember there was a straight flight of stairs, a small landing and then three more steps off to the right that got you to the top corridor? Well, we sat on that small landing and," – Euan was already struggling to keep his face straight – "and we starting blowing on the backs of our hands and making farting noises as loud as we could. We kept cracking up every time someone did one, and our stupid giggling was probably as loud as the noises we were making. I think I must have been about eleven years old; you would have been ten, Ronan, and you seven, Conor, so I doubt if you could make any noises."

"Of course not," said Conor. "I was much more mature than that!"

"Well, you've made up for it since," said Ronan.

"Both Mum and Dad kept coming to the lounge door, and as they opened it we would bolt up the last three stairs and tumble and push each other out of the way so as not to be the one seen – as if it made any difference with the noise we made to escape!" continued Euan. "We knew we would get a belting, but it was such a boring afternoon and the weather was so bad that we must have decided it was worth it. Anyway, as soon as the guests were gone we got called downstairs and got a right walloping."

"I seem to remember you got away with it, Conor. I got a little bit and Euan got the worst as he was the oldest and didn't have the sense to take care of us and set an example for our behaviour," remembered Ronan, finishing the story.

They all had a good chuckle at the naivety of the mischief and the inevitability of the reckoning.

"Yeah, you weren't much of a role model to your two younger brothers, Euan," started Conor. "You also started a fire one summer in a dry field behind a new lot of houses with big wooden fences. We had enough money between us to buy three sausages at the Stockton Heath butcher's shop and we had sneaked a box of matches from home to light a small campfire and cook the sausages on a stick each – 'like Kit Carson used to do', you said."

"Kit Carson, my arse!" interrupted Ronan. "It took us ages to get the small amount of wood we had collected alight; we nearly ran out of matches. We were all puffing and blowing and getting smoke in our eyes and our throats, wiping our eyes with black streaks from the dirt on our hands and faces and coughing all the time. Eventually it caught alight and we had a reasonable heat there and the sausages were soon sizzling."

"That's right," said Euan, smiling broadly at the memory, "but our sticks caught on fire and the sausages dropped in the flames and we had to rake them out with a fresh stick through the ashes at the edge of the fire. All the ash stuck to the leaking sausage fat and we had nothing to clean them with and we kept burning our fingers, so in the end we gave up and pushed them back into the hottest part of the fire to cook."

"Conor saw what had happened to us so he kept his stick and sausage well away from the fire and it hardly warmed up. So there we were," continued Ronan, "the three intrepid frontiersmen, two eating scalding-hot ash-covered sausages with skin shrivelled and black, holding them with our fingers wrapped in our T-shirts, burning our mouths and constantly spitting out charcoal and ash and bits of dry grass – and one of us eating a pink raw sausage which must have been gross!"

"It was!" agreed Conor.

"When we came to leave, we weren't sure how to put the fire out, so you, Euan," said Ronan, "came out with the classic words before a stuff-up! Can you remember what you said – and did?"

Euan was giggling hard by this stage. "Yes, I remember. How could I forget? Something like 'I've seen the Indians in the movies; I know what to do.' I gave the fire a couple of swift kicks. Surprisingly," he said with mock incomprehension, "burning brands went everywhere in the dry grass and we soon had more than enough heat and flame to cook sausages."

"Yeah, we had truly cooked our collective goose," laughed Conor.

"I realized later that the Indians used to kick dirt over the fire – not the fire over the dirt, or in this case a dry field."

"We ended up taking our T-shirts off to fight the flames, and some of the residents were using garden hoses over their fences. Some came around the front and helped us to get it out with spades and wet towels." Ronan too was laughing, remembering their fear and the frantic bashing of pockets of flame with their T-shirts.

As Euan and Ronan battled the blaze they had kept talking to each other about being sent to borstal or prison, and the fear of the consequences was hotter than the fire.

They ordered coffees to give themselves time to relax and ease their aching ribs, and the waiter smiled knowingly at them having picked up snatches of their conversation as he moved between the tables.

"You were very clever though, Euan," admitted Conor. "You made up some story about a group of other kids who were smoking and whom we had supposedly been watching. You told these people that that was what started it, and you said these guys had run off when the flames began and we had stayed to help. I can't think how you got away with that, but you did. It was actually a piece of land that would eventually have more houses on it; and I suspect that some of the residents were glad it had been tidied up, so they were prepared to believe anything."

"And it was the same later with Mum. Same story, and we were almost heroes. The T-shirts didn't matter. We were never allowed to wear good clothes when we went out to play anyway, so Mum just dumped them. Yours was OK, Conor, because Euan had made you stay out of the way as soon as the fire really got under way."

"That was very caring of you, Euan."

"That was me all over," replied Euan.

There were many more stories that came back to them, and they delighted in the retelling and the exaggerations and the embellishments of time and forgetfulness.

They drank their coffees when the waiter brought them in, then settled the bill between them and complimented the restaurant on the food and the service. When they left, carrying their DIY goods, they were waved off with a smile and a request to come back soon. It seemed sincere, and all three realized that they weren't sure when they would be back, keen though they were to see more of everything around.

Chapter 35

They walked slowly back to the Lodge and already the sky over the bay was beginning to turn light pinks and light and blacker greys and look comfortably sullen. Conor went to the car, opened the boot and dropped the things in. Then he closed it up and headed in with the others through the large front doors. They noticed, as they headed up the stairs to their room, that the Lodge bar was open and several people were there, comfortable and chatty.

They got to their room and just idled around for a while: Conor washed his hands; Euan sat in a chair, grabbed one of the brochures they had acquired and skimmed through it; Ronan took his shoes off, leaned back in his chair and looked across the bay. As he finishing drying his hands, Conor came out of the bathroom, walked to the light switches and turned the lights off in the room.

"Thanks!" Euan said. "Quite hard to read in the dark."

"Sorry, Euan. I should have looked. Can I just have a look at the sunset for a minute?"

"Sure."

They could all see through the balcony window how beautiful it was, though it was not quite at its best yet. They stood up, moved closer to the balcony window and looked out.

"Let's go and have a drink at the bar, just for fifteen minutes, and come back. I think it will be fully ripened by then. Yes? No?" Ronan seemed to be getting a second wind.

"OK," Euan and Conor agreed almost in unison.

Euan jumped up, abandoning his brochure, and Conor turned the lights back on and headed out through the door.

"Hey, wait for me!" shouted Ronan, scrambling for his shoes and putting them on as he hopped across the room to get to the door.

A voice came down the corridor: "I have the swipe key, so just let the door lock behind you! God, Conor, what a coup! We've beaten old Billy Whizz to a destination for the first time."

They walked at high speed to the stairs and rattled down them, harmoniously in step like Spanish dancers.

Euan bought three whiskeys and they sat at a table waiting for Ronan.

"A few guests," said Conor, indicating with his head the small number of couples and one foursome drinking in the bar as well.

"No, just casuals dropping in," said Euan. "I asked the bartender. They often have people in here who just want a quiet drink."

Ronan came rushing down the stairs to join them, smiling at their small victory, and they enjoyed the drink and just listening to the conversations around them. Conor had brought his backpack with him and carefully letting himself in, just inside the bar, he gave the bartender the bottle of whiskey back and paid for the drinks they had had out of it, and everyone seemed happy.

Euan and Conor realized now why Ronan had suggested they have a drink at the bar. Knowing what was going on (it was all done below the bar level), they left it to happen quietly, not wanting to draw people's attention to what Ronan was doing and maybe get the bartender into trouble. Ronan joined them sitting in the lounge without a word. They drank quietly, knowing good stories need to brew like a good pot of tea, and, in the agreed fifteen to twenty minutes, they were back in their room, lights off, having got their seats organized before sitting and looking out through the window at a mythical sky.

Chapter 36

While it wasn't exactly a Galway Bay sunset, they were charmed and enthralled by the constant changes to the sky and the sea and the land as they watched the setting sun, in the role of classical painter, magically colouring a beautiful seascape with deft and amazing touches,

"There has to be a God," whispered Euan into the silence.

They had no idea how long they watched for, but the scene changed before them: steel-coloured waves in a silver sea, edged on both sides by the pincered shores of Oranmore Bay; shining rocks off the coast like sculpted black whales of all sizes; a sky of dark clouds, brown and differing shades of grey as well as black streaks; pink and orange-pink flashes mixed in parts with mauve scatterings. All of it went gentiy, intentionally and colourfully down, trickling over the edge of the horizon, following the sun, silently and gracefully collecting the paints together.

"Fantastic?" said Conor, breaking the mood and the silence.

"It's partly the song 'Galway Bay' that makes it that way though," said Ronan. "It was absolutely magical. but I've seen sunsets like that in many parts of New Zealand."

"I didn't want to say it first, but I agree with you, Ronan. I've seen some beautiful sunsets in various parts of Canada too."

"No argument from me," agreed Conor. "I'm the same."

"I told you it's the songs we sing and the songs we remember that drag out all the memories – the long, long soundtrack to our experiences. I must have heard that song twenty times in the house and a hundred times since, and it always has happy memories for me. And so did that," said Ronan, indicating the darkening sky.

"I wonder if Mum or Dad ever saw a sunset in Galway Bay. Dad might have," mused Euan.

"OK, bed for me," said Conor. "I won't be long."

And he went into the bathroom.

Once they had all finished they were in bed. With their eyes used to the dark, they settled into their respective beds to 'sleep the sleep of the just', said Euan.

Chapter 37

It was a spooky night for Euan particularly, and his nervousness showed.

'What a daft time to be out!' he thought. 'Whose idea was it, anyway?' He couldn't even remember what they were supposed to be doing.

The other two, looking pale and wide-eyed, stood looking at the grave under the dark evening sky, covering with cloud a hidden moon.

Euan couldn't for the life of him remember whose idea it was to come out to the grave at this time of night to make a start on the work. He knew he had expressed some concern during the evening about how little time they had left to complete things, but he had felt reassured by his brothers' confidence.

"What time is it?" Euan asked.

He had forgotten his watch somehow in the frantic rush to get ready and drive to the church. Where was the car?

"You've just been walking around the bedroom waking us up and telling us to get out of bed and get ready to make a start – not enough time to finish the job tomorrow, and so on. You said we're not going home the day after tomorrow with it all dug up and unfinished. You just rambled on and on, and you were very insistent."

"I must have been sleepwalking, you daft buggers, and you took me at my word!"

"It was quite entertaining," said Conor.

"Agreed," said Ronan.

"It didn't seem like sleepwalking to me," said Conor. "We argued with you and you continued to push the whole thing about running out of time. There was no changing your mind."

"That's the way it happened, Euan. It was your idea and now you're back to standing on your dignity as the older brother. You wouldn't give us time to think," confirmed Ronan.

"OK, OK, I'm sorry. I must have got really worried about it and it was preying on my mind. So what do we do? What can we do that will save us time later?"

"Not much," admitted Conor. "I'm also having a secret affair with the groundsman and I was going to borrow some tools from him before we headed off to Galway later this morning – spades and that sort of thing – but he doesn't work at this time of the morning."

"I'm sorry, guys. I really don't know what I was thinking. Bloody idiot!" Euan was annoyed with himself for not accepting the confident attitude that the other two expressed yesterday when they said they were sure that everything would be finished 'tomorrow'.

Just then an owl hooted and Euan shivered.

"No big deal," said Ronan.

"Well," said Conor, "we have no tools in the boot of the car. We're not ready for that part yet. We could lift the weed protector and the stones off and put them to the side here. But I think it would be best if we pulled the fuchsia out first – otherwise it will rip the weed cover. It's in reasonable condition at the moment – there's no point in wrecking it. What do you reckon?"

"Yep," said Ronan, "I agree. That seems to be the job that's held things up all the way along, so let's just do it as soon as possible! Happy with that, Euan?"

"No, not really, but I'll go along with what you say. It will make up for my stuff-up."

"Look – just forget it," said Conor. "If we get these few jobs done it will give us a good head start, so you were right. We all need to pull in the same direction. Ronan, you get closest to the base; Euan, you in the middle on the top part of the stump;

and I'll grab the two top branches on the other side of you. They're thick enough to get a good grip on."

"Oooh," teased Conor. "A bit twitchy, are we?"

"C'mon, Conor – I'm getting a sore back. Let's move it!" said Ronan.

"I'm not keen on this, guys! We could wreck the whole thing, and then we'll have a major job on our hands. Wad'ya think?" asked Euan.

"You have the nerve to suggest that after getting us out of bed! We've come out here in the middle of the night and now you want to go back to the lodge having done nothing. You've got to be freaking joking!" said Ronan.

"He's right," agreed Conor. "Come on! Get a grip!"

They all moved into the places that enabled them to get a handhold or two on the stump.

"OK – ready? One, two, three, pull! Pull! For God's sake put your backs into it! Pull!" he yelled, and together they all leaned back and heaved as hard as they could.

Maybe they were all pulling in opposite directions, or they were pulling horizontally rather than at an angle, but, whatever the reason, it wouldn't come out completely. However, they were pleased to see that the dirt around the bottom of the bush had humped and loosened and there was more movement in the stump, though it was very slight.

The three of them stood up, puffing with the exertion and wondering what it would take to get the fuchsia off the grave.

"OK," said Conor, "I hate to waste a good night's sleep. Let's try again. Euan, can you just move more to the middle of us two – sort of between us and lower down? We'll be slightly off to the sides."

"Yeah, sure."

"OK, on the count—"

Euan was impatient and uncomfortable: "Just get on with it!"

"Heave!"

They all tugged as hard as they could.

"It's coming out," gasped Euan. "It's starting to break the

soil. Pull harder and keep hold! C'mon! Pull!"

Slowly but surely they could feel it letting go of the ground, because their hands were coming closer to them and they were standing stock-solid.

"C'mon now! Big effort!" urged Ronan.

"Pull!" yelled Conor.

As he spoke, one of the branches that he was holding bent sharply but didn't break, and he fell against Euan and grabbed the back of his jacket. Euan was overbalanced, but hung on tight, bumping against Ronan, who also felt himself falling backwards; but he hung on too, determined to win the tussle. Euan was starting to crash over backwards and the other two were beginning to fall partly underneath him. But, because they all hung on for dear life, the stump came out of the ground with a final 'sluck' of release, which threw them all off balance and on to their backs. Euan, the last to let go, threw his arms up and back as the fuchsia came up, and he let it go as it sailed over his head.

It was such a sight, even in the dark, and each knew the other was quietly laughing at Euan's predicament.

They restrained him then shook him, and he came fully awake with a start.

"What the—!" he started. "Oh, shit! Shit! That was awful. That bloody fuchsia! I was sure we were there. Am I awake? Which is the dream? Am I out of there or not?"

"We're here! We're here!" said Ronan, shaking Euan to be sure he was fully awake. "What was it? What were you dreaming about?"

Euan wanted to have it out and off his mind: "We all got up to go to the grave. My fault. I mean I was sleepwalking and you didn't believe me. I mean you didn't know. Oh, God, that was scary! Please tell me I'm awake!"

Euan was still shaking slightly and in the pale light he ran his hands across his face and shook his head to clear it. He sat there, occasionally shaking his head. Distracted. Unnerved.

"C'mon, mate – you just had a bad dream, that's all." Conor

was trying to settle him down and bring him back to now. Conor looked at his watch: "Quarter to two in the morning."

"Good!" Euan sighed with relief. "It was a dream, then."

The other two just looked at each other, shook their heads and shrugged with no idea what he meant.

"You haven't told us what it was about yet," said Ronan.

"Did we go to the graveyard in your head?" asked Conor. "We went to pull up the fuchsia in the middle of the night and Dad came up with it? Was that it?"

Euan shivered involuntarily and nodded.

"Ya daft bugger!" said Conor. "This must be like what you did that time as a kid, wanting to go to school in the middle of the night. I bet you've done it since too and you're not letting on, eh?"

"'Ya feckin' eejit!' as Dad would say. Just a bad dream!" Ronan gave him a gentle push as he said it.

"Didn't seem like it at the time." Euan was beginning to feel sheepish and was half-heartedly defending himself. "Not at all." And he shook his head.

Ronan started laughing first, and then Conor, and finally, after looking up and around at the other two and with a relieved look on his face, Euan started to shake; then muffled, contained giggles followed before he burst like a sea explosion into laughter that rocked them all. And as the other two got a picture of what Euan had seen, and Euan relived safely what he had dreamed, they laughed loud and long, each one feeding off the others until they were too tired to laugh any more.

"Every time we mentioned the fuchsia you got that nervous look about you. I wondered what was going on," laughed Conor. "You dreamed what you had imagined every time we talked about it. You obviously built it up in your imagination as a scary thing to do, and so it's come out now. You scared us all witless there for a while."

"Yeah, well, so much for the early start tomorrow," said Euan. "That's not likely now, is it, with the back of the night broken in two like this?"

Conor wanted to get back to bed, so he was in a generous

mood: "It doesn't matter. We agreed we wouldn't get a chance to do much in Galway other than look anyway. While half a visit is better than none, it's not as good as a long visit; so we'll see what we can do. That's the best we can do."

Ronan sprang into action: "Right! Do you want some help to put your bed back together?"

While Euan collected the pillows, Ronan and Conor tidied up the bundled-up bedclothes into some reasonable order.

"Are you both ready?" asked Conor.

They were very soon back in bed, and he turned the lights out and made his way carefully to his bed.

Conor spoke into the darkness: "You'll have to give us the full story one day, you know."

"Mmm" was the only reply he got.

"Go to sleep. It's late, or early – whichever way you look at it. There's still lots to do tomorrow though," said Ronan.

"Like what?" asked Euan.

"Like replanting that fuchsia on someone else's plot," replied Conor.

There were sounds of muffled giggles smothered in blankets.

"Fuck off, ya eejits!"

And, as the darkness closed in, they fell backwards into sleep.

Chapter 38

Conor was the first one to stir. As usual with a broken night's sleep, he felt foggy-headed and more tired than he wanted. They had done a lot in the few days that they had had together so far, and it wasn't over yet. He wished now they had planned for a few more days together.

It amused him as he thought of the number of nights they used to have disturbed when their two girls were babies, two years and three months different in age, and he and Tessa would take it in shifts to see to them during the night. When they had colds was the worst. And yet he was always able to bounce off to work and do his job as principal at his school in Highgate. Or was he just looking back forgetfully? Had time smoothed out the bumps in the difficult times of sleepless nights?

Now his kids were much older and they were sparky girls who gave as good as they got from him or Tessa; it was often more than a fair match. He loved the time with his kids and the laughter and jibes that were so much of their conversation. Tessa often chided him for having passed on his 'wicked wit' to his family.

His head soon cleared and he knew his energy would return. He looked at his watch and was surprised to see that it was 9.40 a.m. – much later than any of them intended to sleep. He raised his head slightly and twisted to look at both of his brothers, still asleep. Ronan was snoring softly; Euan was quiet as a headstone. He decided to let them sleep. While they had had some very amusing times and had enjoyed each other's company, there was no doubt that they were of an age that recovered less quickly from exertion, and the emotional toll was a stealthy drain on their energy.

'Let them sleep,' he thought. 'They can have until 10 a.m., and then I'll make a cup of tea. What a few days!' he thought to himself. 'I was planning on a quiet life now, but I met up with these two nutters, whom I have to confess to being related to. I expected we would gently travel this lovely country, admiring the countryside and breathing the afterlife of Mum and Dad. Instead, it has become one big rocket launch, the stages breaking away one after another in quick succession until my head feels weightless this morning, and my brain is having an out-of-body experience. How did I get into this?' he asked himself, lost in his thoughts about how well they had got on together, the fun they had had, the thoughts of the past and the hopes for the future they shared. Why did we leave it so long? Thirty years! I swear I'll never let this happen again.'

'That's because you'd be over ninety, and you won't make that,' sneered a tiny self-mocking voice in his brain, somewhere out there in space.

'Smart bastard! We do need to get our wives together and visit each other's countries and meet each other's families somehow. He was missing Tessa badly and really looking forward to catching up with her and the kids in just under a week.' He stared at the ceiling, hands under his head and lost in his thoughts.

"What are you thinking about?" asked Ronan, quietly enough not to wake their sleeping brother. "Last night?"

"No, not at all," answered Conor. "I was thinking about us and what a good time we've had, and what good company you both are – well, reasonable, anyway. I was thinking we should have met up again years ago. But I'm over it. You can't change the past, but you can plan the future."

"So what's the plan?" asked Ronan.

"I don't have one. I've never really had one involving family, other than my wife and kids. I think it's a good time for us all to widen the circle now that our kids are all grown-up and moving out; and we need to involve our wives too. I don't know – just spend time together doing things like this, only slower and less crazy. We're too old for this, aren't we?"

"I'm not so sure. I could take a bucketload of this."

Conor looked across to see if Ronan meant it. Looking at the glint in his eyes and the turned-down lines of his mouth, he guessed he did.

"I don't think it would be any different if we met up, even with our wives as well." Euan had woken up without them noticing and he joined seamlessly into the conversation, suggesting he might have been awake for a while. "You two are such mad sods."

"Oh good morning, bodysnatcher! Where does that place you on the insanity scale?" Conor was unable to resist.

Ronan realized he had to catch the philosophical moments quickly or they suffocated in jokes: "We should just keep planning and see what happens. If you and Tessa decide to have a holiday in Greece for a couple of weeks, give us both a heads-up early, and one or both of us with our wives may be able to join you for part of the time on our way to somewhere else. We could at least have a few days together as we cross flight paths. Anywhere in Europe, Catherine and I would be keen."

"Sounds like a perfect holiday ruined!" teased Conor. "No – just kidding! It's a good idea."

Ronan continued: "And if you and Maria were off to the States, or even South America, we'd be keen on that too, or even some part of Canada. I've heard a lot about British Columbia and Vancouver Island. Not the whole time together, but just a week or so. Does that sound like a plan?"

"Sure does to me." Euan was already thinking about it.

"Yep, we'd go along with that."

They waited for a smart ending from Conor, but it didn't come.

"OK – it's a very loose plan, but it's tighter than anything we've had for the last thirty years. Sometimes all six of us might be together, sometimes four, sometimes maybe only two, but at least we'll be trying rather than orbiting around our own shrinking worlds," concluded Ronan as he eased himself out of bed and over to the tea-and-coffee station.

"Talking about shrinking worlds, I need to go to the bathroom."

Conor was out of bed with surprising agility and locked the door as he went in.

Ronan didn't bother asking what they wanted. They got the same as they had asked for the night before, only without the insulting remarks.

It took longer than they expected to get all three of them through the ablutions process – a study in time, space and movement as well as an example of immovable object meets irresistible force when Conor and Ronan collided while racing for the bathroom. Euan popped in for his shower while the other two admired the carpet from close up.

Euan was the one to remember to put some of the brochures from the church into his bag to help them with their sightseeing in Galway.

It was 11.15 a.m. before they were ready to leave the room and head downstairs. Breakfast had finished at 9.30 a.m., so they decided to wait until they got to Galway to have a brunch and then a meal in the evening to fill them up. They were greeted with a sunny smile and a cheerful wave from Kathleen as they came down the stairs.

"Good morning, me darlin'," said Conor in a mock Irish brogue. "You're a delight for old eyes."

"Good morning, Conor," she said, flickering her eyelashes at him and speaking in a mock English accent, teasing.

"Is Colin working today?" asked Conor.

"Yes, he is. He's just working on the hedges around to the left as you go through the doors. You'll see him."

"OK. We're out for the day and we have no idea when we'll get back."

"That's all right, because we have—"

But they were all out through the door before she could finish. She shrugged and went back to checking the booking details for the evening. Euan was striding hard to catch up with Conor.

"Who's Colin?"

"He's the caretaker/groundsman here. Good sort," muttered Conor.

"That explains it," said Ronan.

But Conor was already calling out, "Colin! How are you, my friend?" Conor waved his hand to give Colin a chance to work out which direction the shout was coming from.

Colin was a study in groundsman's dress as he peered out with squinted eyes from under his flat cap. His two hands, like old tree roots, were wrapped around the handles of a pair of hedge clippers, which he held in front of him in an unintentionally menacing stance. His jacket was an old brown-orange tweed, the colour of autumn leaves, and his dark shiny trousers were tucked inside black gumboots like wetted tree trunks. You could lose him in the grounds if he stood still for long enough to use his camouflage.

As they approached he recognized Conor and his face for all seasons cracked into a landscape of stubble and bush, mounds and dips and etched promontories, and the standing stones of some ancient teeth clung like the centuries of tales.

"Well, well, you old bastard! What are you doing back here? I thought last time was your last! So you've come back again, have you? And who are these two gentlemen? Are ye goin' to—?"

Conor interrupted him: "I've come to see you. Last time was not my last – obviously I've come back or I wouldn't be standing here. My brothers. Yes, we are, at the end of the day. There – that answers all your questions."

To Euan and Ronan's surprise he seemed to have followed all that and to be quite satisfied with the answers.

"Now," continued Conor, "can you ask them one at a time, but before you start . . . how are you, my good friend?"

"Ah, sure, I'm in fine fettle," said Colin, his grin getting bigger as they hugged and clapped each other on the shoulders and back. He looked at the two brothers and held them with a rough, coarse grip, giving a handshake that was all knuckles and bones. Each time his blue eyes twinkled and pierced under the awnings of his brows, they knew he had seen all he needed to see. His smile relaxed and then spread and he welcomed them in and showed them early warmth and friendship.

"It's true, then, what they say about the youngest child, isn't it?"

"I don't know, Colin. What do they say?"

"That they're always the ugliest," he replied.

"Get off! How do you know I'm the youngest?"

"I just answered dat," said Colin as he broke into a cackling phlegmy cough.

Ronan and Euan chuckled at the familiarity of the exchange.

"What are ye after from me now, lad?" he asked Conor.

"We're going to Dad's grave together to tidy things up. I just want to borrow some tools from you if I can: a couple of spades, a rake, a couple of small lump hammers – or any kind of hammers, really – some scissors or shears to cut some ground cloth. Em, what else? An old sack or some large plastic bags to put the tools on to in the back of the car – the forecast is for rain later on and we've made enough of a mess of the car already. Is that OK with you?"

"You don't have to ask that. You're welcome to whatever you need," Colin said. He looked mildly hurt.

"Thank you, my friend. You're a grand man."

"Come and get them, then. I'm not carrying them for you."

And he moved gruffly off to his work sheds.

They came out looking like plunderers and looters, handles and blades sticking out like thistles, and trundled over to the car.

"Do you have a couple of large towels to spare, then, if it's going to rain on us?" Conor realized he was pushing his luck.

"Da ye want the clothes off me back as well?" asked Colin, smirking.

"If you have any spare—" began Conor, but he received a look from Colin as he went back into his shed, and Conor shut up.

He was out again in no time.

"Here," he said, and he handed over two large but dirty old towels that had seen better days. "They've been used and they had a wash last year, so they'll be grand." And he winked.

"Thanks, Colin," called Conor over his shoulder. "I'll drop them in to you tomorrow morning early, before we fly out to England. OK?"

Colin just waved, picked up the hedge clippers from the ground, where he had thrown them, and then slowly turned and went back to his work.

They piled the tools and bags, sacks, towels and smaller implements into the back of the car; the rake was long and stuck up into the ceiling of the car from behind the back seat.

They got in themselves. Conor in the driving seat and Euan taking the passenger seat; Ronan in the back with the rake handle.

"How do you come to get favours there?" Euan was curious as to how Conor regularly attracted helping hands and warm welcomes.

"He lives in a small cottage just off near the trees by the road into the village. You can't see it from here. Both times I've been here he's come into the bar of an evening and sat by himself. I thought he might like a bit of peace and quiet, but I went over the first night to just say hello. We were the only two in the bar. We sat talking until they closed, and he shambled home and I staggered off to my room. Geez, he could drink, and yet you couldn't tell the difference between the early evening and when he left to go home.

"He's a great talker and he has views about everything – Ireland, God, gardening, you name it. He has that lovely easy grace when talking, and he told me some wonderful stories about his youth in Ireland. He's always lived near Galway and only moved house once – just to be nearer to work. I think they keep him on because he's a national treasure.

"It's funny, but I know more about his life and his family from a couple of long conversations, than I know about Mum's and Dad's. I wonder if that's always the way. You always ask strangers about themselves when making conversation, but the conversations of the home are usually more practical and incident-sized so as not to take up time. He treated me like an old friend the second time I was here, and the same just now. He's just a lovely complex man of simple pleasures."

"He's certainly very trusting," agreed Euan.

Ronan knew differently: "I got the impression he knows whom he can trust. I doubt that just anyone would drive away with a boot-load of his tools."

Conor moved the car gently away and pointed it in the direction of Galway town. The shy sun shone overhead in fits and starts as slow strolling clouds passed in front of it at regular intervals. It was warm and they were looking forward to some lunch and seeing some sights.

Chapter 39

They were soon on the outskirts and once they had mastered the crush of the driving, with no direction or destination clear in their minds, they found a similar place to park near where they had parked the day before. Then, with jackets safely in their backpacks, they made their way through the streets to the square. There was no sign of rain in sight.

The square, as they already knew, was a beautiful place, even in driving rain. In the opaque sunlight and a comfortable temperature, it was even more beautiful. They found that half the population referred to it by its 'old' name, Eyre Square, but it seemed the other half preferred the name The JFK Memorial Square. Others told them that JFK Memorial Park was a part of Eyre Square. In the end they didn't think it mattered, because whichever name they used everyone seemed to know where they meant.

But the day didn't turn out as they expected. This was the end of their time together and they had the feeling that they were skimming the surface in order to see as much as they could before the day closed in. Both these factors combined to make them realize that, in some ways, it would have been better not to bother at all. It was almost worse than seeing nothing, which would have still left the excitement of anticipation and the possibility of future time together. This way, it seemed final. They were absorbing nothing because they were cramming in too much information. They rushed to get to the next attraction, like tourists whose only concern is to tick things off on their list rather than to live and breathe the life of the place and the people, at least for a decent time.

They loved the fountain in Eyre Square with the corroded copper-coloured iron sheets, which they realized represented the sails of a classic Galway hooker – a traditional fishing boat. They knew it from the shape and colour and what they had read about it in the brochures from the church information shop.

They stopped briefly for lunch in a very pleasant café and filled the gap that a lack of breakfast had left. They were soon back in the tourist race.

They left out as much as they saw because they realized they were never going to get it all done. They missed the seaside suburb of Salthill, but walked about three kilometres down to Claddagh, the old fishing village, now the harbour and dock area of the town. It was a busy, lovely place. They really only picked there because of the line in the song: '. . . watch the moon rise over Claddagh . . .'. They had never known what the word meant before; now they did.

While there they thought about visiting the museum, but it was too full of fishing history, farming implements, military history and weapons and early photographs of Galway and the fish market at Claddagh. The brochure also indicated there was a hooker displayed inside, and they paused for a long time wondering about whether or not to go in; but in the end they decided to put it on the next trip list because there was going to be just too much to see and they knew they would never get out.

They walked past the famous Spanish Arch and Euan read from one of the brochures about the history of the old walled city of Galway. The wall was partly destroyed by Cromwell, the bane of Ireland, in 1651.

They wandered close to the harbour, where swans moored in the water like regal miniature barges, and they sat for a time on a bench next to a grassed area close to a stone wall acting as a breaker down by the docks. They knew the day was slipping away from them, but they still held on as tightly as they could; in a sense they were holding on to each other's company as well.

Euan told them there were daily passenger ferries to the Aran

Islands, but that only served to increase their disappointment as it was another opportunity they would have to miss.

'Another time,' they silently promised themselves.

They did, however, visit the National University of Ireland, where Irish is the language spoken on an everyday working basis. This in itself fascinated them, but they never heard any Irish speakers because they simply stood inside a huge quadrangle which, with its massively imposing clock tower, was an exact replica of the layout of Christ Church, one of the colleges of Oxford University. Ronan and Euan in particular were in awe of buildings so old that spoke so much of the past and held the secrets of the future. They came from places where most things seemed to be of the present or from a very recent past.

Despite their need for haste, they still found themselves on a leisurely walk around the streets, just taking in everything around them, hoping somehow the history and life of Galway would seep in through their pores and become a part of them. The locals drifted along equally casually, unaware of the envy of visitors like themselves. It's the same in every country, with visitors wishing to be locals and always thinking someone else is so much luckier. As they talked about it, it somehow made them more aware of the choices they had made, and in the end they found happiness in what they had done and the paths they had taken.

They were getting tired being on their feet by the time they decided to head back to Oranmore.

"It's up to you guys, but I think we could get something light and quick to eat at the Lodge and then go out to the grave. It's coming up to six thirty and I can feel a little bit of rain starting up again. What do you want to do?" asked Conor.

Euan spoke up quickly: "We can't eat at the Lodge. The restaurant isn't open tonight."

"Who says it isn't?" asked Ronan.

"There was a sign on the door this morning, and the bar's closed as well," answered Euan.

"Bloody hell! I never saw that!" Conor seemed quite put out. "Why?"

"I don't know. I don't run the place. A notice near the bar said the bar was closed tonight. I never saw any reason. I don't suppose they have to give one." Euan didn't think it was such a big deal. "It's just as easy to get something here, have a drink and then go straight to the graveyard. That was the original plan, wasn't it?"

"Agreed!" concluded Ronan. "It'll probably be quicker in the long run. It won't take long, Conor. Come on – let's find something cheap and cheerful, then we can head back and get started."

It didn't take them long, and they were keen to be on their way, so they didn't need to linger over the fish-and-chips-and-hamburger meals though the place was crowded and the food came more slowly than they would have liked. They didn't complain because while fish and chips seems the same the world over there is always something more romantic about eating them in a different country.

The rain had set in again and was falling in a steady downpour though it wasn't cold. To save themselves from a soaking they put on their rain jackets and made their way to the car, staying under the shelter of shop awnings as much as possible. They jumped straight in and drove off on the road to Oranmore. It was almost 7.20 p.m. and they were keen to get it finished. Within a very short space of time they were outside the church and looking out through the car windows at the rain. It had slowed down a little, but it was still going to soak them all.

"What do you think?" asked Euan. "Shall we wait and see if it stops?"

Euan was always prepared to wait; never impulsive. He was measured in his responses to challenges.

"It never stops! You know that!" said Conor.

Solid logic every time.

"So we're going out there? Is that what you're saying?"

Conor was exasperated with their luck. Just a couple more hours and they would have completed the job. "What do you think, Ronan?" he asked.

"Simple," he replied. "We have no choice. It has to be done tonight. It's the only time we've got. I'm not coming back in the morning and working myself into a sweat just before getting on a plane. Anyway, it will still be raining in the morning."

"OK," said Euan, "just a quick change before I go out there."

And he started taking off his shoes and socks followed by his trousers.

"Hey, whoa!" Conor was alarmed and puzzled. "What are you doing?"

"We've got to catch a plane tomorrow and I don't want a whole pile of wet clothes in my backpack. It's not cold out there, and so I'm getting down to my daks and the raincoat – minimum soaking. I suggest you do the same."

Euan was clearly serious as he continued to take off his polo shirt and fold up (roughly) his socks, trousers and top and put his jacket back on.

As he saw their hesitation, he reminded them, "Time's moving on, guys. This is our last chance to do it together. C'mon! It's not cold. Get your shoes back on; leave your socks off."

Once he had decided, Euan would not be turned back. He attacked the situation with a feeling of doing something daring for a change of pace.

"C'mon, Conor. He's right."

And Ronan did the same quick change as Euan had managed in the front.

Conor reluctantly followed, complainingly, the lead of his brothers and soon they were all sitting there in underwear, shoes and raincoats and with the windows thoroughly fogged up.

"I hope no one is out there to see us," complained Conor.

"There's no one out there as silly as us bastards, so you don't have to worry about that." Euan was amused by Conor's obvious discomfort. "Anyway, this weather is bringing the darkness on quicker, so we have extra cover."

"Extra cover?" shouted Conor. "There's no extra on me!"

"C'mon! Out of the car!" said Ronan, and he was gone and the door slammed behind him.

The other two followed and were drenched by the time they

got around to the back of the car, where Ronan waited. They opened the boot and pulled out all the things they would need for the task ahead.

"Not the towels and the plastic bags!" yelled Euan above the noise of the rain drumming on the car roof. "We need them to be dry for us when we finish! You can forget about spraying the weedkiller around as well."

And he put it back in the boot.

"I think I'd rather stay soaked than wipe myself with those towels!" shouted Conor.

Ronan was already heading into the churchyard, spade and weed-proof roll over opposite shoulders. Euan, always practical, put the towels into a corner of the boot and spread the plastic bags all over the base of the boot. Conor held the boot down for him to keep him and the inside as dry as he could. They quickly closed the boot, picked up all the other gear they needed and followed after Ronan. When they arrived they dropped everything on the ground by the graveside and stood looking down.

"Right! Where shall we start?"

They decided in the end that they should cut the existing weed protector in a line from the fuchsia to the front of the grave at the headstone end.

"If we pull the fuchsia up and it tears up the cover with it, all the small stones will go everywhere," argued Euan.

The others agreed. And when it was done, using Colin's shears, Conor and Ronan tore at a corner each, digging deep into the ground with their fingers. They pulled it up and around the fuchsia, stopping occasionally to push stones along on top of it, drawing it down towards the foot of the grave, keeping as many stones as they could in the carry bag they were creating as they pulled carefully but forcefully. Before they got to the end they both grabbed the other two corners and scrabbled and lifted those up and pulled until they were able to hold two ends each. They lifted it all up like a carry bag and laid it carefully on the ground away from the grave – a harvest of stones with a couple of weeds dangling underneath.

"Didn't seem to be anything to hold it down except the weight of the stones," observed Euan. "No clips or pegs that I could see. It just seems to have been tucked in around the edges like a bunk bed. Still, it's lasted remarkably well."

"Right, now for the fuchsia." Conor looked gleefully across at Euan.

"I'm cool," said Euan. "I'm over it. Let's get on with it. It's not getting any lighter – the rain or the night-time."

His nightmare of the night before had had a cathartic effect, and the ridiculousness of it had settled his practical mind back on a real plain. It was darker than it usually was at this time of the night, and there was every chance that it would become too dark to work if they didn't get the job done quickly.

Without seeming to even think about it, they all grabbed a piece of it and pulled as hard as they could. They were on wet soil now and it was hard to get a firm footing, which meant a lot of slipping and falling over, so before long the backs of their jackets were covered in mud. Because of the rain, the ground was softer and, in spite of their frequent slipping, there were clear signs that the fuchsia was moving. None of them made a sound, other than grunts and the odd few words not appropriate for a graveyard. They just kept picking themselves up, grabbing hold again in desperation and trying to keep on their feet. They felt the ground shifting slightly under their feet and made a last huge effort as the crumbling, piling soil creviced at their feet and the uneven ground began to create brief moments of purchase. Ronan pushed rather than pulled as the fuchsia moved more towards the other two; and then it was up and out, pulling clouts of soil with it.

They were overjoyed. They laughed and hooted with joy and a sense of achievement as they sat on the small grave surround, oblivious of the rain and the soaking ground. In their minds this had always been their biggest challenge, but the urgency to get it done had focused them and in the end it seemed easier than they ever expected. The relief flooded in faster than the rain. They couldn't get the smiles off their faces.

Ronan was the first to throw mud – a big, thick wad of it that had come up with the fuchsia. It hit Conor in the chest and spread out across the front of his raincoat.

"You bastard!"

Ronan just had time to put his head down as a sloppy clod came heavily, drippingly back across the grave to catch him on the top of his head. Euan laughed with delight at his aim, wiping his hands on some of the soaked clean grass behind him.

Before long they were standing up and – all caution tossed aside – they were hurling mud and filth at each other and splattering each other's jackets and hands and faces with dripping mud. Their emotions had been tightly coiled, and the release was a powerful unwinding. They didn't care about the few clothes they had on; they simply laughed as the last remains of anxiety washed away.

Euan held up his hands in surrender. "Whoa! Whoa! That's it for me, guys. Lots still to do and time's moving on."

A couple of intended mud packs slid unused to the ground.

"And look – the Gods are smiling on us! The rain is easing." Ronan held his hands palms upwards as if to prove it. They couldn't see because the sky was as black and thick as the mud, but they could hear the diminished clickety sounds of rain on their jackets.

"Right. What next?" Euan was back to his busy, organized self.

Conor took control: "Let's use the spades to flatten the soil on the top."

He passed a spade to Ronan and kept the other himself.

"It's too wet to use the rake, so, Euan, if you can walk around the inside edge of the grave and press down the soil as hard as you can with those big feet of yours that will help to hold the clips in place when we push them through the cloth."

They busied themselves as best they could, though the narrow space they worked in meant they had to move out of each other's way several times. By the time they had finished it was better than they had expected, and it was level and hard though a little muddy on the top. It had dried quickly once the heavy rain had stopped, and they were surprised. Euan looked pensive.

"Wouldn't it be better if we put the old sheet on first and the new one on top just for a thicker coverage?"

He looked at the other two and they looked back, annoyed at how they had missed the obvious.

"The trouble is we have the stones on top of the old piece of cloth. We will need to tip the stones in the clean grass off to the side here." Ronan indicated the ideal spot.

"Let's just do it."

Conor grabbed two corners, Euan grabbed the other two, and they carefully tipped the stones on to the ground in such a way as to keep them as closely piled as possible in a clean grassed area. They placed the old cloth over the top of the grave, pulling the cut end around the cross. The old piece was a good size, and they pushed the ends and sides as hard as they could into the ground using the spades gently so as not to tear the already damaged cloth and so as not to create a thin drain all along the inside edge of the grave, which would collect water. Euan was all action.

"New piece!" he said as he grabbed the fresh piece of covering cloth. "It feels like it has small holes in it." He was puzzled and uncertain because it was too dark to be sure. "Is this the right cloth?"

"'Course it is! If it was plain plastic the rain would just pond on top of the grave. This cloth lets the water run through." Conor thought it was obvious.

"And lets the weeds grow through too," said Ronan. "However, we can't help that, can we?"

Conor agreed. "No, we can't, and I'll be back again sometime anyway. Don't worry about it. Let's just do the best job we can with what we've got."

Euan was soon in control again: "It's a generous size, so there's plenty to tuck under all round, but leave a little extra again so we can push it down on the edges with the spades like we did with the old piece."

They soon had it done, and even in the blackness of the night they could see it was a good job as the grey concrete surround, now pitch-black in the ever fading light, emphasized the neatness of the grave top.

"Don't forget the pegs to secure it," Ronan reminded them,

and he went round pushing the pegs through the double thickness of the folded-under cloth while the other two used the lump hammers gently to knock them down as far as possible, with the loops pressing on the top of the cloth. It felt and looked very secure.

They then set about collecting handfuls of the stones and sprinkling them around the top. They picked up every single one as far as they could see, but they still looked a bit sparse.

Euan couldn't hide his disappointment: "I wish there were enough stones to almost fill it to the inside lip of the grave surround. They looked like plenty when we lifted them off, but now it doesn't look quite so full."

"Hmm," said Ronan. "Maybe we flattened the top of the grave too much, or we should have replaced more of the soil the fuchsia pulled out."

"It's a good job, guys. It could be better, but it will do until I have time to get back here. Don't start fretting now."

Conor began picking up the tools and scraping them against each other to get some of the mud off and then dragging them through the clean, wet grass to clean them off some more. The others cleaned up their share and stood briefly to look at the grave one more time – maybe for the last time for two of them. They didn't know. Sometimes what you want and what you get don't match up. They all said a quiet goodnight to their dad – a silent fond wish – and went back to the car. They piled the tools in, careful to place them on the plastic. They wiped themselves as well as they could with the two towels that smelled of earth and mown grass, took off their muddy jackets, piled them on top of the tools in the back and jumped into the car wearing underwear and shoes only. They had two towels between the three of them. They felt cold and damp all over.

Conor squinted at his watch as the lights faded inside the car: "Looks like it's ten to nine. We'll be able to have a warming shower before nine."

They were soon under way, driving back to the Lodge. They were tired after their day and satisfied, and a gentle warmth crept over them.

"We'll have to put our jackets on when we get back," said Euan. "Might need to wipe them off with the towels in the car park before we go in. I'd hate to make a mess all over their foyer carpet."

Ronan laughed. "Whatever we do we're going to look a sight!"

The others laughed too.

Within minutes they turned into the car park and, as they came to a halt, stared in bewilderment at the Lodge, which was completely blacked out. It seemed darker than when they were at the graveside.

They just stared for a while and then Euan spoke up: "There you are. I told you the bar and the restaurant were closed. They haven't got anyone staying other than us, as far as I can see."

Conor was bemused. "So they've closed up for an early night. Good on them, I suppose, but it's never happened before when I've been out here!"

Ronan salvaged a benefit from it: "Well, we'll be able to creep in quietly and up to our room without having to put on any of our wet, dirty gear. There's no one around to see us, so let's go before anyone does arrive."

He grabbed the room keys from the glovebox and scrambled out of the car. The other two were right behind as they slammed the door and went around to the boot.

"Leave it," said Conor. "Forget about the towels and drying ourselves. If it stops raining I'll come and get them later on and see if we can get them cleaned and dried somehow. C'mon – we'll be in in no time and up the stairs so fast the drips will evaporate off as steam."

They all agreed and ran for the door quietly in case anyone was around.

Chapter 40

"They're here! They're here!" whispered Mrs Doherty noisily, like a one-woman football crowd. "I saw the car lights pull into the car park. Now shush, everyone! I can hear them at the door!" she yelled into the silence. "Are you ready with the player, Niall?"

Niall's finger had been paused over the 'pause' button for some time, ever since he saw the car headlights.

"Rory, get to the lights, man. Get to the lights!"

Rory was already in his position by the lights with his hand over the switches.

The three of them entered quietly after opening the front door, not wishing to wake anyone up and have them see them in such a dishevelled state. They were ready to bolt for the stairs when suddenly a song they all recognized began its sombre introduction and brought them to a startled stop. Then the full force of the lights filled the room and they stood there stage-struck.

Looking at the whole scene, it was hard to say which group was the most astonished.

Euan, Conor and Ronan stood inside the door and stared in disbelief, hands covering their soaked dignity, looking around the group gathered there and all hoping that they were sharing the limelight in one of Euan's dreams.

Mrs Doherty was aghast and stood there ready to faint, mortified and ruined; and The Three Tenors sang out, unaware of the stunned audience and the consternation they had unwittingly caused.

There are moments in life which are just too ridiculous for words, and the only way to deal with them is to extend the bounds of credibility so that it becomes the stuff of legend, providing decades of table talk. Added to that was the residual emotion of their farewell to their dad, and now his theme song rang out. As the starlight gathered around them, in their minds the crowd became an auditorium of people and the three extra tenors stood there on 'stage' under the lights in their 'formal' gear, and joined in singing a final song of tribute to their dad for all they were worth.

Mrs Doherty had gathered her composure and all the strength of a vengeful woman facing a ruined night, so she tried shouting over the top of six enthusiastic voices: "Turn it off, Niall! Turn it off!"

Niall stood there with a grin on his face as wide as Galway Bay and turned the volume up while his other hand covered the 'stop' button.

"Rory, do something!" she whispered loudly through pursed, frantic lips that, mercifully, were almost closed. "Do something and don't just stand there!"

Rory looked across at her briefly as a smile he had almost forgotten how to use began to spread across his face and into his eyes like the morning sun along the hilltops.

"I will. I most certainly will."

He crossed the floor, walked up to the three new tenors and made it four. His voice was strong and true, and he was cradled into the group as they all sang in release.

He looked proudly round at his son, who had just entered behind them with his fiancée. They too were laughing quietly, Danny with no idea of what was happening, planned or otherwise, while Bridget wondered who had changed the plans that were so carefully prepared for their entry into the Lodge tonight.

Rory contemplated it as a distinct possibility for him as Mrs Doherty eyed him malevolently and kept pointing abruptly to her heel as if he were a dog that had forgotten its training.

"Sing up, will you!"

Euan, forgetting his remaining dignity, raised his arms like a conductor and the whole crowd of them sang, bar one.

The song finished playing, but they sang on, afraid to let go of a moment like this that would never come again in quite the same way. The song would forever be etched on their minds and this place, this time and these people would become part of a magnificent story among the many in their lives.

Conor caught a glimpse of Kathleen, head back, singing and laughing and giving the thumbs up to the boys on centre stage, who returned the gesture.

Only the serious and proficient could get that last note! The whole was a crescendo of accidental harmony that simply boomed around the lobby unaccompanied, and when it finished there was a silence and a sense of love and loss mingled with great joy. Three souls had been lifted and three heads were bowed for the final fall of the curtain.

And then, like being jolted awake, they came to their senses, clapped Rory on the back and ran for the stairs chased by applause and whistles and cheers that tumbled back down the stairs behind them as they ran for their room, fumbled for the card key and fell in the door laughing and hooting. They pushed it shut behind them, knowing they would never dare do anything like that again and feeling amazed and perplexed by the madness and the relief that had given them such courage.

The shower gave them a wonderful feeling, and they all spent a long time under it – far more time than they usually did. Soon they were dried and in the equivalent of pyjamas for each of them, warming nicely and feeling contented as they sat near to the large window in a comfortable chair or on a bed, looking out across the bay and cradling a beer.

There was a sudden knock at the door, and for a moment they all froze as they looked from one to the other to see who was the most acceptably attired to answer the door.

There was general agreement: almost simultaneously they said, "You go."

Ronan got up off the bed to open the door while the other

two continued to look out of the window and sip their beers.

Kathleen's face was outside.

Ronan was surprised, but tried not to show it: "Hello, Kathleen. Can I help you?"

"Yes. Hello there, gentlemen," she said, waving to the two other occupants of the room, who turned around to return Kathleen's greeting. "Well done tonight. You stole the show!"

"Thanks! Didn't mean to."

"Thank *you*! We could hardly walk up the stairs in silent dignity, could we?"

"I've come up to grab your wet clothes, including socks, and your boots. I'll have them clean and dry for you by the morning." As Ronan stood there inactive, she insisted: "C'mon, love – it's not a big job. You can't pack them in your bags tomorrow in the state they're in. Did you not think to wear raincoats? Where are your jerseys and jackets and things?"

"They're in the boot of the car. They were too wet to wear to walk into the Lodge, soaked as they are."

Kathleen was very persistent: "Give me the keys, then." And she held out her hand. "Give me the keys!" she insisted. "I'll get them dry and cleaned as well, and I'll have the keys at reception for you in the morning. C'mon now or I won't have time to get them done for you."

Ronan was embarrassed and the other two were looking around at him, enjoying his discomfort. He gave in and went to pick up all their wet clothes from the shower floor – the boots as well – and took them to her standing just outside the door.

"And the car keys?" she asked as he handed her the few clothes.

"Oh, sorry. Forgot."

He picked them up from the bench top and handed them to her.

"Like squeezing leather dry," she muttered as she took them from him.

Euan and Conor shouted questions to Kathleen over their

shoulders, not willing to stand up.

They learned about the birthday party they had gatecrashed, how the candles were lit and how the conversation had all been about the singing and nothing about the birthday. They refused her invitation to come down and join the group, even though she said she had been asked several times, by all sorts of people, to come up and get them.

"Please yourselves," she said, and went off with their clothes as Ronan closed the door behind her and went back to join the others.

"Well, that was quite a belated, but grand, send-off for our dad, wasn't it?"

"I think our Oscar-winning performance downstairs was the highlight."

"'Highlight' might be stretching it a little bit."

"Mum and Dad deserve the Oscars, not us. Winning performers as parents!"

"Yep, much more deserving than some of the plonkers who get them for making millions and showing the public how to have many wives and lots of spoilt, unhappy children."

"It does have a lot to do with role modelling, doesn't it? We had two of the best."

"You're right. They should have an Oscars awards ceremony for great parenting."

"There'd be too many nominations."

"Yes, there would – the unrecognized millions that preserve our civilization. Maybe they should be on the Queen's New Year's Honours List, then."

They could hear the sounds of the party downstairs drifting upstairs to the door of their room, but they weren't tempted. This was their last night in Ireland and a time for recall. And there was plenty to fill their minds. They pondered how much they had done in only a few days, and smiles lit their faces involuntarily as they remembered some of the things that had happened and the songs they had heard and talked about and sung that took them back so timelessly to moments in their childhood.

They finished the few beers.

"Not taking them on the feckin' plane" was Conor's conclusion.

They rolled into bed, and for all of them it was like they had struggled from a great depth of water to reach the surface again; and tonight, just as they felt they couldn't hold their breath any longer, they had burst through into clear air. They gulped in the life-giving freshness as guilt and anxiety, uncertainty and fearfulness were drained from them forever.

They were soon asleep and, if they dreamed, they could not remember their dreams in the morning.

PART SIX: DEPARTURES

Chapter 41

Conor woke gently from a peaceful sleep, thinking he was the first to wake. He looked at his watch and was surprised that it was 7.30 a.m., and he knew they should be moving soon and getting ready for dropping the car off and catching a plane back home. He liked the sound of the word, though he realized that it wasn't home for his brothers and suddenly understood how hard it must be to put a place to the word 'home' when you have had more than one.

He got up on one elbow and looked to see if either of the others was awake. Euan's bed was empty.

'Must be in the loo,' he thought, but the bathroom door was open and there were no sounds from inside.

He eased himself from his bed and made his way over to the window. He drew in his breath in amazement at the three neat piles of clean underwear, socks, jerseys, jackets and jeans, and, when he felt them, even the boots and shoes were dry. He was very pleasantly surprised and could only surmise that Euan had quietly gone downstairs for some reason and they had been given to him to take upstairs to their room, where he had sorted them. But where was he?

Conor's question was soon answered as he walked across to the window and looked outside on a misty morning scene that was graceful and serene. The sea was calm, the rain had stopped and a gentle breeze blew on to the shore and playfully fingered the trees. A strengthening sun picked up jewelled water drops in the grass and hedges, and it looked for all the world like a painted scene with only irregular surface disturbances to give away that it was real.

Euan was down near the car with the boot wide open, and he was with Colin, who had a wheelbarrow and was collecting the tools they had borrowed from his shed. He was being given everything they had taken for the digging, and also included were things unused or left over, like weedkiller and ground cloth. It seemed the towels and plastic bags had done a good job because from where he was standing looking out through the window the boot seemed remarkably clean as Euan pulled it down and closed it. Only ever happy when the plan was being carried out. Chaos and spontaneity were not his sports.

And then they shook hands and Conor thought he saw Euan give Colin some money. He was annoyed that Euan had broken a friendship based on generous help for its own sake, and not based on payment for services. He promised himself to have a word with Euan as soon as he could find the right time and place.

He turned back from the window and, on his way into the shower, woke Ronan as he went past his bed.

When Euan arrived back there was a bustle about the room as Ronan showered and the other two packed their bags. Ronan made a cup of tea as Euan showered, and in their own offhand, efficient way they were all ready at about the same time.

"Thanks for collecting the clothes and sorting them for us," said Ronan.

Euan replied casually, "I collected them, but Kathleen had already sorted them."

"That's a worry," said Ronan. "She remembered what each of us was wearing, and even remembered which pair of underpants belonged to which one of us."

"Don't get excited, mate. She probably guessed rather than recognized." Conor smiled. "Maybe she matched character to underwear."

"So how would she guess yours, then?" asked Ronan.

"Sexy, old, with a large suggestive pocket caused by a frequent tenant," answered Euan for Conor.

"And yours, Ronan?" asked Euan.

And Conor answered for Ronan: "Loud, 'dare to take your eyes off me', 'look, but don't touch'."

"And yours, Euan?" asked Conor.

Ronan answered, "Entry denied, restricted access, press to play."

Each had tried to identify some aspects of character on the basis of 'underwear maketh the man' with mixed results.

"Are we bothering with breakfast?" asked Euan to try to drive things forward.

They looked at each other, and Conor advised that they would get nothing on the plane and that it would be close to 5.30 p.m. by the time they got back to Conor's place and unpacked and sorted themselves out; so breakfast would be worth a serious thought.

They headed downstairs and stopped at reception to leave their bags while they got breakfast.

"Thanks for the washing and drying, Kathleen," said Ronan. "I don't know how you managed it. Really grateful. Thanks."

"Sure, you're welcome, all of you. The secret is a drying room as long as a football field. Bit of soaking, some washing, drying and then the presses out the back. Easy job."

"It won't have been, but we really appreciate it. Do we owe you anything for it?" asked Euan.

"You don't have to pay for every kindness." Conor's tone was surprisingly curt. "Can we get breakfast, Kathleen?"

"Aye, you can. Find some places and I'll come over and see you in a few minutes."

Euan was surprised at Conor's outburst, but decided to say nothing.

"Can we settle the bill?" asked Conor, taking out his wallet.

"All done, me darlin'." And she glanced at Euan.

"Oh, I see. Big spender again, was it?" And Conor glanced at Euan with a scowl on his face.

"Maybe a thank you would have been kinder, Conor." Ronan intervened before any more could be said, and Conor just grunted and walked to a table.

There were no signs of last night's celebrations, so the staff must have had a late and busy night. The tables had all been set out for the morning, so the other two went over and sat down with him. Kathleen had hurried away to ready the kitchen, not really understanding what was going on.

Ronan hated situations where sullen grunting and moody silences replaced dialogue, so he moved to find the cause of the sudden change of mood.

"What was that all about, Conor? Do you have a beef with Euan?"

There was silence.

"Aw, c'mon – we're not going to finish like this after all the fun we've had and the friendship we've rediscovered. What is it?"

"I'd like to know too, buddy. Have I said or done something to upset you?"

Conor came straight out with it: "Why did you pay Colin this morning for us borrowing his tools? It doesn't work like that. Doing that changes the relationship."

"I didn't pay Colin for lending us his tools," answered Euan.

Kathleen came up and the conversation stopped.

"Right, gentlemen, what can I get you for breakfast?"

She sensed the tension and was keen to let them get on with things, so she took the order quickly and went away to the kitchen. Conor waited until she was gone.

"I watched from the room window this morning and I saw you give him money after he put all the tools we had borrowed in his wheelbarrow. So what was that, then?"

"Oh, I see." Euan smiled rather sadly. "That money?"

"Yeah, that money."

Euan looked at Conor sadly. "We were all pleased with what we'd done at Dad's grave, but we kinda agreed that the stones were in short supply, and, Conor, you said that you would fix it next time you came back. I've spent most of my days here trying to get rid of the feeling that I never really did enough to help you with the funerals when Mum and Dad died—"

"I said not to—" Conor began.

But he was firmly interrupted: "Would you mind listening? If you hadn't brought this up, I wouldn't have to explain myself to you and re-scratch the old scabs. I got up early just to help out and return the tools and other bits and pieces to Colin so as to save you both the trouble. When I got down to reception Kathleen had all the washed and dried gear sitting there in three piles, so I thanked her and collected them and brought them back up to the room and left them where you found them when you woke up. I went back down to catch up with Colin. I didn't bother with a shower, to save you from being woken up."

Conor shifted uncomfortably in his seat while Euan continued: "I found Colin and we chatted and I told him about last night – all of it. He laughed and swore a lot and said something about 'mad feckers'. When I mentioned about the stones he said he knew where to get them and would be happy to fix that for us so that you wouldn't need to come back so soon. He was clearly joking with that last comment, so don't take offence." The last bit he said with an ironic smile on his face as he looked at Conor. "It started the usual argument. 'I couldn't ask you to do that' and 'I'd do dat for you lads,' etc., etc. 'OK,' I said, 'but I insist on paying you for the stones.'

"'Now, dat's a deal.'

"We shook hands and I gave him a note – I don't have to tell you how much, but it was fair and still left both of us in the other's debt, which is the gap that ongoing kindness on both sides can narrow. Your friendship with Colin remains on the same footing as before, and I would never dream of changing that."

Conor was looking really uncomfortable by now; and while Euan felt he should be enjoying his brother's embarrassment, he wasn't. Ronan was silent, a thoughtful, admiring look on his face at the ongoing revelations of Euan's thoughtfulness.

Just at the right time Kathleen arrived with three Big Bay Breakfasts and a rack of toast, and another young kitchen hand passed out the tea and coffee.

"Paying the room bill was my way of saying thanks to you

both for being such great company over the last few days. You've both paid for other parts of the trip, so I thought it was my turn. I was nervous about this whole thing and didn't know how it was going to go, but it has been outstanding and we've just got along like . . ." Euan was struggling for the right word.

"Brothers?" offered Ronan.

"Yeah, sure – like brothers . . . and great old friends. My way of saying thank you," he repeated. "I apologise if that upsets you."

Euan was finished. He didn't know what else to say. But neither did anyone else at first, so they stirred their drinks, avoided eye contact and buttered some toast while the dust settled.

"I'm sorry. I should have trusted your judgement more. I also should have known better by now, having seen how you do things over the last few days. I don't know you absolutely well enough yet and the lost years have caused that. I misjudged you on the basis of how many times you beat me up as a kid." There was a smirk on Conor's face as he said that, but he also needed to own up to his mistake. "I'm really sorry. I shouldn't have said what I said without checking first. I really should have known better. I won't get it wrong again."

"Accepted. While I have no regrets that I beat you up a lot, it clearly didn't sort you out because you're still a cheeky bastard with no respect for your elders. We would know each other better and learn to trust one another more if we had had more time as adults together. You change a lot from being a kid and your values grow and some of the rubbish falls away, but we haven't been here to see that happen to each other. It's felt like getting to know one another all over again."

"I know. I'm sorry. I think we do trust each other after even this short break. Family members have to trust each other. The older you get the more you realize that. That's what I think, anyway."

Ronan exhaled as if he had been holding his breath for the whole span of the conversation. He felt relieved and glad that the last few bits of reserve and misunderstanding, which distance had magnified over time, had finally been laid to rest.

"It's been a very comfortable few days. I've felt like we're old friends, and I felt like that on the way to the airport to catch the plane to Ireland. That's a real testament to the bond that there is between us, and I think that comes again from Mum and Dad constantly reminding us of the value of family."

Euan carried on as he remembered things: "That's right. We used to fall out and fight—"

"Most of the time, and I was usually the one getting thumped," interrupted Conor.

"And one of them would say 'Blood is thicker than water' or 'You'll appreciate each other one day' or 'When everyone else has given up on you, your family will still be there.'

"They had it right and I think, without really trying, we've got it nearly right as well."

Ronan was surprised at where the conversation had led them to.

"As long as this doesn't mean that we can't send insulting emails to each other and I can't tell you when you're talking crap – which will be most of the time." Conor looked serious.

Ronan knew now it was just the usual style that Conor adopted. He would still be there when he was needed – kindness itself.

"Nothing we could say will stop the steady stream of drivel that you send nor the crass comments you make to all and sundry about all and sundry."

They smiled and ate their breakfasts in silence and reflected quietly on how far they had come. When they had finished, Ronan was the first to stand up.

"I suppose the breakfast was included in the bill?"

Euan nodded.

"Thank you, Euan," said Ronan.

"Yes, thank you," added Conor. "Much appreciated."

"Yeah, yeah. Don't need to overdo it, you smarmy bastards. Let's get going."

They said goodbye to Kathleen and each got a hug when she came round the front of the reception desk; she seemed to do every job in the hotel and was everywhere. Colin arrived as they walked out through the door and down the outside steps. They all got a firm handshake and a smile that warmed a cool morning, and Conor got a sharp but affectionate clout on the back. They turned around as they headed for the car and waved to the two of them standing together on the steps.

"Great people!" said Conor.

The other two agreed, unreservedly, and as they waved it was a farewell to the Lodge and to Ireland, to everyone they'd met and to everything that had happened as well. But some things would never leave.

"You driving, Euan?"

"No, you can."

"Can I have the keys, then?"

Conor was back to his old self. He caught the keys tossed to him, pushed the button to open the doors and lifted the boot. They put all their gear in and went to get in. Then they glanced back once more at the Lodge, and to their surprise Kathleen and Colin were still there. One last wave and they drove away.

It wasn't too far to the airport, but it took an easy hour and a bit. Following the signs they made their way round to the rental drop-off area and found the company yard. They drove in and Conor and Ronan went inside while Euan emptied the boot and gathered the bags together. He looked after them while the other two sorted out the car.

There were two or three people in the yard, but there was no one in the office.

"We just have to wait," said Conor. "They come when they're ready."

"We're quite early for a 1.45-p.m. flight, aren't we?" asked Ronan. "It's only just after 11.30 a.m."

"Wait and see," said Conor sardonically.

Ronan bowed to his greater experience and held his peace.

Conor turned out to be right. Neither Euan nor Ronan had considered that the car would need to be checked to make sure that pieces hadn't been wrenched off or dents put in the bodywork or fires started in the engine or cow shit used to decorate the inside. It took a while. Then they had to sign it all off to make sure neither party could claim later against the other.

"The wheel trim on that wheel was missing when we picked it up," said Ronan, telling them that he had pointed it out before driving away in the car several days ago.

"That's fine, mate, it's—"

"I know – covered by insurance. I was told that when I picked it up. Thanks."

It was well after 11.30 a.m. by the time they were bundled into a van with several other would-be flight passengers and driven to the departure area to get organized to catch their planes. It turned out they arrived only a few minutes before checking-in time.

As they sat in the departure lounge they were unable to fend off the sense of gloom that settled over them, though the gloom was only on the surface. Underneath was a deep sense of satisfaction with the time they had spent together and how it had gone, and the relationship that had grown between them without trying.

It was better than any of them had expected, and they felt sadness at the looming separation, knowing they would soon be heading off in different directions. When they had first talked about their get-together, and set the dates and the times in England and Ireland, it had seemed so far away and such a long time to be with people who had shared each other's company in only very patchy ways over the last thirty years and more.

It could have all gone badly wrong or awkward, but it had been the best time they remembered together as adults and they didn't want it to end. It was like being a kid again, mourning the loss of a Christmas which was all over before it had properly got started.

Conor got up quite suddenly and said, "Right, guys, grab your gear. We need to head down to the boarding lounge because we know about the Pamplona Bull Run once the call for boarding passes goes across."

He was right, and the queue and the incoming tide was only just behind them as they lined up.

The trip back across to England was uneventful and sparse. Try as they might, they could not clear the gloom. Even Conor's humour about anything and everything seemed to have deserted him.

PART SEVEN: ARRIVALS

Chapter 42

By the time they had landed it was just after 3.25 p.m., and they walked rather gloomily from the plane to the exit of the arrivals lounge. They had each come to terms with the memories and the fun and the possibility that they might never be back either to visit the graves or to visit Ireland together. They were old enough and experienced enough now to know that no matter how many plans you make, life has a way of butting in and changing it all.

"How are you, Jimmy?" shouted Conor as Jimmy appeared just outside the door, car keys in his hand and a big grin on his face.

The other two hadn't even noticed him until they heard Conor call out. Conor hugged Jimmy, and Jimmy held him briefly and patted both shoulders. The other two felt obliged to do the same – after all, he was a friend of Conor's.

"How was it?" he asked as they walked towards the car.

"Great!" said Ronan. "Loved it, every minute, and we had such a good laugh." He patted the front pocket of his jacket, where his new wallet was.

"Yep, she was fantastic all right," agreed Euan.

"He was asking about the holiday, not the couple of times you slipped away and we couldn't find you," quipped Conor.

They reached the car, piled their bags in the boot and climbed in, and they were soon under way and out on the road after paying the parking fee.

"What about you, Conor? I suppose you're sad now it's all

over?" Jimmy was nothing if not persistent.

"Yeah, really sad in one way, but really glad in another to be getting rid of these two. Tessa will be back soon, and that's a bonus anyway. I couldn't even try to tell you the trouble I've had with them. I doubt that you would believe me."

Conor's humour was, for once, unconvincing, and he stared out through the car window.

"I'm sure you'll try to tell me about it sometime soon," nodded Jimmy, and he glanced across at the sombre face of Conor, eyes fixed on a distant horizon.

The rest of the journey was completed in silence, apart from the soft 'slur' of the tyres and the whisper of the traffic on the roads. All sounds seemed muffled to the occupants as they closed their senses to clear their imaginations. Jimmy too was silent, knowing that he would simply be interrupting the settling process that each brother, in his own way, was going through. They were soon outside Conor's front door.

Jimmy helped them get their bags from the boot and handed Conor's car and house keys back.

"Jimmy, my old friend," said Conor, "I owe you one."

"No, you don't," answered Jimmy. "It doesn't work like that."

Conor smiled at him. "Sorry we were such poor company on the way home. Didn't tell you anything, did we?"

"I learned more on this return journey than on the way out to the airport. The stories I can wait for. See you, guys." And he shook hands with Ronan and Euan. "I told you, didn't I?" was his parting comment before he walked across the road to his home.

"I think he reads too much," said Ronan to break the awkward silence. "He's full of plot and themes and characters."

Conor opened the door and they all went inside. The house was cosy with the early autumn sun shining in. Slowly and almost reluctantly the gloom started to lift to match the weak sun and Euan and Ronan relaxed, sensing this was another home where they would always feel comfortable and welcome even if they weren't sure that they belonged any more.

"Don't wait for me to tell you where your rooms are. You can't have forgotten in a few short days."

Conor headed upstairs with his bag, and the other two followed.

The rest of the day was quiet. Ronan went for a long walk – further than they had walked when they first arrived. He drank in the sights and sounds of England, intoxicated with its beauty, drinking as if it was his last drink and pondering the strange and quite separate fates that they had been dealt – the different roads they had taken – and yet, in a funny kind of way, the similarity of the place of ease they had all arrived at.

They all knew how important their parents had been to their lives even after they were gone. They had subconsciously modelled most of their experiences of parenting with their own kids; their wives had had similar childhoods, and they too added their own uniquely different skills with identical love. They all realized that the best things in life were family, and with a strong family it doesn't matter where you live. It will be home.

They had all come to accept that there was a soundtrack to their lives. Ronan never stopped convincing them of it, and he smiled to himself in amusement as he remembered how he had found a song or a tune to partner every experience they had. He still hadn't solved the meaning of life, but he was pleased and contented.

Euan and Conor stayed in the house though Conor wandered outside to look at the garden which he knew was tidier than when he left. Jimmy was a good friend, and friends were important to him. Conor would get the house ready for Tessa's return and catch up with his kids when his brothers were gone. They would fill a vacuum, he thought, and overfill it. He wasn't looking forward to tomorrow, and he knew it would be hard to maintain his feigned casualness towards his brothers. He had been comfortably surprised by the strong bond that had grown between them in such a short few days together. He knew he shouldn't be surprised, but he was.

'I'm losing my touch,' he thought. 'This is the first real sign that I'm getting old. And I have all those other things to think about that the aged philosopher has been planting in my head for days.' He smiled, knowing the questions had always been there; now he would give a little more thought to the answers.

Euan sat inside, comfortably sprawled on the settee, looking through some of the pamphlets they had picked up in the various places they had visited, brief as most of those visits had been. He found himself staring at photographs of places miles away from where his mind was now. He was exhilarated by the success of the trip. He had felt that same satisfaction of being the older brother, though their wanderings had cut that period of his life short the first time he experienced it. He felt like their guardian for no reason he could put his finger on except that they needed to be looked after, like two village idiots, and he was old enough to do it. He laughed at how they had been like kids again, and then, as soon as he thought it, he saw that they had never stopped being kids. It was the way they had been taught. 'Don't be naive, but don't lose your sense of wonder and excitement' and 'Once you stop being playful, then you might as well dress in tweeds' and 'The pages are open and if you close them too quickly you won't finish the story and you'll never know how it might have ended.'

In different places their minds crossed over. There were brief moments when they considered identical things and shared the same values, never realizing that in spite of the differences they were close together as they pondered the love they had known and the experiences they had shared.

PART EIGHT: FINAL DEPARTURES

Chapter 43

They always seemed to be rushing, and after a good night's sleep they moved around at high speed with their thoughts always distracted from the urgent. It was a surprisingly chill morning with a thin veil of mist hanging in patches around the houses.

'There's an autumn coming,' thought Conor gloomily.

They grabbed a quick breakfast of scrambled eggs on toast – enough for long flights; not too much to fill them before the meals started up on their respective flights. Then they were rushing around again, checking everything. They had the usual anxieties that they had forgotten something and they checked every part of their rooms and the bathroom and all their documentation at least ten times.

"Don't worry," said Conor from behind his paper. "If I find something belonging to you, I'll throw it in the rubbish anyway or sell it to an antique shop. Either way, you'll never see it again or know that you left it behind."

He was amused by them flitting across his vision and their constant drumming beats up and down the stairs.

They packed the car, the bags bigger and more full than they had been when they left for Ireland. As they backed out of the drive and turned on to the road, Jimmy was on his front lawn waving them off, standing with his arm around his wife.

"I presume that's his wife?" asked Ronan as he pushed the button to lower his window.

"That's Sandra," answered Conor.

"Bye, Jimmy! See you, Sandra!" Euan and Ronan both shouted while Ronan waved out of the window and Jimmy and Sandra waved back from their manicured garden.

They had the car radio on on the way to the airport, and caught the nine-o'clock news. Euan and Ronan listened intently to the newsreader talking about English cities and European and world affairs. Events in Canada and New Zealand were beginning to make headlines in England and overseas. They were of sufficient interest, and it was a strange thought that these places were important in other people's worlds. They mattered to millions, not just their own citizens, and place names in Canada and New Zealand were becoming more widely known worldwide.

'Ticket to Ride' by the Beatles started after the news, and Euan turned the volume right down. He sat there thinking, 'When you live a long way away from a place you sometimes think of it with more affection than those who are living there going through the hard grind of making a living. From a distance the weather seems milder, the queues less busy, the hassles mere inconveniences that you get everywhere. Distance puts a romantic gloss on any memory, whether of people or events or countries. He found it hard to work out which was the true impression, and in the end he realized it didn't matter that much any more. He had exorcised his demons. In the old saying 'Home is where the heart is' he knew that, for him, the 'heart' was family.

He relaxed and enjoyed the journey to Heathrow. Euan looked behind and caught Ronan's eye, and for a brief second they held each other's gaze. A smile passed between them and they knew that each of them had come to the same understanding.

Conor refused to drop them off at Watford, and insisted when they tried to argue the point. From there they turned up the radio and occasionally punctuated the journey with snippets of conversation.

"You came a long way for such a short break, Euan," said Ronan. "I'm looking forward to another break and I'm looking forward to seeing Catherine and the boys."

"It's not that far," answered Euan, "and anyway it was worth it. How long will you go on calling them 'boys'?"

"Probably forever because they'll always be the same number of years younger than me as when they were born. They'll always be my boys."

Euan screwed his face up at Ronan's logic. "And by the way," he said, carefully emphasizing the last word, "I'm longing to get home too." And he winked at Ronan.

Within two hours they were parking at the airport, heading into the international terminal and checking flight details and gate numbers on the screens against their tickets. Ronan and Euan went to check in their luggage and came back to stand again in an awkward island in the middle of swirling crowds.

Ronan put one hand down the neck of his jacket and pinched and pursed his face into that of a crone. "When shall we three meet again, in thunder, lightning or in rain?" And he capered in front of them.

"Mad bastard!" was Conor's only response, while Euan looked on amused.

"We have to keep talking and planning," said Euan, "and we can't leave it this long again. You'll be looking bloody ugly in your late eighties, if we leave it till then." And he indicated Conor. "We talked about a holiday with all our wives next year or maybe later, all meeting somewhere in Europe for two or three weeks, maybe?"

"Yes, we did, so let's keep working on it," agreed Ronan, and he looked expectantly at Conor, who was unusually quiet and simply nodded. He realized then that because they had all lived worlds apart for many years, life would always be a series of arrivals and departures in more ways than one.

"Right – I'm going," he said. "I don't want to drag this out and I know what you two sentimental old bastards are like. I suggest we all leave it here. I'll be in touch – I promise!" he added as he saw the doubt in their eyes.

He reached out to shake Euan's hand.

"You're kidding me!" said Euan, and he stretched out, held on to the hand, pulled Conor to him and gave him a huge hug while pinning his arms to his sides.

"Get off me! Ugh! I can't breathe!" And he wheezed to prove the point. "You squeezed the breath out of me. Made my eyes water," he muttered at the end.

"Thanks for everything," said Euan, holding him further away, and he put his head down to avoid looking at Conor. "You're a top guy, though you hide it well. Give my love to Tessa and the family."

Conor touched his forehead against Euan's, but didn't trust himself to speak and looked everywhere except at him.

To distract himself and to give Conor some space, Euan grabbed Ronan and Ronan knew what Conor had meant as the lack of air left him stranded.

"You too, Ronan. Loved the company and the ideas, mate. Good luck with the search, my friend. Love to Catherine and the boys when you catch up."

And he stepped away.

"Thanks for everything, Euan. We could have fallen into an inescapable hole of bad jokes if you hadn't rescued us with common sense. Safe travels. Give my love to Maria and the kids."

Ronan allowed his hand to slip from Euan's shoulder, and he stood awkwardly, head bowed.

Conor found his voice again: "See what I mean about making your eyes water?"

"Yeah, I see what you mean," said Ronan, and he grabbed Conor and held on. "I shall miss the jokes and the rudeness. You've been very generous. Love to do a trip with you and Tessa, like we said. Take care and keep in touch."

"I will." He still saw the look of doubt on Ronan's face. "Honestly, I will! This trip was my idea, remember?"

Ronan looked reassured.

"I've enjoyed the friendship between us. Love to your family too." Conor was almost whispering and his voice wavered. Then he changed: "I told you that you two old buggers would get sentimental. Right? So now piss off and go and annoy your own families!"

He touched them both briefly and loped away, a slight stoop reappearing in his gait as he disappeared into the crowd.

Ronan and Euan looked at each other, smiled through blurring vision and moved off to their respective departure lounges. There was no hurry any more now all was said and done. They slowly walked backwards until, after a brief wave, they turned away and never looked back.

There was no more to say. It had all been said well before the parting, and each of them found waves flooding them with memories of their time together. While it had been brief, they had found a bond that they now knew had always existed and that, hopefully, would get all their families closer together in the future.

As they walked in separate directions, though closer than they had ever been before, they all seemed determined in their minds not to be apart from each other again for so long. What would be next? Searching out their brother's grave? How would they know? It would have to wait. So, pleased beyond belief at how well it had all gone, they independently pinned their shoulders back, lifted their heads contentedly and, against the backdrop of memories, they each sang together the soundtrack, silently in their hearts. The silent song of family – the song they would always sing.